The 

Summerland Affair

WORDSWORTH ROMANCE

The Perfect Pirate

AND

Summerland Affair

MARY EDWARDS/JUNE SUTTON

WORDSWORTH EDITIONS

The paper in this book is produced from pure wood pulp, without the use of chlorine or any other substance harmful to the environment. The energy used in its production consists almost entirely of hydroelectricity and heat generated from waste materials, thereby conserving fossil fuels and contributing little to the greenhouse effect.

First published by Robert Hale Limited

This edition published 1994 by
Wordsworth Editions Limited
Cumberland House, Crib Street, Ware,
Hertfordshire SG12 9ET

ISBN 1 85326 509 8

Printed and bound in Denmark by Nørhaven

The Perfect Pirate

This book is dedicated to
Betty Irish
For always believing in me.

One

Her breath tore raggedly from her throat. She held it silent for a numb, terrifying moment and listened. Listened hard as pain throbbed through her heaving chest. Footsteps still followed. One, two, maybe three pairs of leather-soled shoes pounded down the dusty track.

There was little time. They were getting closer. Scraping her shoulder-length auburn hair away from her face and tucking it behind her ears she began to run again. The midday sun beat down on her head and perspiration trickled down her back, soaking her white cotton blouse until it clung to her body like a second skin. Her lungs were close to bursting point and it took every ounce of will to make herself keep going. But fear was a powerful spur and, although she did not know where it was coming from, the will was there, spurring her legs to carry her on towards the tiny village, her only hope.

She had to find somewhere to hide, a dark corner to crawl into until her pursuers had passed by, given up the chase, returned to the villa. There must be somewhere! Please let there be somewhere, she begged.

Slipping and sliding on a patch of loose gravel, she reached the first dusty white buildings and almost lost her footing. Reaching for the wall to steady her balance, she rounded the corner into a narrow cobble-stoned street flanked by two rows of low adobe houses with red pantile roofs.

In the next moment she hit a brick wall. At least it had the feeling of a brick wall. On a panic-filled scream she found herself flying through the air. A large hand clamped tightly over her mouth and sound became impossible. Then she was bundled down a narrow alleyway between two houses and pushed through a doorway into a darkened room smelling strongly of spice and decay.

He held her tight, her captor, as he leaned back against the closed door, adding their combined weight to keeping it tightly closed. She was not sure if he meant to keep others out, or herself in! Her heart was beating a rapid tattoo beneath the brawny arm pinned across her chest, holding her to, what seemed under the circumstances, a gigantic body with such great strength that movement was impossible. His other hand was still clamped over her mouth, so firmly that she feared her jaws would be permanently crushed together and she would never speak again.

But she did not give in easily. She wriggled as best she could within his grasp and attempted a scream. The muffled, mumbled moan, lost beneath his salty tasting palm, would not have woken a sleeping mouse. His hand tightened, covered her nose and made a good job of almost totally cutting off her breath.

She continued to wriggle and kick, finding strength in panic, causing his fingers to close more forcefully on her cheeks in an attempt to stop any further noise, and, like a steel vice, the arm around her middle closed in. She did not have the power to stop the second moan, this time of pure pain, as she felt her ribs turning to chalk, along with her jaw.

'Keep quiet!' was grated close by her ear. The first words he had spoken. He was English! He spoke in fluent Spanish, but his accent was clearly southern England. The knowledge gave her some comfort, though in their present position, she was not sure why it should. Then, after a short pause, he added, 'I'm on your side!'

The urgent rattle of masculine footsteps running over the ancient stones in the narrow street outside rang out with menace. Each clattering footfall shuddered through her veins like a jolt of electricity. They were too close for comfort, far too close for comfort. The sound wiped away any chance she might have had of considering the man's last words. At that moment the need to hear those footsteps keep going right on past her hiding-place was all that mattered. That she was being held against her will by a total stranger was forgotten.

Breathlessly she listened, silently begging her pursuers to keep running, willing their steps to keep on going until she could not hear them any longer.

Seconds stretched into seconds, moments into eternity. Finally they had gone, their noisy treads dying into the distance, leaving behind a blessed silence.

Drawing a deep breath of grateful relief, she relaxed visibly, unconsciously allowing her head to fall back easily against the man's chest. In the silence her breathing echoed and her ears became filled with the rapid thump, thump of her anxiously racing heartbeat vibrating from each erratic pulse-point.

Slowly her captor removed his hand from her mouth, little by little, pausing before he took it completely away. 'Are you going to keep quiet now?' he asked, questioning uncertainty in his perfect Spanish vocabulary.

'If you let me go,' she replied in English to see what his reaction would be; more than a touch of the Dempster spirit, which Aunt Maeve would have called hot-headedness, being revealed in her impetuous manner.

'Then keep quiet,' he repeated, reverting to his native tongue without showing any evidence of surprise that she was a fellow countryman. 'They won't be far away.' He released the body-hold he had on her very slowly, very carefully, as if dealing with a dangerous animal that might turn on him at any moment.

The instant she was free she sprang across the room and out of reach, bumping into a table and sending a chair tippling noisily to the floor in the dim light afforded by the shuttered windows.

'I said ... *keep quiet*!' he ground through stiffly clenched lips, folded his arms and leaned back against the door with a breathy, long-suffering sigh.

She had expected him to follow her across the room. That he had not, threw her somewhat off balance. The only reason she could find was that he was intent on keeping himself in a position to prevent her escape.

'Who are you?' she demanded hotly, fixing his shadowed face with hostility that, although he could not clearly see, he must have sensed. For a low rumble of ironic laughter burst from his lips.

'Does it really matter at this moment in time?'

'Of course it matters!' she spat. 'You leap out of nowhere, take me by surprise ... by force ... and ... and push me in here.' Her hands made agitated circles in the air as she grasped for words hidden within her fear and anger. Her eyes danced around the room in despair. In the darkness it looked seedy, but she imagined it would look a whole lot seedier by daylight. A luxurious penthouse it was not! And he most certainly was not the smooth sophisticated type. 'Who are you? And why have you brought me here?' She attained an assurance of voice that concealed the unwelcome thoughts filling her head. Thoughts that doubled uncomfortably in the following silence. He seemed to be weighing her up ... much like a wolf contemplating its next meal!

But then he moved abruptly from the door. 'Jay Rutherford, at your service,' he announced with heavy sarcasm, taking her completely by surprise when he did not try to pounce on her. 'Forgive me! I was under the impression you were in need of a little help. Obviously I was wrong. So ... ' pulling the door open he extended his hand towards the slice of sunlight which bombarded the inner dimness like a flash of lightning and made her eyes crinkle in a frown, ' ... please, feel free to take yourself off to wherever you wish to take yourself off.' He flicked his hand with disdain towards the open doorway, dismissing her with equal rebuff.

She took a step forwards, then hesitated. What should she do? Was he playing with her? Taunting her with the false security of offering a freedom he thought she would not take ... ? And would not allow her to take if he was wrong and she attempted to set foot over the threshold!

What was wrong with her? Her feet had turned to lead. The door was open. She could walk out. So why didn't she do it?

The devil you know etc., she recited to herself, silently looking at the man standing in the searching beam of sunlight from the doorway, for the first time seeing him clearly.

He was older than she had expected, thirtyish she imagined. He was tall ... well she had known that ! But he was exceptionally tall, and broad with it. He had the shoulders and muscular build of someone accustomed to heavy manual work; and the tan of someone who did that work outside. His hair was blond and, she thought, short. But then he turned his head slightly, as he nodded towards the open door, asking her silently what she was waiting for, and she could see that the sleek, pale hair was pulled back into a ponytail which reached down between his shoulder-blades.

Dear heavens, she thought, swallowing back the gasp of astonishment that rose in her throat, what was he?

Dropping her gaze to the long athletic legs did nothing to boost her confidence. They were bare beneath the frayed edge of scruffy denim cut-offs. The sleeves of his dirty blue shirt had been ripped out, also leaving rough, frayed edges, and all the buttons were missing, except one close to his waist, which exposed a vast amount of very masculine chest.

She stopped there, not wanting to believe the rest. The long hair was bad enough, but no, not this! A large wild-eyed eagle's head peered out of the open shirt front, fiercely daring closer inspection.

The ponytail could have made him a hippy: a product of the swinging sixties, one of the 'love' generation; gentle people who wished to be left to their own devices. But today her luck was out. With the ponytail went the tattoo, and had he been wearing a large gold ear-ring he would have been the perfect pirate.

The devil you know, she decided, most definitely was preferable, and strode out of the door without a by-your-leave. She would take her chances with Sebastian Font and the men from the villa. Her departure, surprisingly, went unhindered.

But she did not get far. It being siesta-time, the little Spanish village lay sleeping in the height of the midday sun and the street was deserted – which was fortunate, enabling her to hear her pursuers returning. They were calling to each other as they searched around the houses on the route back through the village, making no attempt to keep their whereabouts secret.

They obviously did not consider she had the ability to escape them, she told herself bitterly, realizing that if she did not move quickly they would soon see her standing there like a dummy.

It took only a moment to reach a decision. After all there really was not much choice. She turned and ran, finding both relief and annoyance that, when she reached the door, he was standing holding it open, confident that she would be coming back.

'Can I come in?' She hovered on the doorstep looking sheepish.

Silently, and with an infuriatingly knowing smile, he motioned her in. Then he closed and locked the door behind her, leaning back against it as he had done before.

She stood in silence, embarrassed, not knowing what to say. How to explain why she had come back? She was not sure she knew the answer herself.

Then a pair of heavy footsteps came into hearing, getting closer, closer. Approaching the darkened house, their hiding-place. The next moment she was down on the floor, huddled beneath the window. The man, who had pushed her there, huddled by her side, holding her down with one arm and motioning her to keep silent with the other; an unnecessary order as the unseen owner of the footsteps loudly rattled the closed window shutters. Every nerve in her body leaped six feet up in the air and she froze, fearing the unseen pursuer would break the catch and get in, or detect their presence as he tried to peer through the narrow slats of the closed shutters.

A second pair of footsteps joined the first, then a third. Voices could be heard, including *Señor* Font's voice, loud, angry. She had never heard him sound so frightening, so aggressive. Her heart was beating so loudly she feared they would hear it. The window shutters clattered and trembled from a violent jolt as someone hit out with a frustrated fist, and she almost cried out loud in the sudden shock of terror, biting her lip to hold back the noise as her body jolted and trembled as if it, too, had had a mighty blow.

Feeling her fear, the man's arm tightened around her, his free hand swiftly, yet silently, closed over her mouth as before.

This time she did not struggle but held on to him, fingers clutching at the dirty shirt and the warmth of his body beneath, needing him, forgetting the way he looked, forgetting she knew nothing about him. At that moment all she needed was the protection he readily offered, the comfort of another human being in an hour of need. She could not remember ever having needed anyone as much as she needed this stranger right now.

It seemed an eternity before the men outside moved away. All the time they sat there, two strangers huddled beneath the window of a dingy room – clinging together like two lost children, she thought, as the silence stretched longer and the reality of the situation settled on her.

Embarrassed she tried to sit up, to push away from the man and end the bodily contact that suddenly seemed so intimate, far too intimate. But he held her there, refusing to allow her to move one inch. His hand remained clamped over her mouth and her eyes widened as they peered up at him questioningly.

He merely shook his head, a slow emphatic order to remain still, unmoving, in total silence until he was convinced the men had gone. Her green eyes carefully watched his shadowed features, seeing and feeling the studied concentration as he listened for the slightest sound, the tiniest evidence that the men outside were still there, playing tricks, feigning departure and waiting for them to give themselves away ... Waiting for her to give herself away, she corrected. *Señor* Font and his friends did not know she had found an ally. She shivered at the thought that those three angry men had been looking only for her, for one defenceless girl. She looked at the man she had just considered to be her ally. She hoped she was right, and shivered again.

He was definitely the type to have on one's side. He was big and strong and if he was possessed of any fear he kept it well concealed. He was in control. Instinctively, she realized he knew exactly what he was doing ... He had obviously been in this situation before!

The last thought was both depressing and worrying. Fortunately she did not have long to dwell on it. In one easy motion the man jumped to his feet and pulled her up with him.

'We have to get you out of here,' he stated unnecessarily. No one knew better than herself that she had to get right away from there, from the Villa Romano and Sebastian Font, its owner. In reply she merely nodded sagely.

'Do you have anywhere to go?' he asked, picking up a large bag and moving quickly round the room throwing things into it.

'No,' she replied flatly, wishing the light was better and she could see exactly what was going into the bag.

He turned at her reply. 'Nowhere?' The frown on his face was evident in his voice, and she grimaced. It seemed incredible even to herself, but as from that morning she had nowhere to go. She was homeless. 'Where do you live?' he continued, almost as if he had been privy to her thoughts.

'I ... ' she paused uncertainly, ' ... lived up at the villa.' She nodded towards the hillside beyond the dimly lit wall, where the white-stuccoed Villa Romano nestled amongst the olive groves, orange-trees and grapevines like a sparkling sunlit jewel set in the dusty hillside.

'You have no one you can go to?'

She shook her head, unable to keep the grim, ironic smile from her face at the incredulity and, she suspected, slight annoyance in his voice. It seemed he was beginning to regret having played Sir Galahad.

'I'm the children's nanny ... er ... ' hesitating she grimaced, ' ...*was* the children's nanny. I had been there for eighteen months. But there was not much chance to meet anyone outside.' Until today she had been happy in her job. Very happy. So much so that she had never realized just how cloistered an existence she was leading. There had been plenty of parties at the Fonts' villa, plenty of entertaining guests, many holidays to exotic places. But when she looked back, she realized that no matter what the Fonts had been doing or where they happened to be, their life had revolved around the same group of people, mostly business associates from *Señor* Font's lucrative winery.

It was the man's turn to shake his head then. 'I knew I should never have got out of bed this morning.' He sighed heavily, plonked the bag noisily on the table, zipped the fastener, rested his hand on the top and stared at it for a long moment of total silence.

'Well you can't stay around here,' he finally said. 'So you'll have to come with me.' He looked up, narrowed eyes piercing the uncertain disbelief upon her features. 'I suggest you don't bother to raise any objections,' he hurriedly put in. 'Not unless you can come up with a better idea.'

At that moment she had no ideas, better or worse. But wasn't she playing with fire, agreeing to go with a total stranger?

Taking her prolonged silence for assent, he turned for the door, swinging the bag from the table. 'Come on then.' He carefully unlocked the door so there was no click, then hesitated, looked dubiously down at her. 'I hope you can manage not to fall off the back of a motorbike. I don't suppose you have ever been on one before!' he added drily, swung the door open with a silence that she would have thought impossible of the old cracked wood, and stepped outside into the narrow sun-filled passageway.

Feeling that what she was doing was slightly insane; that so far all the events of the day had been slightly insane; knowing better than to speak out and make any sudden noise, she followed him out. She tried, not very successfully, to focus on the broad capable shoulders and pretend the long blond ponytail hanging down the middle was not really there.

'Now ... *who are you?* And what happened?' Pulling the top off a can of lemonade he handed it to her, then took a can of lager for himself from the small refrigerator in the galley of the boat to which he had taken her.

'I told you. I *was* the Fonts' nanny,' she replied a touch acidly. She was having definite second thoughts about agreeing to come with him, now she had seen his 'home' as he called it: the *Rosy Rita*! A large motor cruiser, moored up with the local fishing fleet. It smelled of diesel oil and fish and looked as if a good douse with clean water would not go amiss.

He took a long pull at the lager in his hand, then leaned with one arm high on the side wall of the cabin, bending his head to see out of the small oblong window. Without looking at her, he asked, 'Don't nannies have names?'

'Rhea Dempster,' she replied, giving him no time to pass comment, before adding, 'And who are you?'

'Jay Rutherford,' he replied simply, and she recalled he had told her before. 'J. Rutherford at your service,' he had sarcastically announced, before throwing her out ... or at least suggesting she should leave. Which was as good as throwing her out.

'Am I allowed to know what the "J" stands for?' she enquired haughtily.

'Jay as in bird.' He did not take his eyes from the window, but a smile pulled at his lips, hinting that it had not been an uncommon mistake to make. She also realized he was watching out of the window to see if they had been followed, making sure their hasty departure on the noisy motorcycle had not been observed. A cold shiver trembled over her spine. What had she got herself into?

For a long moment she watched him worriedly. She studied his calm stance, the steady gaze, almost able to feel the sharpened instincts that throbbed through his head. He knew exactly what he was doing, what he was looking for. He was one of them ... maybe on another side ... but definitely the same breed.

'And what does Jay as in bird do for a living?' she asked, trying to conceal the uncertainty she was experiencing by being flippant. He was no stranger to a situation such as this. He had done it all before.

It was a disquieting feeling. He looked the rough-and-ready criminal type and that, she was afraid, was what he was seeming more and more to be. She hated the thought that she might be consorting with a criminal, yet at the same time wished she were more like him, more able to cope with the situation. If she had been, she would not be there with him now. She would have made her own decisions and acted on them. Instead, her own *naïveté* had put her in a position just as dangerous as the one he was supposed to be helping her to escape from.

'This and that,' he replied easily, drained the last remnants of the lager and threw the can into a red plastic bucket on the floor. 'Fishing trips ... pleasure trips ... You pay the fare, I'll take you there,' he quipped humourlessly.

Rhea shivered again. So where did that leave her? She could not pay any fare! She could not raise so much as one peseta! All she had was herself and the clothes she stood in. Everything else was at the villa and going back to collect it was right out of the question.

'What happened?'

Rhea, startled visibly from the depths of her depressive thoughts, splashed the untouched lemonade down herself and on to the floor.

'I had an argument with *Señor* Font,' she said, a little too quickly, as she brushed the liquid from her blouse and skirt, then took a large, nervous gulp from what remained of the lemonade. Not being accustomed to drinking out of a can, she succeeded in spilling it down her chin.

'You made a good job of that,' she muttered self-consciously, dusting further moisture from her blouse before it soaked in, even though most of it already had.

Leaving the window Jay went to the cupboard, took a glass and handed it to her with an expression that said he thought she needed a nanny herself.

'What was the argument about?' Taking no notice of the spillage on the floor he watched Rhea empty the can into the glass before she spoke.

'Oh ... you know.' She gave an all-encompassing shrug and turned to stare out of the window where previously he had stood. She did not want to tell him the truth. It was too risky. Maybe ... just maybe ... if *Señor* Font found she had not breathed a word to anyone, he might let her off. After all, he had always been kind to her, pleased with the way she looked after his children. That must stand for something. But if he found she had told the first person she had come into contact with ... well she was asking for trouble.

'No, I don't know.' Jay's voice tightened. He moved up close behind her.

Rhea did not look up, but knew by some sixth sense he was back on guard, watching over her shoulder for any sign of trouble - though she was not sure how he would know when it was coming. The Costa del Sol in the height of the season was anything but quiet and the quayside at Fuengirola was teeming with holiday-makers, not to mention the growing number of local fishermen who were moving in to get their boats ready for the evening's catch.

'You owe me an explanation,' Jay pointed out insistently at her protracted silence.

'*Señor* Font made a pass at me. I refused him. He got angry.' The age-old story seemed to be the safest bet.

Not for Jay Rutherford. 'Come on!' he drawled with exaggerated cynicism. 'You're trying to tell me that Font and his two sidekicks were combing the village for you like madmen, just because you refused to give in to him!'

Rhea winced at his bluntness, then asked herself what she had expected of someone so rough.

'Yes,' she retorted stiffly, and with more primness than she had intended, or wanted. 'I do not do that sort of thing!'

Throwing his head back, Jay gave a bark of laughter. He had not missed the warning in the last remark. 'And I do not go around seducing little girls. Neither, would I have thought, does Sebastian Font. But if he does, I really don't see him charging around like an enraged bull.'

'I am not a little girl,' she flung back hotly, stretching to her full five feet three inches. He thought she was making the whole thing up; that it had been a childish attempt at attention-seeking.

'How old are you? Eighteen? Nineteen?'

'Twenty-one,' she grated through clenched teeth, wondering why she was even bothering to answer him. She would have been the first to admit that most of her actions today had been more in keeping with a ten-year-old.

'Forgive me. I was a couple of years out,' he replied drily.

Silence followed, and, not knowing what else to do, Rhea studied Jay once more, the rough-looking man who had been her saviour. An air of assuredness pervaded him. Oh to be half as assured, she silently wished. She imagined he never made a move unless he was totally convinced it was the right one, at the right time.

It had been the right one, and the right time for Rhea, when he had jumped out on her and carried her to safety with such swiftness she had found no time to protest, or her pursuers time to see. She had thought he was attacking her, and even afterwards she had wondered why he had been so forceful. Now she knew the answer. He had known exactly what was happening – that she was running away from those men and that he had to get her into a hiding-place without the men seeing. Had he tried to do so by any other means, Rhea knew she would have made a noise about it, objected, thinking that he was perhaps another of Sebastian Font's bullies. He had saved her. Had he not been there, she was sure she would have been caught. Not having possessed the stamina the men had shown, she had known she would not have been capable of outrunning them for much longer.

She owed her life to this man. But now she must leave. To stay would be foolish. 'You pay the fare, I'll take you there.' His words echoed in her head. He was not the type of man to do anything for nothing, and she had no money, nothing of value ... only herself. There was only one way he could extort payment from her ...!

'Thanks for the help back there. I appreciate what you did,' she hesitated briefly, not wanting to rush her farewell and make it obvious she was aiming to leave ... aiming to take off.

She sauntered towards the steps leading out on to the deck, the only exit, the only escape route. She wanted it within reach before he realized she was going. 'But I think it is time I got out of your hair, left you to do ... ' she shrugged and her smile was forced, '... whatever it is you have to do.' Half turning, she placed a hand on the wall to steady herself as she took the five steps to freedom.

'Where to?'

Rhea stopped on mid-step. She had not expected a time-wasting enquiry: a hastily reached-out hand pulling her back, yes; a rapid lunge as he grabbed her bodily and threw her back into the cabin – even straight on to the bunk so he could reap his payment there and then – she had also been expecting. But not the most simple, most reasonable question in the circumstances, so unanticipated that for a moment she was unable to think of a reply.

'Where are you going to?' he repeated, watching her seriously as she hovered half way up and half-way down the wooden steps, delving the inner recesses of her numb brain for some reasonable answer.

'To get the first plane home.' The words came tumbling from her lips without consideration.

One dark blond eyebrow rose the smallest fraction. But enough to make Rhea take a backwards glance at what she had said.

'What with?' Jay voiced the question at the same time that it formed in Rhea's own mind. 'Where are you hiding your money?' His gaze travelled pointedly from her head to her feet, taking in the cotton blouse and skirt, lightweight in deference to the climate, the blouse having one small pocket, obviously empty.

With the air of someone who, although having only just thought of it, had decided it was a brilliant idea, Rhea replied, 'I will go to the British Embassy.'

Jay did not reply. His frowning gaze remained riveted through the window and Rhea began to have second thoughts. Where was the British Embassy? Was there a British Embassy? Of course there was! There had to be ... didn't there?

'And what will you do when you get home?" Jay enquired, not turning to look at her. 'Does your father have a fortified castle?'

'What do you mean?' Rhea looked anxious. What was he doing? Deliberately trying to frighten her?

'Are you going to tell your parents what happened? Or will you pretend everything is fine ... ? Keeping up the pretence until one dark night someone comes to spirit you away?'

He *was* trying to frighten her! They wouldn't. They couldn't.

'Men such as Font are not to be messed with,' Jay continued. 'They have connections all over the world. A single phone-call will get a job done.'

He did not specify what job. There was no need. Rhea knew exactly what Jay was inferring and, after the morning's interlude, she knew it was true. If Sebastian

Font wanted her out of the way, there would be someone around willing to perform the service for the right price. And Sebastian Font had the right price.

'What can I do?' she asked, stepping back into the cabin, placing herself in the hands of Jay Rutherford,the stranger who, she suddenly realized, was her only hope.

'It would not be safe to go home right away,' Jay replied, looking thoughtful. 'That is exactly what they will expect you to do and the airports will be the first places to be covered. I don't trust Gibraltar either. You being a Brit, they're bound to keep an eye out for you trying to get there.' He paused, as if thinking out some entire plan inside his head before putting it into words. Rhea's heart did a sickening drive. He seemed to know what Sebastian Font would be thinking and doing. She was not happy with the thought, but had to admit that Jay's mind worked in the same devious way as that of a criminal, which she had found that very morning her employer to be.

'I'm pretty certain they did not see us leave the village. If they did we should know about it very shortly.' He glanced round at Rhea, just as his words sent a tremor through her veins. 'The safest place to be at this moment is right under their noses, the last place they will expect you to be.'

'Stay here?' Rhea questioned, the uncertainty of her voice entering the gaze she cast around the dirty cabin.

'Yes,' Jay replied, taking little notice of her concern. 'You can stay here until the heat has died down. Then I'll take you across to Morocco and get you on a plane from there.' He hesitated, looked questioningly at her. 'You can go home to your parents ... ?'

Rhea was not sure why she did not lie to him. But something touched her deep inside and she felt a swell of deep gratitude to Jay Rutherford for his concern, which, despite her misgivings about his appearance, seemed to be very genuine. 'I don't have any family,' she blurted out.

Jay groaned, passed a sweeping glance across the window, then returned to her face as if he did not want to believe what he was hearing. 'No parents?' he questioned.

Rhea shook her head and Jay groaned again.

'Do you have anyone?'

'An aunt.'

'That's all?'

'That's all.'

There was a long silence. Jay returned to his observation of the outer world through the window; once more his mind was working overtime. Though this time Rhea had the feeling he did not like the conclusions he was coming to.

'Will this aunt take you in?' Jay finally asked.

'I could go to her cottage. But Aunt Maeve is in a nursing-home at the moment.' How Rhea wished she had heeded the inner cry that had told her she should go home and look after her aunt after the serious heart operation. Rhea had known it was her duty to return and nurse her only living relative. But the lifestyle of extravagance she had become accustomed to while living with the Fonts had been too hard to give up. She had succumbed to selfishness, she told herself, and now she was paying for it dearly.

But Rhea did not have long to ponder on her guilt.

Jay suddenly turned. 'Get on the bunk and cover yourself with blankets,' he ordered briskly, hurrying out of the cabin before Rhea could raise any objection.

For a moment she stood, too stunned to move. Then, realizing Jay must have seen some of Sebastian Font's men coming, she dived onto the bunk and pulled the blanket over her head.

Two

The throb of the old cruiser's engine pounded through the wooden hull, entering Rhea's ears, head and body. Her heartbeat quickened and she willed the engine to share its heightened rate. The motion of the boat seemed so slow, too slow, as she sweltered beneath her blanket cave. She longed to peep out, see what was happening, but fear held her still.

It seemed like an eternity before the engine stopped. For an awful moment Rhea felt her heart might also stop, convinced that they had been caught.

'It's all right,' Jay assured, lifting the blanket from Rhea. 'They must have been checking the harbour on the off-chance. No one has followed us out.'

Rhea did not speak, could not speak. For a moment she felt like screaming at him, or hitting him for putting her through that for nothing.

Calmly Jay turned away, rummaged through a chest beneath the opposite bunk and came out with a pair of his own shorts and a tee-shirt. He dropped them down on the bunk. 'Put those on,' he ordered. Then he pulled one of the galley drawers open. 'And fix your hair up in some way to make yourself look different,'he added, handing Rhea a rubber band before leaving her alone to make the transition.

Rhea gazed at the shorts and massive tee-shirt. This was like a bad dream. It couldn't really be happening. She was ordinary, a children's nanny, not some playgirl to get mixed up with villains and crooks.

Pinching herself proved what she already knew. It was true. Everything had happened and she was not about to wake up and breathe a sigh of relief.

Resigned to her fate, she slipped out of her clothes and into Jay's.

'Why don't we move from here?' Rhea asked with more than a touch of impatience. Two days' imprisonment on Jay's boat was proving more than she could handle. If Jay was so concerned about her welfare then why didn't he take her right away from Spain, not keep her sitting about one mile out at sea? There he seemed content to watch every boat which went in and out of the harbour through a pair of high-powered binoculars.

She was also fed up with feeling ridiculous going around dressed in his borrowed clothing. She was still wearing the same white shorts held up with a canvas belt tied tightly round her middle, plus the baggy yellow tee-shirt with Kawasaki emblazoned across the chest. At least it was Kawasaki when Jay wore it. On Rhea's meagre frame it looked more like 'wasa', the beginning and end being lost somewhere in the multitude of folds under her arms.

'Because this is the safest place for you to be.' Jay's reply was brief, delivered with the same lack of concern which had characterized all his other replies.

Frustration and annoyance, along with a large helping of real fear for her own safety, exploded in Rhea.

'How can you be so unconcerned?' she flung hotly. 'You don't know what Sebastian Font is! Or what he does.' She paused, taking a ragged breath. 'They are murderers,' she uttered; the disbelief she herself found in the truth echoing in her voice. 'Murderers,' she repeated. 'And ... and I ... I ... 'she hesitated, not wanting to speak the words, fearing to admit that which she had tried to hide, tried to deny.

'You are at the top of their hit-list,' Jay elaborated for her.

'Yes,' she replied defeatedly and turned quickly away. She would not show her fear, she ordered herself, gripping the side rail in search of extra strength.

When Jay's hands rested on her arms the shock was only mild. Rhea had heard him move, heard him come up behind her, though she had not expected him to touch her.

The coolness of his fingers against her burning flesh had a strangely therapeutic effect. Within only a moment Rhea was fighting the strangest urge to turn into his arms, fall completely under the influence of those large, capable hands.

'You're safe now,' he assured her, his voice breaking the spell of his touch and stopping Rhea from making a fool of herself. 'They don't know you're with me. They will never have expected you to stay right under their noses.'

'How do you know?' Rhea questioned, her voice heavy with the weariness of her thoughts. 'How do you know what they will or will not be thinking?' She did not really want to know the answer. She was sure it would point to Jay being cast in the same mould, being one of them, a criminal.

For a long moment the only sound was the gentle slap of the clear blue Mediterranean on the *Rosy Rita*'s dinghy hull. Rhea thought she sensed an almost imperceptible tightening of the fingers against her arms. But it was so slight she assumed it was only in her imagination.

'Are you ready to tell me everything?' Jay finally asked, ignoring Rhea's previous question.

Rhea grimaced inwardly. Since the first day, Jay had not pushed her for further explanation to what had happened at the villa. She had assumed he had, after all, been content to believe her feeble story. But now she had thrown her previous lie to the wind.

'There's no point in involving you,' she replied, feeling a need to keep Jay out of the whole nasty business. He was already involved too much, just by being with her.

'If they do find you're here and I have to reap the consequences, I think I have a right to know why,' Jay pointed out.

Rhea turned to face him and Jay let his hands fall to his sides. 'You said they would not look for me here,' she challenged, feeling cold on her arms where his hands had previously been, and shivering.

'I don't think they will. But you have to accept that they will still be looking for you and will be for some time to come,' Jay replied and, misreading her shiver as one of fear, pulled her into his arms, cradling her there with a gentleness that seemed so alien coming from such strong arms.

A tremor rippled through Rhea's body. She looked up into his face, into his eyes. She was safe, protected. It was the strangest notion, yet one Rhea was so very sure of. She felt that while she was with Jay nothing could harm her, nothing hurt her.

'Are you going to tell me everything?' Jay prompted, looking into her eyes with a persuasiveness that she felt might melt her.

'Yes,' she whispered, looking quickly away before all sense diminished.

'The Fonts had two children,' she began, as she pulled away from Jay and turned to look out over the sea. 'Marcos, the baby, and Eduardo, five and beginning to find his feet ... in a playful sort of way.' She smiled with the fondness of her memories. They had been lovely children and she had loved them. 'One of Eduardo's favourite games is ... er was,' she grimaced at her own slip of the tongue; it seemed incredible to her that she would never see the boys again, 'hide and seek. The villa is very large and old and has many staircases, corridors and rooms, a bit like a rabbit warren. That morning,' she continued, knowing there was no need to specify which morning. 'Eduardo was up to his usual tricks. He ran away from me while we were out in the garden. At first I could not find him. Then I noticed a small open window. It was on the stairway leading down to the cellars and the office where *Señor* Font conducted all his business. The garden in front of the window had been recently watered and I could see Eduardo's small footprints going straight across. I didn't know what to do. We were not supposed to go anywhere near *Señor* Font's office when he was working but I was worried for Eduardo's safety. I guessed he would have gone to hide in the wine cellars. It's dark and he could have been hurt.' Rhea paused, taking a breath as the memories came flooding back, bringing pain.

'I decided I had to go after him,' she began once more, then hesitated again. If only she had gone round the villa and in through the door none of this would have happened. But she had feared doing that would have got Eduardo into trouble. To spare the boy a telling-off she had squeezed through the window and crept down the old stone stairway. 'I had to pass the door of the office before I could get to the cellars. Unfortunately the door was open and I stopped. I wasn't doing it to listen, just to wait my moment to dart past,' she quickly added before Jay condemned her for her stupidity. 'There were two men with *Señor* Font and one was pacing the floor in thought and would have seen me ... did see me,' she corrected with a sigh, looking out over the sea to a group of fishing boats, all the regrets of her foolish actions mirrored in her green eyes.

'Did you hear any of what they were saying?' Jay questioned calmly.

'Yes,' Rhea nodded her head, wishing she had not.

'Tell me,' Jay urged when Rhea remained silent, his voice hardening as he repeated the request.

Rhea looked unsure. 'Why?' she asked. Why should Jay want to know? It was the actions of the men that were more important to Rhea, not their conversation.

'In order to keep you safe I need to know everything,' Jay pointed out, his voice once more calm and gentle.

'There was an Englishman,' she began, not totally convinced she was doing the right thing. 'I don't know who he was. He could speak fluent Spanish but his accent was clearly English. He was the first I heard and he said "Everything has been taken care of ... There's nothing to worry about ... The new warehouse is fully operational", or something like that,' she added with a shrug. She had not taken too much notice of what they had been saying.

'Then *Señor* Font mentioned a name, something like "Karam", and the Englishman replied "A convenient accident." Rhea remembered that part clearly; the implication of the words had not been lost on her and she recalled how a shiver of horror had trickled down her arms. The same happened now and she looked anxiously at Jay, one part of her wanting him to tell her she had got it wrong, the other part knowing he could not because she had not got it wrong. The words had only one meaning.

'I can't remember everything after that. There was some joke about the new warehouse being so watertight it was beneath a lake. Something about polythene bags with holes in.' Rhea scraped her fingers through her hair, trying to remember. 'No ... I can't remember anymore.'

Jay nodded sagely and Rhea frowned. He seemed to have understood more than she, who had actually been there.

'Then what happened?' Jay prompted.

Rhea gave an eloquent shrug. 'That is when I was seen. The man who had been walking the floor spotted me standing there.' Coldness rippled over her skin along with the memory.

'What did he do?' Jay queried, with a lack of emotion that made Rhea want to scream at him. How could he act so calm and unconcerned when she was burning up inside with the recalled terror of it all?

She ran her fingers through her hair once more. 'He pulled a gun from his pocket and lunged for the door.' Her voice was jerky, disjointed, her mind's eye seeing once again the moment when the dull grey metal object had slid from beneath the man's lapel.

'And what did you do?' Jay asked gently.

Rhea looked incredulous. What did he think she had done? Hung around for the party?

'I turned and ran,' she half spoke, half gasped. 'I didn't think about what I was doing. I couldn't think. I just did ... acted on instinct. And my instinct was to get out of there,' she concluded heatedly, directing her unfulfilled anger at Jay.

'You know the rest,' she finally added, calmly, all emotion washed away to leave a strange emptiness. She was glad it was over, that she had finally told someone. But she did not exactly feel the cleansing of the spirit she had expected, now that her burden had been lightened by pushing a small part of it on to Jay Rutherford's more than adequate shoulders.

Then, quite unexpectedly, all the tensions, fears and frustrations of the past few days erupted in noisy sobs. Rhea broke down in tears.

Jay was quickly by her side. He pulled her into his arms, held her there. 'Let it out,' he coaxed. 'Let it all come out.' He rocked her gently against the warmth of his large body, her head rested against his chest.The rhythmic beat of his heart pulsed close to her ear, soothing away all her fearful memories.

Rhea felt so safe, so protected by him and she lifted one hand, placing her open palm over his heart and pledging her gratitude to the fates that had sent Jay to her in her hour of need. But then she looked up, her eyes following her hand and she could see the caricature of a fierce wild-eyed eagle where her head had rested, its open wings and long talons, spreading from beneath her hand, ready to pounce on any unsuspecting prey.

Rhea removed her hand, slowly pulled away from him. She had been forced into a position of having to put her trust in Jay but she must not forget what he was. Despite having become unexpectedly reliant on him, she must not forget that he was perhaps a petty crook.

The following morning Rhea woke early and found to her surprise that Jay was sleeping on the bunk opposite. He was more accustomed to spending the night out on the deck.

He looked so peaceful and Rhea quietly watched him. Once more the question 'What is he?' leaped into her mind. This time an answer came, one Rhea was not sure she wanted to hear. *The man she was becoming more and more attached to!*

No, she denied. It was only the situation. Jay had

saved her life and it was only natural she should feel gratitude towards him. It was nothing more.

A smile pulled at Rhea's lips as she imagined Aunt Maeve's reaction if she turned up on the doorstep with a man with a tattoo and shoulder-length hair.

No, it was nothing more than gratitude, she reaffirmed, and got up and began to make breakfast.

'We're running out of food,' Rhea announced as they sat on the deck in the morning sun, eating the cheese omelettes she had prepared.

'I have to go ashore today,' Jay replied, taking Rhea by surprise. 'I'll bring some back.'

Rhea did not like the implications of Jay leaving the boat, leaving her alone.

'Alone?' she questioned, just to make sure she had got her facts right. 'Can't I come with you?'

'No.' Jay chewed thoughtfully on a piece of omelette for a moment. 'It wouldn't be wise. You'll be safe here.'

Rhea wanted to object. She knew that in time she would, although not forget, be able to live with and come to terms with what had happened to her. But at the moment she still felt she needed Jay around to make her feel safe.

Keep hold! she instructed herself firmly. It was humiliating to feel so helpless and dependent. Pushing her cowardice aside, she asked calmly, 'Why do you have to go ashore?' and put her plate down on the deck, the half-finished omelette suddenly unpalatable.

'Work,' was Jay's brief reply.

'Work?' Rhea questioned. 'You said the boat was your work. How can you have anything to do on shore?'

Jay finished the last bit of omelette before proffering a reply. 'My main source of income is from the boat. But I do other things. And, as my main source of income is tied up at the moment,' he added pointedly, pausing just long enough for Rhea to feel the heat of embarrassment creep up her cheeks, 'I need the job because I need the money.'

Shame engulfed Rhea. For so long she had wallowed in the luxurious lifestyle of the Fonts that she had forgotten ordinary people had to work for a living. Not only was she putting Jay at risk by being there with him, she was also interfering with his livelihood.

'What is this job?' she asked, anxious to know it was not something illegal.

'Bit of car maintenance. Oil change etc. You will be perfectly all right for the couple of hours I'll be away.'

This time Rhea agreed with him, outwardly if not inwardly. She did not want to be left alone, but the sooner she got used to being less reliant on Jay the better for them both.

Even so it was with increasing unease that Rhea watched Jay preparing to leave.

'Carry on as if I was here,' Jay instructed as he fetched the oars from over by the cabin wall. 'Do a bit of sunbathing. Walk round the deck.' He dropped the oars over the side into the dinghy, then turned back to Rhea. 'Make the boat look lived-in rather than looking as if you're trying to hide away. But don't put your own clothes back on,' he warned, looking at her for a long, steady moment.

'Aye, aye, Captain,' she joked, trying to lighten her own mood.

Jay smiled. 'You'll be all right, kid,' he said and to Rhea's humiliation stepped forward and gave the hair on the top of her head a fond, paternal ruffle. 'I'll be back before you know I've gone,' he promised. Then he dropped his holdall over the side and followed it into the swaying dinghy.

'Try and catch some fish to supplement the larder,' Jay called the final instruction as he began to row away.

'Aye, aye, Captain.' This time Rhea added a mocking salute to the gibe which made Jay laugh as he moved quickly across the water.

Rhea watched until Jay had reached the shore, the fatherly farewell she had just received grating on her womanly senses. He was not that much older than she was. There had been no need to pat her on the head and call her 'kid'!

It did not take Rhea long to catch five sardines: three large ones for Jay and two smaller for herself. She washed them and put them in the small refrigerator. Then she went to put the fishing tackle away.

Despite the boat looking so unkempt and grubby, Rhea marvelled at the way Jay had a place for everything. It all looked such a mess, but move anything or fail to replace something in its proper place and Jay complained.

At that moment it was a habit which Rhea found annoying. The fishing rod had to be threaded behind several cans of engine fuel and propped against the cabin wall. There were quite a number of cans and where Jay's height would have allowed him easy access, Rhea's small frame was having to stretch to its limits.

Just then two home-bound fishing boats went by. The swell they produced caused the *Rosy Rita* to rock and roll, almost sending Rhea crashing face first into the fuel cans.

She grabbed with one hand for the cabin wall to steady herself. The other hand tried the same, but she was still holding the fishing rod and the action smashed the rod into the cabin wall and jabbed it down hard against the deck.

Oh heavens! She had the awful suspicion that she had broken the rod. Her heart was in her mouth as she regained her balance on the still-unsteady deck.

A quick check proved the rod still intact, although the bottom was fast, stuck on something on the deck behind the cans. Rhea tried to work it free but it would not budge. The fuel cans were hindering her progress so, grumbling to herself, she lifted them away to find the end of the rod had gone through a hole in the deck. At least Rhea hoped the hole had been there before and she had not just made it.

Rhea got a better purchase and carefully, so as not to snap the slender shank, she pulled and wriggled until, with a jolt, it finally came free.

But Rhea's victory was short-lived. The end of the rod was still encased in wood. A piece of the deck timber had come away with it.

'Oh no!' she gasped. Jay was just going to love her for breaking his boat. Despondency growing, Rhea prised the rod free. She looked at the piece of wood in her hand. It seemed clean-cut, she realized, brightening, as if she had removed a whole part, rather than broken any off.

Quickly she kneeled down and studied the hole. Her spirits rose. The hole was also clean-cut. She could fit the piece back and Jay would be none the wiser.

A couple of oily pipes ran beneath the hole and there was an old rag protruding out of the side of the hole. Rhea tried to fit the rag flat so that the top would fit back neatly. The rag sprang up again and Rhea tried again. Again it sprang up. So, aiming to give herself just enough material to tuck around the pipes to hold it down, Rhea pulled carefully on the rag.

But the action caused the rag to move more than Rhea had intended. With the clunk of a heavy object, the bottom of the cloth rolled open.

In the next instant Rhea's hand leaped away as if burnt. It flew to her mouth, catching the gasp which rushed from her throat. A hot, sick feeling expanded deep inside her.

Concealed, in what Rhea had imagined to be nothing more than an oily rag, was a large bundle of bank notes ... and a gun!

Three

It was early evening by the time Jay returned. The 'couple of hours' he was to be away had turned into seven and Rhea was so concerned for his safety that the fright experienced on finding the gun had been pushed aside.

She should leave, she told herself, make an escape while Jay was out of the way. For whatever Jay was doing on shore, Rhea could be sure of one thing ... no car was being attended by his hands!

But despite her sensible reasonings, some indescribable emotion made her fear for Jay. Despite everything she wanted to see him safe, needed to see he was safe. So she waited and worried, willing the black and orange dinghy to appear, begging for Jay's safe return. A safe return which, in the moment of its realization, turned her legs to jelly and the blood in her veins to liquid fire.

First Jay handed over two boxes lying in the bottom of the dinghy. He did not speak and Rhea matched him, praying the tell-tale tremble in her hands was not obvious to Jay.

'Get the car finished?' she enquired as Jay finally boarded the *Rosy Rita*, the tautness of distrust in her voice.

'Yes,' Jay replied dismissively. But the slight pause before speaking and the long moment of interested eye contact told Rhea her manner had not gone unnoticed.

'Have you been all right?' Jay asked, changing the subject.

'Yes,' Rhea lied. The concern in his voice had been so genuine and she held her tongue against blurting out the truth of her find.

'I couldn't help being longer than planned. I got a few problems,' Jay continued.

'With the car?' Rhea questioned, cynicism returning with the reminder of the lie he was playing out.

'Yes.' He turned away and began to secure the dinghy rope to the cruiser's rail.

Rhea looked at his hands and grimaced inwardly. They were not perfectly clean, but there was no sign of oil or grease, the accoutrements of car engines. Neither did the khaki shorts or green tee-shirt bear any evidence of having had greasy hands wiped down them.

He could have worn overalls, a small voice somewhere at the back of Rhea's mind tried to insist. But it was a very weak voice.

'*Have* you been all right?' Jay repeated suspiciously, turning to pick up one of the boxes filled with food.

'Yes, fine,' Rhea replied to his retreating back with a sigh of resignation, as he carried the box into the cabin, giving her the distinct impression he was making himself busy because he did not want to get involved in a lengthy discussion.

Rhea picked up the second box. 'How long do you intend keeping me here?' she queried, struggling down the steps with the heavy box, so full it seemed they now had enough food for a couple of months.

Jay shot her a sceptical look. 'Until it is safe for you to leave,' he replied, and returned to stacking the empty cupboards with the fresh supplies.

'And *just* when might that be?' Rhea dropped the box down on the table, infuriated by his dismissive attitude.

Jay stopped what he was doing, turned to her, hands on hips. 'The sooner the better,' he returned, making it quite obvious he would be as pleased as Rhea when that day came. 'I'm not keeping you here for my benefit. I have plenty to do without having to act as nursemaid.'

'Then why don't we make it right now?' Rhea lifted her chin defiantly. He did not want her here. She didn't want to be here. So why prolong the agony?

'Because Font's men are all over the place,' Jay enlightened her simply.

Rhea looked uncertain. Was he telling the truth? How could she believe anything he said ... after finding the gun? She really could not believe Sebastian Font still had a posse on the look-out for her. Naturally some of the men would be about, they lived in the area. But she felt it was now time to take her chances. Staying with Jay Rutherford was beginning to appear to be of equal danger.

Stuffing the provisions from her box into the cupboard with indecent haste, Rhea made up her mind. Jay could take her back to shore tonight, under cover of darkness.

The last can safely stored, Rhea turned to Jay. 'I want to leave,' she insisted, gaining a confidence she was far from feeling.

Jay was silent for a long moment. Rhea lifted her chin, her eyes glaring in defiance of the refusal she could see building behind his rigid stare.

'It is ridiculous just sitting here waiting,' she continued. 'You have made it obvious you don't want me here and you said yourself they would not have expected me to stay here. So it should be safe for me to go back into town now.'

'And just where do you intend to go?' The timbre of Jay's voice showed clearly what he thought of the silly demand.

But Rhea's idea that she would get herself back home ... how she did not know ... then go to the nanny agency which had found her the position with the Fonts and find another job in another country – America or some other place that was miles away from Spain – seemed so contrived, even to herself, that she hesitated a moment too long before speaking.

'You haven't got any idea, have you?' Jay blasted, the unexpectedness of his fury taking Rhea aback so much that words failed her.

Jay found no such difficulty with his own words. 'You little fool,' he blazed. 'The moment you set foot on that land,' his head jerked stiffly to indicate the direction of his words, 'the jungle tom-toms will leap into action. Font has the entire Costa del Sol sewn-up. You won't have to wait until one of his thugs finds you. He has contacts all over the place, every strategic point. The airport, hotels, bars ... you name it, there will be at least one seemingly bona fide employee who is also in Font's pocket, earning a nice little backhander for informing him of anything or *anyone*,' he stressed to make his point clear to the incredulous Rhea, 'who they think he might be interested in. So for now you are going nowhere!'

'Don't be ridiculous,' Rhea spat. He was trying to frighten her and she would have none of it. She began to wonder if she was his hostage, rather than he her saviour?

'You have no right to keep me here against my will,' she declared hotly, anger at her own frightening thoughts spurring her on. She stepped forward, glared determinedly into his eyes. 'I will not stay here,' she hissed through tight lips. 'You cannot make me.'

'Now listen to me,' Jay ground through equally tight lips, his eyes burning into her with hypnotic fire. 'You are not leaving this boat until I say you can. I have stuck my neck out for you. It would have been far easier for me to have kept my nose out and looked the other way. But I chose not to do that because I cared what happened to you. I don't like to see great bullies picking on people smaller than themselves. And I still care enough to have no intention of watching you throw everything away by going back before *I* think it is safe for you to do so.'

Rhea's mind clung to the word 'care'. Did it mean Jay cared for her? Oh how she wished! No, stop it, she ordered herself. Jay was a crook, a criminal ... the gun proved it ... and she must not forget it.

She covered her face with her hands, wishing, wishing, wishing. But how could she care for a man of Jay's type? Slowly she dropped her hands, all anger gone, just a deep sadness left behind.

'I had a slight accident today,' she began, turning from him, unable to look in his face as she spoke the words. 'The fishing rod got stuck in a piece of the deck. I pulled it out.' She hesitated, unsure how to speak the rest. 'I found the gun,' she suddenly blurted out.

The silence stretched to eternity. Rhea waited, praying Jay to give some reasonable explanation for needing a weapon. She began to wonder if she had just done a rather stupid thing ... letting Jay know she knew about the gun could prove fatal if, after all, he was keeping her hostage for some underhand reason.

When Jay moved, it was with unexpected gentleness that he pulled her into his arms. 'Look, love, the men we are dealing with will stop at nothing. The gun is there for our defence only. I would never use it without good reason.'

Rhea looked up into his eyes, wanting, needing, ready to believe his every word. 'I'm sorry,' she murmured. 'Sorry for mistrusting you. Sorry for doubting you. Sorry for being there and causing you so many problems. I'll never forget what you have done for me and I'll always be grateful, even if I don't always show it,' she added, looking sheepish.

Jay smiled. 'There's no need for gratitude. It's been a pleasure ... even if *I* don't always show it.' His smile turned to a grin. 'I wouldn't have missed it for the world.' Slowly his head descended.

Rhea knew he was going to kiss her before their lips touched and she was ready, allowing his mouth to meet her own with no resistance. It was sweet, gentle, loving.

Rhea felt her mind soaring on the softest cloud of warm air, high into the heavens where she had never been before.

'Oh, Jay,' she murmured, resting her head against his shoulder. 'Why can't we go right away from here, somewhere they will never find us, and forget all about Sebastian Font and everything connected to him?'

'We will, love, one day. When it's safer. It won't be much longer now.'

Rhea looked up, savouring the word 'love', as a shadow crossed Jay's face. 'What's wrong?' she questioned uncertainly as he moved back, releasing her from his arms.

'I'm sorry, Rhea. I should not have kissed you.'

'Why?' Rhea was too stunned to say more.

'I am old enough to know better,' he replied, stunning Rhea further.

'Don't be silly,' she gasped. How old could he be? 'You can't be much more than thirty!'

'Thirty-three,' he responded sombrely.

'So ... ? That's only ...'

'Twelve years older than you,' he pointed out before Rhea could do her sums. 'It's too much, Rhea, and this situation is not allowing you to think straight. You might do something you would regret later and I would not want that on my conscience.'

'I'm old enough to know my own mind,' Rhea asserted, bristling at the accusation that she was not capable of handling her own feelings.

But Jay would not be moved. 'I'll do the fish with a salad,' he informed her bluntly. Then turned to thread his large form through the low door and vanished into the cabin.

How could he think of food at a moment like this? she wondered, staring at the empty doorway, lost in the dejection of his dismissive manner.

Rhea did not venture into the cabin until Jay called that the meal was ready. She sat on the deck and nursed her bruised ego. She was angry with Jay, but she was more angry with herself for allowing the intimacy to take place. After all she hardly knew him and she had not only allowed it to take place, but been a willing partner in the action. But she *had* wanted him to kiss her and the reality had been just as enjoyable as she had imagined it would be. Unfortunately the kiss had not held the same magic for Jay ... or he could not have acted the way he had.

The meal was conducted in silence. Rhea picked at the two sardines on her plate, breaking them up so that it looked as if she had eaten more than she really had. She noticed, sadly, that Jay was having no such problems with his digestive system. He had soon polished off his full plate along with two large hunks of bread and cheese.

'Why do you wear your hair long?' Rhea finally asked, unable to stand the silence a moment longer and leaping on the first safe subject that came into her head.

'Because I like it,' Jay replied, watching her carefully, as he asked, 'Why, don't you like it?'

Rhea shrugged. 'It isn't very masculine,' she replied, realizing as she spoke that it had been a foolish statement to make. Hair or no hair, Jay Rutherford was one of the most masculine men she had ever met.

Jay grinned crookedly. 'What about the tattoo?'

Rhea shrugged once more. She had always felt that men who found it necessary to sport tattoos were trying to prove something. Yet she could not see how Jay fitted into that category. 'If you like that sort of thing it's none of my business,' she said, thinking it better not to put another slur on his manhood.

'Exactly,' Jay emphasized. 'You do not like my hair or the tattoo. I am not the sort of man you would look twice at if we met on a busy street. Yet if I walked around the table and kissed you, you would put up no objections.'

'Just you come and try it!' Rhea warned, his arrogance fuelling her anger. Just who did he think he was?

'I'm not trying to insult you, Rhea,' Jay pointed out kindly. 'I just want you to see the situation for what it is. You don't know me, Rhea. You know nothing about where I come from, what I do. Fate has thrown us together for the time being. But it won't be long before we are parting, probably never to see each other again.'

Rhea's chest tightened at the thought. Never to see Jay again! It was too painful to consider. But consider it she must. Knowing nothing about Jay did not matter. She just knew that her feelings were something more than gratitude for a safe port in a storm. But unfortunately Jay did not return those feelings. She was no more than a friend to him ... perhaps not even that, she unwillingly accepted. 'I'll try to behave myself in the future,' she joked in self-reproach, to hide her real emotions.

'I promise to do the same,' Jay returned, getting up from the table and moving down the cabin before Rhea could see the forced grin slip from his face.

Reaching the bunks, Jay hooked up the makeshift screen he had erected for Rhea to dress behind and informed her he was going to go swimming.

The lack of a swimsuit was the only reason Rhea did not follow Jay out on to the deck. A swim in the cool evening sea would have done wonders to perk up her flagging morale. So she stayed behind and did the washing up before venturing out.

It was that brief interlude when the sun had vanished below the horizon but the night sky was not yet fully born, when everything looked grey and the line between heaven and earth was barely discernible.

Rhea struggled in the lack of light to find Jay. His blond head was not easily picked out in the dull water. But she finally spied him, swimming strongly out towards the shore. She sat down to watch him, hoping he was planning on returning and not thinking of making a quick exit.

Her emotions were on the boil. She wondered how she could be so sure of the feelings that were growing for Jay. She tried to tell herself there could be no future with a man like him, a pirate, a gypsy of a man who would move his boat and live wherever he happened to fancy at that moment.

Just then Rhea's silent contemplation was interrupted by the roar of a noisy engine. Rhea turned to see an expensive speedboat roaring towards land. She watched it for a long moment as it skimmed across the water, kicking up a frantic shower of silver spray. Then terror struck!

Rhea's head spun round, back to where Jay was swimming. His arms carved the water, head down, quite oblivious to the approaching danger. She spun back to the boat flying across the water with rapid speed. Right on course for Jay.

For an instant her mind spiralled. She jumped up. She had to stop the boat, make them change direction. In the next moment she was standing one foot on the side bench, the other resting precipitously on the side of the *Rosy Rita*'s hull, Jay's safety the one and only thought filling her mind.

Rhea waved her arms madly. She shouted. She screamed. She did everything she could think of to attract the attention of the two young men in the expensive boat.

But the men only waved back, laughing and calling out jokingly as they sped past the *Rosy Rita*.

'No!' Rhea screamed, terror for Jay throbbing through every part of her body. The next instant the speedboat's bow wave hit the *Rosy Rita* with a mighty thud. The boat heaved, her bow diving low in the water. Before Rhea knew what was happening, she was tossed high in the air, performing a perfect full roll before hitting the water with a breath-stopping crash.

Under normal circumstances Rhea was a reasonable swimmer. But with the shock of the unexpected entry into the water draining her senses, plus Jay's overlarge tee-shirt becoming waterlogged, stretching out of all proportion until it wrapped around her legs in a tangled swathe, making movement increasingly more difficult, she found getting back to the boat not as easy as expected.

Her arms struck out at the water, but the more she struggled the further away the boat seemed to be getting. On and on she tried, until her arms ached, becoming like lead. She had to make it, she ordered herself. It was ridiculous. The hull was only a few feet away, the anchor-line even nearer.

Jay's tee-shirt and shorts became heavier and heavier, the sodden weight dragging her down. The water seemed to be rising, inching its way into her ears, her mouth, nose and eyes.

She tried to scream but water filled her mouth, cutting off her breath. She began to sink. Realization returned and she grasped for the air, popping the surface like a cork from a bottle. She gasped in relief, taking a large gulp of fresh air and struggling for the boat once more.

Once again the water claimed her strength and her body began to submerge. Her legs kicked and her hands clawed savagely at the water, willing herself to find the strength needed.

With one final pull her hand reached out, her fingers closing around the anchor line. The second hand reached out and she heaved herself upwards. But the strain on her weakened body proved too much. Her head spun dizzily. Unconsciousness claimed her senses and, unable to stop them, her hands slipped slowly down the taut metal line. The sound of the water filled her ears and, realizing this was her last chance, she found from somewhere the strength to scream out, '*Jay!*'

Four

The next moment Rhea thought her end really had come. She was grabbed around the waist from behind and, visions of a giant octopus entering her terrified mind, she struggled, finding strength in fear.

It took a while before Jay's insistent voice broke through the misty dread of her mind.

'Stop it, Rhea. You'll get us both drowned,' he insisted, the urgency of his voice telling Rhea it had not been the first time he had spoken.

She stopped fighting. 'Jay?' she questioned, disbelief in her voice as she craned her neck round to see him. Her head spun with the action, but a wave of relief swept over her weary body and she willingly relaxed, falling into the protection of his arms.

'Oh, Jay,' she murmured feelingly, her relief doubling in the knowledge that he was also safe. She felt like crying but knew this was neither the time nor the place. She hoped he had enough strength left to get them both back to the boat.

Jay had no such reservations. He pulled Rhea round, took a firm hold on her and began to drag her towards the boat. She kicked her legs and moved her arms, attempting to help even though she was not totally sure where her limbs were going.

'Keep still,' Jay ordered. 'Just let yourself float.'

His tone clearly told Rhea she was being more of a hindrance than a help and so she obliged, becoming still, feeling herself being pulled through the water with a speed that belied her previous anxiety over Jay's own state of fitness after such a long swimming session.

Jay took her round the side of the hull. 'Hold on to this,' he instructed, fastening her arms around one of the old rubber tyres that hung over the side. He clamped his hand over Rhea's for a long moment to ensure her grip, while his other arm remained around her body in support.

'Can you hold on?' he asked. He looked worriedly into her face, not taking his hand away from her life-saving grip. 'You only have to hold on for a minute ... Sure you'll be all right?' The uncertainty of his expression extended to his voice and Rhea attempted a smile of reassurance. But it came out all wrong.

'I'll be all right now,' she replied. But the anxiety on Jay's face told her she had not been very convincing.

Slowly he removed his hold on her, then hesitated a moment, obviously expecting her to sink.

'Don't move an inch,' he warned, making Rhea grimace. Where did he think she was going? For another long moment he watched her, assessing her capability of doing as he had instructed. 'If you feel yourself slipping, shout.' With the final instruction he turned, grabbed a rope hanging down the side of the steep hull and, with the speed and agility of a chimpanzee, climbed up the side and was back on the *Rosy Rita*'s deck.

He remained there for only a minute. Grabbing a life-jacket he dived back into the sea, his arms reaching around Rhea before she had time to realize what was happening. Jay had the life-jacket over Rhea's head and fastened inside a minute. It had a lifeline attached and he wound it round his wrist.

Rhea's head began to revolve once more, her senses spinning in the relief of feeling the life-jacket supporting her, and the knowledge that she was securely attached to Jay. She was only half-aware of Jay leaving her in the water to climb up the rope once more, only half-aware of being lifted and bumping against the hull as Jay used the strong nylon line to haul her up the side and on to the deck.

But she was aware of the flood of gratitude towards Jay for saving her life. Attempting to express that gratitude, she tried to stand up on her shaking legs. Her knees buckled beneath her weight and her head bounced in unison with the *Rosy Rita*'s rolling deck and she gave up the struggle for consciousness, falling into Jay's readily outstretched arms.

Slowly Rhea opened her eyes. A blanket of blackness hung above her, filled with tiny dancing lights.

Why were the stars moving ? she wondered groggily. Her senses slowly returned. She looked around, moving her head carefully, recalling the instability of earlier. She was lying on the *Rosy Rita*'s deck. She blinked, opened her eyes wide as her confused gaze focused on a head of long blond hair, a silvery glow radiating all around it.

Did all the angels have Jay's face? she wondered. She stared at him blankly for a long, silent moment.

'Rhea!' A breathless voice echoed in her dulled mind. 'Come on, Rhea ... Wake up, sweetheart. Wake up!'

A hand touched her face, brushed her cheek so gently, so fondly. Rhea blinked again. 'Jay?' she questioned, unable to believe the caring voice and loving actions. She thought there were tears on his cheeks, then came to realize they were only drops of water. He was wet all over from the sea, just as she was. She shivered both from the frightening memory and from the sudden awareness of her wet clothing.

'That's one to be put down to experience,' she quipped, failing to find the dry humour she had intended. She carefully eased herself up on to her elbows, lifted a hand to her slowly clearing head and watched the rapid rise and fall of the eagle on Jay's chest giving evidence of the exertion of getting her inert body back on board. Then she looked up, her eyes resting on his hair.

Rhea had never seen Jay's hair hanging loose before, free of the rubber band that created the long ponytail. It was hanging like a veil of golden satin around his shoulders and giving off a strange aura of light around his head. He really did look like an angel with a heavenly glow. Rhea's confusion increased, planting a frown on her face.

The reaction put a smile on Jay's face and, obviously relieved with her return to the land of the living, he sat back on his heels. The movement revealed his silver halo had been nothing more than the brightness of the deck light's glow, hidden behind his head of angelic hair.

Rhea wanted to laugh. But she had the feeling that if she gave way to any emotion she would end in tears.

'I thought you were going to be killed,' she said, reliving the horrific moments of watching the speedboat closing in on Jay.

'You were the one in danger,' Jay pointed out, a frown of incomprehension wrinkling his brow. He looked intently into her wide-eyed stare, as they were both overwhelmed with the shared knowledge that things could have turned out very differently and this moment might never have been shared.

The mental pain of his thoughts flickered over Jay's face. He pulled Rhea into his arms, held her tightly, as if to let her go would be to lose her. The persistent beat of his heart thumped in her ear as his chest lifted and dropped against her cheek. A small tight smile found its way to Rhea's lips. She was safe and protected. Safe with Jay. Protected by his embrace. She wrapped her arms around his neck and tears filled her eyes.

Why couldn't she have met Jay in better circumstances? she asked herself. Yet she knew that Jay was right when he had said that, had fate not thrown them together, she would not have looked at him twice.

Burying her face in his damp chest, Rhea allowed her emotion to surface.

'It's all right,' Jay murmured reassuringly. 'It's all over.' He rocked her in his arms as if she were a small child. His hand stroked her hair, caressing away all the hurt and confusion she was finding such difficulty dealing with.

Jay continued to hold her until both her body and mind were in a state of relaxation.

It was not until Rhea began to shiver from the cold that Jay slowly released her. He lifted her to her feet and helped her into the cabin, then left her there to change into a fresh pair of shorts and tee-shirt he provided.

At first Rhea thought Jay must have gone swimming again and a moment of panic filled her as she scanned the inky black water.

Then she saw him; his almost invisible outline as he sat silently in the darkness at the boat's bow. His long pale hair, picked out by the dim glow of the single mooring light, once more gave his head a ghostly effect, a celestial candescence. Rhea smiled, recalling how he had looked when she had first regained consciousness ... like a guardian angel!

Jay did not turn and for a time Rhea silently watched him. She wondered what manner of fate could turn out to be so blessed, yet so wretched at the same time. Rhea's blessings had been a hundredfold when Jay had stepped out at her, rescuing her from Font's men. She dared not think where she might now be if Jay had not been there. Her knight in shining armour!

Stuffing her hands into her oversized pockets she moved down the deck.

'Thanks,' she said self-consciously, 'for ... for saving my life.' For the second time, she added silently, realizing how much she was beholden to Jay.

Jay turned as if only just becoming aware she was with him. For a long moment he stared into her face, the solemnity of his expression exaggerated by the shadow of the night.

'Are you all right?' he asked, taut concern in his voice.

'Yes,' Rhea replied humbly.

'Whatever possessed you? You could have been killed,' Jay insisted, raking his fingers through his damp hair in evidence of the strength of his emotion. 'If I had not heard ... If I had not seen ... '

'I thought the speedboat was going to hit you,' Rhea quickly put in, eyeing him curiously. He thought she had gone into the water by her own choice, she realized, cringing mentally from the idea that he thought her stupid enough to go swimming fully clothed.

'I was trying to get their attention,' she added flatly. 'Make them change direction.' Her voice diminished. Once more her own *naïveté* had led her to do the wrong thing. She stared out across the black sea, half wishing she had drowned. It would, at least, have got her out of Jay's hair.

Jay moved so quickly that his large presence, suddenly right before her, startled Rhea. She took an involuntary step backwards, stunned when he reached out and took hold of her arms. His eyes, clouded with concern, looked deep into her own.

'You got thrown in?' he questioned anxiously, incredulously.

Rhea nodded. 'I stood on the side and when the speedboat's bow wave hit I got tossed overboard.' She gave an ironic smile. Just as it would seem she had been tossed overboard when it came to Jay Rutherford himself.

'You could have been killed!' The emotion of his words were in the arms that reached around her.

He held her tightly, pressing her to the protective warmth of his body.

Rhea looked up uncertainly. Emotion spilled from his gaze and a tremble rippled over her skin. Pulling her hands free she rested them on his shoulders, looking into his eyes, an invitation on her lips: an invitation Jay could not resist. He kissed her slowly, lovingly. The kiss deepened, all the fears of the evening adding power to their emotions. For the second time Rhea felt she was drowning. But this drowning was too sweet to be fought against.

But then, exactly the same as before, Jay ended the embrace. He cast Rhea away with a ferocious growl, much like the sound of a wounded animal.

Rhea looked stunned, unable to comprehend his sudden action. He turned away, clenched his fists and looked up at the star-filled sky as if seeking some greater guidance.

'What's wrong?' Rhea asked, numbed by his rejection.

'Go away, Rhea,' he growled.

But Rhea would not be so easily put off. Her feelings for Jay were too great to be put aside so lightly. She reached out to him. 'Jay ... ?' But she was given no time to complete her sentence.

'Go away!' he repeated. He would not look at her.

With increasing hurt, Rhea watched his fists fasten tightly around the cruiser's rail, her own hand dropping despondently to her side.

'It should never have happened. Go away and forget it did,' Jay ordered.

Forget! She could never forget! 'No!' she retaliated,

cut to the core by his unexpected volte-face. 'I knew what I was doing. It is *you* who seems to have the problem,' she taunted angrily, the rage of her hurt prodding her onwards.

'You don't know what you're talking about,' Jay returned, glancing cool dismissal over his shoulder. 'You're nothing but a kid,' he added crushingly.

Kid! Rhea wanted to scream. She reached out. This time she did take hold of his arm, pulling him sharply round. I am not a kid, she wanted to bellow. Instead she looked icily into his eyes. 'Look at me!' she instructed. 'I am a woman. And maybe if you looked more like a man you would see that for yourself.'

Jay shrugged her hand away. He turned to face her squarely, hands resting on his hips. His expression was grim, cool as the errant breeze that came suddenly from nowhere, whipped Rhea's hair across her face and tossed a single strand of Jay's long locks across his top lip, giving the impression of a long droopy moustache. At another time Rhea would have laughed.

'You don't know me, Rhea,' Jay insisted, swiping viciously at the wayward bit of hair.

Rhea pushed her own hair nervously behind her ear. 'Maybe I know enough,' she attempted to protest, but her voice was not convincing, even to herself.

'Leave it, Rhea. Go to bed,' Jay ordered, turning his back on her once more.

Go to bed! Sent packing as if she were a naughty three-year-old. But, Rhea dejectedly became aware, there was no point in staying to prolong the fight. Jay was immovable. There were times when he was so nice, so full of concern. And there were times when he was so cold and aloof that she had the distinct feeling he came from another planet.

'Good-night, Jay,' she tossed flippantly, turning to walk away with her head held high, refusing to allow him to see how much he was hurting her.

Throughout the night Rhea lay staring at the flaking wood on the panelled ceiling above her head. Sleep was a million miles away as she attempted to come to terms with the ebb and flow of her emotions, her feelings for Jay. The only time she closed her eyes was when she heard Jay coming down into the cabin. Then she feigned sleep, moaning softly and turning over as if in the deepest slumber, to hide her face from his view when she felt he was standing over her, looking down on her for what seemed like an eternity.

When she was alone again, Rhea rolled over on to her back, once more staring at the flaking wood. Her earlier irresponsibility returned to plague her. Humiliation rose hot and red in her cheeks. Never had she acted in such a shameless way, so forward, almost begging Jay to kiss her again.

The potentiality of Jay's influence over her was suddenly frightening and disturbing. Despite his present coolness, despite his making it quite clear he did not reciprocate her feelings, she had foolishly made it equally clear that she desired him.

Rhea did not know how, or when, but she did know she had to get away from Jay ... before it was too late.

At daybreak Rhea was no wiser as to how she was going to make her escape. Though Jay, himself, was soon to change that.

He had stayed out on the deck all night, leaving Rhea alone in her bunk. She was still there when he came half-way down the steps. Bending his head so he could see her without coming right into the cabin, he called, 'Are you awake?'

Rhea pushed up on her elbow and looked at him, but did not speak.

'I have to go ashore again. I'll be back around lunch-time,' he informed her. Then he turned and vanished before Rhea made any reply.

Jay was going, leaving her alone on the boat. Today Rhea did not object. This was her chance!

With a flash of inspiration she knew exactly what to do. Leaving the boat would mean she had to run the gauntlet of Sebastian Font and his men. But, despite Jay's theory that half of Spain would be on the look-out for her, Rhea was of the opinion that her ex-employer would no longer be looking for her in these parts. Had Jay not come to her rescue, she would have got as far away from Spain as possible, and Sebastian Font would be an idiot not to have had the same thoughts. He would assume she had got herself back to England by now and would not expect to find her walking around the Costa del Sol.

Convinced by her own reckoning, Rhea waited until she could hear the splash of the dinghy's oars carrying Jay away. Then she got up.

She went on deck and watched Jay until he had

reached the shore, moored the dinghy and gone off into the town.

When she was sure he had gone about his business and was not in a position to see the boat, she returned to the cabin. There she threw off Jay's clothes and dressed in her own red skirt and white blouse.

The next part she did not like. But if she was to succeed it had to be done. She hesitated only a moment. Then, searching out a pen and a scrap of paper, she quickly began to scribble:

'IOU £300.00. Signed Rhea Dempster.'

She stared at the paper in her hand. It seemed a lot of money to take. But she did not know how much she would need to get to the airport and she needed to have enough left for the plane fare when she got there.

With the note in her hand she hurried out on to the deck. Her heart was hammering a polka by the time she had cleared away the fuel cans and removed the loose bit of wood. She kept glancing over her shoulder, assuring herself that the orange and black dinghy was not coming back.

Lifting the bundle of notes very carefully, anxious not to touch the gun, she counted out fifteen twenty-pound notes. She stuck the IOU inside the roll and returned it to the secret compartment. Then she secured the wooden panel and replaced all the fuel cans. She wanted everything left just right, nothing to be seen that might give away Jay's valuable cache, should anyone come to the boat before Jay returned.

Casting aside the small voice that told her *she* had no

right to be taking Jay's money, she stuffed the folded notes into her blouse pocket.

The next part was not so straightforward. Rhea needed a boat to come by. Later in the day the sea would be filled with small craft, but it was still early morning and most of the tourists would be lingering over breakfast, if not still in bed.

For the second time that day fate smiled on Rhea. She had only been on deck for five minutes when a late home bound fishing boat came puttering along.

It looked to be in a worse state of dilapidation than Jay's cruiser. But Rhea did not mind. It only had to get her to the harbour.

She waved and called until the fishermen saw her and brought their boat alongside.

'Will you give me a lift?' Rhea asked in broken Spanish, adding a winning smile and a lot of arm waving gesticulations. She wanted to look and sound like a tourist.

The Spaniards were only too willing to help and Rhea was soon on board, standing amongst baskets of sardines, squid and crabs. Breathing a whole lot more easily, if not exactly inhaling rose-scented air, now she was actually on her way to dry land.

Rhea continued speaking to the men using snippets of Spanish, throwing in the odd English words and many vague hand signals. She was well aware that the locals, after seeing some of the idiotic things the holiday-makers got up to, viewed all tourists as slightly insane. They would think nothing strange in finding one such tourist had got herself stranded in the middle of the sea, as the many laughing asides, passed from one weatherbeaten face to another in quick-fire speech they assumed Rhea could not understand, only went to prove.

From the harbour Rhea went straight to the *cambio* to change her English pounds into Spanish pesetas. She had no time to waste. Now that she was on her way she wanted the journey over as soon as possible. In the safety of the boat she had been convinced Sebastian Font would no longer expect her to be in Spain. Now, feeling unprotected, vulnerable and very alone, she was having second thoughts, and felt the urgent need not to hang around for too long.

After visiting the *cambio* she purchased a red leather shoulder-bag to make her look more like any other homebound tourist at the airport, a purse to keep her money safe and a comb to make herself look half-respectable – all done with equal haste, her heart pounding every time she felt a pair of eyes looking her way.

Then she found a taxi to take her to the airport.

Feeling a little more secure in the confines of the car, she found her thoughts turning to Jay. She wondered just where he had gone to? What *job* he was doing at that moment? She still could not equate the Jay Rutherford who had rescued her in her hour of need with the Jay Rutherford who, it seemed, earned his money by being on the wrong side of the law. She sighed with the weight of her thoughts, hoping she could be wrong, wishing he could be simply someone who preferred to do his own thing rather than conform. But the amount of money he had seemed to disprove that theory.

As the taxi left the town, taking the road to Malaga, Rhea began to wish she had left a note for Jay. She had been too wrapped up in the need to succeed in getting away, and had not thought about letting Jay know she had left of her own accord. She hoped that when he returned to find her gone, he would not leap to the assumption that Sebastian Font's men had found her and taken her. Besides, it seemed very ungrateful just running away without saying thank you for all he had done for her.

The airport was crowded, bustling with people going in every direction. Rhea pushed through the crush of bodies crowding the doorway without a second thought, believing in safety in numbers. The end of her journey was in sight and she greeted it with both joy and sadness. She wanted more than anything to feel the safe English ground beneath her feet. But now that wish was coming to reality, she did not want to leave Jay.

With a sharp reprimand to end her thoughts there, Rhea looked along the line of reservation desks. She had to get a ticket on the first available plane and she had to sort out the lack of a passport and any identification ... the results of having had her handbag containing all her personal papers stolen, she felt was the most convincing and least damning explanation.

It was all neatly worked out inside her head. The art of deception, it seemed, came easily when one's own safety depended on it.

But the art of deception was not enough. Rhea was less than half-way across the crowded terminal.

'Hello, Rhea!' A hand rested on her arm and she was brought up short.

Rhea found herself looking into dark brown eyes glittering with cruel amusement. Her heart stopped. The breath in her lungs threatened to choke her. She could not believe they had still been watching out for her. Yet the reality was staring her in the face.

It was a number of seconds before she managed to speak. Then only a shaky, 'Carlo!'

She looked around in helpless desperation, though she was not sure what help she expected to find in the crowd of strangers all too busy with their own problems.

'*Señor* Font would like a word with you, Rhea,' Carlo informed her nastily.

'I won't go with you,' she retorted, attempting to pull her arm from his painful grip.

'Oh but you will, Rhea,' Carlo insisted, and to prove his point, his free hand pushed the metal butt of a pistol, concealed inside his pocket, into her ribs.

'You would not dare,' Rhea challenged, but even as she found the confident words her body froze. Suddenly she believed Carlo capable of anything. Sebastian Font wanted her out of the way and he would stop at nothing to get what he wanted.

It was the last thing in the world Rhea wanted to do but, with a gun pointing at her heart, she was powerless. Her only retaliation was the murderous glare she riveted to Carlo's darkly smirking features, as he 'escorted' her through the crowd and out into the Spanish sunshine.

As they stepped through the airport doors a car skidded to a halt right in front of them. Rhea was pushed into the back between two men. Carlo sat in the front passenger seat. For that Rhea was extremely grateful, having had no wish for Carlo's close proximity for the duration of the drive.

As they spun away from the airport, Rhea worried where Jay might be. She realized, sadly, that she had undone all his good work. All the planning and scheming to keep her out of sight, which he had worked out so expertly, she had thrown away within minutes of being let loose on her own.

They were in the hilly countryside, rushing past olive groves and *bodegas*, before Carlo turned round in his seat.

He gripped Rhea's chin cruelly, staring long and coldly into her face. 'Well, little Miss Perfect finally stepped out of line!'

Rhea glared at him icily. Carlo had a few old scores to settle. On many occasions she had rebuffed his advances.

'So, what have you got to say for yourself?' he taunted, dark eyes laughing at her discomfort.

Rhea deepened her glare to one of Medusan quality and jerked her chin from his grasp. It was too late to care for her own safety now. Whatever they were going to do to her, they would do to her. The sooner the better, was her only hope, as she spat into Carlo's face, 'Whatever I have to say will be said to *Señor* Font ... *Not* his poodle!'

Carlo would have hit her then. It was only Andreas, the driver, whose hand reacted far more quickly than Carlo's, that stopped the assault, knocking Carlo back against the passenger door before he could strike Rhea.

There followed a tirade of hot Spanish expletives, only brought to an end when Carlo's attention was caught by something through the back window.

'How long has that been there?' he asked.

'About two miles,' Andreas replied, and the two men on either side of Rhea turned to see what was following.

Rhea did not turn. There was no need. Whatever, or whoever was following was not coming to her aid. There was only Jay who would do that, and he had no idea where she might be, even if he realized she was no longer on the boat, which she doubted yet.

'Give it two more,' Carlo instructed.

The driver nodded and the car fell silent. Rhea shivered, suddenly apprehensive, wondering what they were planning to do.

When Carlo muttered something to the driver which Rhea did not catch, she could only assume the two miles must have been covered. She shivered again. Suddenly she was desperately frightened, not just for herself. The men were going to take action against some innocent person who just happened to be going the same way. They were mad, she realized, insanely playing with lives for no good reason. She turned around then. But as she did the car took a sharp bend and the road behind was lost to view.

Immediately the driver slewed the car sideways across the narrow road and stopped.

Rhea's heart leaped into her mouth. Ice crawled down her spine. The silence seemed interminable. Her breath stopped, she could not breathe, all she could do was sit and wait, wait until the mystery follower came round the corner and crashed into the waiting vehicle, or veered off the road and smashed into the rocky hillside. Inside she screamed. She was trapped with four deranged men and could do nothing about it.

But the terror Rhea had felt at that moment was nothing compared to the terror she was about to feel.

All in the space of an instant, far too quickly for Rhea to do anything other than scream out his name silently in inward horror, Jay's motorbike came hurtling round the rocky corner.

An ear-splitting screech of brakes and a cloud of smoke from burning rubber was followed by a mind-jarring clash of metal upon metal. Of their own volition, Rhea's terrified eyes lifted to the car's roof, automatically following the unseen course of Jay's body as, like a shot from a cannon, he was hurled bumping and banging right over the top of the vehicle. Then he hit the ground on the opposite side with the sickeningly dull thud of soft meeting hard.

The most mortifying silence Rhea had ever heard filled the long seconds that immediately followed.

Five

A groan shuddered from Jay's semi-conscious body. Rhea clenched her teeth, feeling his pain as if it were her own. She moved the second arm, lying it straight by his side. She was not sure she should be moving him at all. But the men had just dropped him in a heap and she wanted to make him more comfortable.

She knelt by his side, wishing she had more knowledge of first aid. Her heart was pounding and her hands trembled in fear of the possible extent of his injuries. There was a large gash on his temple, spilling blood down the side of his face and neck. One hand was badly cut and one ankle looked odd, crooked and out of place.

It was broken, Rhea unwillingly acknowledged, not wanting to believe it was true. If Jay was put out of action they had no chance. She looked around at the four stone walls of their prison, dark, dank, smelling of years of decay and neglect. With Jay fit or not, they had no chance of escape, she realized sadly. They could be left there forever and no one would find them.

'Oh! Why did you follow me?' she asked his inert form, guilt expanding within her. If she had not been so foolhardy as to run away none of this would have happened.

Jay groaned again, much louder than before. Rhea bent closer to him, hoping the sound heralded his return to a conscious state.

'Jay?' she questioned uncertainly.

Jay did not open his eyes. But he raised his hand to his injured head and grumbled eloquently.

Rhea smiled and thanked the heavens. Jay was back in the land of the living.

'Don't do that,' she warned, taking a firm hold on the hand that was probing none too gently and getting dangerously close to the open wound.

'Rhea?' Jay tried to pull his hand free, but Rhea held tight, needing the reassurance of his touch.

'I'm here,' she replied, also feeling a bursting need to reassure Jay, make him feel safe ... as safe as anyone could be made to feel in a prison dungeon.

Jay blinked. Then he blinked again and struggled to focus on the grey stones above his head. 'What happened? I can't see clearly. Is it night?'

'It's dark in here,' Rhea was quick to reassure him, praying that it was only the dim light that was hindering his sight. 'All the windows are shuttered,' she explained. The narrow windows running around the top of the high walls were too narrow to let any real light in, even if they had not been covered by heavy wooden shutters.

Jay peered into her face, concern on his own. 'Are you all right?'

'Yes,' Rhea nodded, smiling her relief that his questions were sensible, his voice free of any drunken slur that would indicate concussion, his mind alert enough to worry about her well-being. 'There's nothing wrong with me,' she assured him. 'How do you feel?'

'As if I had an argument with a double-decker bus ... and the bus won.' He pulled his hand free of Rhea's then and tried to sit up.

'I don't think much of the central heating,' he joked drily, giving up the painful struggle to sit upright and being content to rest back on his elbows, though Rhea could see even that was causing him discomfort. 'It's cold enough for snow down here.'

'Don't try to move any more,' Rhea warned, fearing that extra damage might be done to his injuries. 'You might have broken something,' she unthinkingly added, then wished she had not spoken. She wanted to play the situation down, not turn it into a major drama which would lead Jay to take control. She had to keep calm, she ordered herself. She had to keep in control for Jay's sake.

For a long moment Jay did not speak. Rhea's words had turned his eyes downwards to his ankle. Rhea pretended she had not noticed. There was nothing she could do about any broken bones at this moment, so there was little point in worrying about them.

'It was a car,' she suddenly said, attempting to draw Jay's attention away from his ankle. 'But it did win,' she added jokingly, trying to lighten her own depression, as well as Jay's.

'Where are we?' Jay looked concerned as he gazed around their surroundings, before turning back to Rhea. 'Do you know?'

Rhea gave a twisted grimace. She knew exactly where they had been put. She knew only too well every nook and cranny of Sebastian Font's home.

'The Villa Romano!' she announced with heavy sarcasm. 'You have now become one of the privileged few to get a private tour of the ancient wine cellar,' she added mockingly.

Jay made a second inspection of the dark impenetrable walls, resting his gaze significantly up on the large wooden doors.

'They're locked,' Rhea remarked unnecessarily. Jay had not been conscious to hear the heavy bolts being drawn across when the men left, but she knew he would know they were locked up, prisoners.

Jay did not respond. He looked into her face, a frown deepening. 'What did you think you were doing at the airport?' he asked.

'Going home,' Rhea replied flatly, dropping her eyes, unable to look him in the face. She did not need Jay to point out that this was all her own doing.

'Why?' he demanded. 'Why did you have to go on your own? Couldn't you have waited for me?'

'You wouldn't have taken me,' she retaliated, wondering how he had the nerve to suggest he would have. His blatant refusal still echoed in her ears. 'You would not let me leave the boat,' she added for good measure, just in case he had forgotten.

'Look in my pocket,' he instructed, riveting her with an expression that demanded she comply.

Rhea leaned forward and slipped her hand into the breast pocket of his shirt. She withdrew a long white envelope, folded in half.

It was not sealed down and Rhea lifted the flap and pulled out the contents. There were some bank notes, she did not count how many, and one plane ticket: Malaga to Birmingham.

For a long time Rhea gazed numbly at the ticket lying in her hand. Jay had gone to the airport himself to provide her with the very thing she had wanted. The very thing she had been in the process of doing for herself.

'You were at the airport?' she asked, realizing now that Jay must have seen everything. She had wondered just how he had known she was in that car.

'Yes, Rhea. You had to go.'

'Yes,' she agreed quietly. She had to go. But why? Because of Sebastian Font? Or because she had made her feelings for Jay so obviously clear? The latter had been her own reasons, so why did it hurt so much to think Jay was of the same opinion?

Jay made a final effort to get himself up into a sitting position, but his attempted laughter at the groans accompanying each move did not fool Rhea. Her anxiety for him returned and, turning away from her own despondency, she quickly returned the ticket and money to Jay's pocket. Then she jumped to her feet and began to look around, seeking something which Jay could lean against to make him more comfortable.

'What's that?' Jay asked, as Rhea leaned over the side of a large ancient wooden tub.

'The wine press,' she replied, turning away from the empty tub. She had hoped there might have been something inside but, apart from a few years' worth of dirt and dust lying in the bottom, there was nothing.

'They made the wine here ... a long time ago,' she

explained, feeling the need to say something as she took her search to a heap of old sacking thrown into a corner.

The sacking was filthy and Rhea sorted cautiously through it, getting ready to leap out of the way should anything 'live' leap out of it.

But, despite being dirty, the old sack bags were perfectly dry and would make good bedding material for Jay to lie on, providing him with a barrier to the cold stone flaggings. She gave a number of sacks a good shake to rid them of some of the dirt, engulfing herself in a cloud of dust as she did so.

Then she hurried back to Jay, her arms full of sacking. 'I look as dirty as Ed – !' Rhea had been about to make the observation that she looked as dirty as Eduardo when he had hidden in the wine chute, but the reminder of the old chute brought her up short.

'What's wrong?' Jay asked, his concerned expression following Rhea's gaze across to a pile of old wine casks stacked against the wall.

'I think I have just found a way out,' she said, and quickly began to arrange the sacks in a thick layer next to Jay. 'Just get yourself on these. They will keep you warmer while I get help.'

'Get help!' Jay repeated, his entire attention focused on Rhea as she helped him wriggle over to the makeshift bed. 'Is there a way out?'

'For me there is,' Rhea replied, hoping she was right. The old chute was very narrow ... and what if it had been filled in?

'Where?' Jay demanded.

'Over behind those casks. There's an old chute in the

wall. They used to drop the grapes down for pressing. It isn't very wide but I'm sure I will be able to squeeze up.' She hesitated, looking sadly over the length and breadth of Jay. 'You are too big,' she added, wishing there could be some way she could get Jay up the chute as well as herself. But even if he had been perfectly fit it would have been impossible.

'If you can get out,' Jay said insistently, 'take this ticket and get on that plane.' He pulled the envelope from his pocket and thrust it at Rhea.

'And leave you here?' she gasped. The idea was unimaginable to her. She would have left Jay on the boat, knowing he was safer without her. But leave him now! At the mercy of Sebastian Font and his thugs ... ! Never! She did not know how he could expect her to agree.

'Yes,' Jay was doubly insistent. 'You *must*.' He waddled the envelope in front of her nose. 'Take it,' he ordered. 'You must go, Rhea. You must not try to drag anyone else into this.'

His tone, his attitude, his expression all frightened Rhea. Slowly, and disappointingly, she began to understand.

To Rhea 'help' had meant going to the police. Jay had understood that too, and his present manner indicated the police were the last people Jay wanted to get involved with.

He preferred to take his chances with Sebastian Font, she realized, her fear for him growing, as she stared silently at the envelope in her hand. The air ticket. The money. Jay was giving it all to her. He was telling her to go and leave him to his fate. She glanced up at him. Cool insistence poured from his silent gaze and she turned away, knowing she had no choice. There was only one line of action open to her!

Folding the envelope she quickly slipped it into her pocket. She looked at the new red shoulder-bag lying on the floor, also containing Jay's money. In the light of what she now knew she felt twice as guilty for taking Jay's money. But now was not the time to get involved in lengthy explanations, even apologetic ones.

'Well, wish me luck,' she said with false lightness. Then she hurried over to the wine barrels before Jay could reply.

'Can you manage?' Jay asked, watching her struggle with the heavy wooden casks.

'Yes.' She did not look round. Jay was in no condition to help even if she could not have done it herself.

Rhea finally succeeded. With a gasp of relief she rolled the final barrel aside. She peered up the opening now revealed in the stone. A faint glimmer of light illuminated the old chute's filthy interior and it looked much narrower than Rhea remembered.

In fact it appeared altogether different from the times Rhea had peered down from the top to pull Eduardo out from his favourite hiding-place. She recalled the large beetle once caught in the fabric of Eduardo's tee-shirt on one such occasion. A shudder trickled down her spine.

'Is it clear?' Jay asked impatiently. 'Can you make it?'

'Yes, it's clear,' Rhea replied and, pushing aside her distaste, reached her arms up into the opening.

'Look after yourself, kid!' Jay called.

Rhea did not reply. A tight lump constricted her

throat. There was not another word in the English language designed to put her in her place more than that one. But oh, how she hoped she would hear it again from those same lips.

Rhea wedged herself into the narrow channel like a cork in a bottle. Her back was pressed against one wall, knees and hands pressed to the other. She inched her way upwards. The process was slow and painful. The old rough stones grazed her skin and tore at the fabric of the blouse on her back. But she had to go on. Jay had saved her life on two occasions and, now she had the chance to repay him, she could not let him down.

Half-way up she paused. She peered upwards, checking her progress. She hoped the wooden planks covering the outer hole were still loose, had not been nailed down as they should have been. Something tickled her cheek and, stifling a scream, she swatted it away. She heard a noise and listened, then heaved a sigh of relief, realizing it was only the pounding of her own anxious heartbeat.

She pushed away again, straightening her spine and nudging her hands and knees upwards, calling on all her strength to keep her going to the top, reminding herself that she had got Jay into this; she must get him out.

In reality the climb lasted only a few minutes. To Rhea, the long, difficult struggle stretched to eternity. Twice she feared her strength would give out. But thoughts of Jay imprisoned down below urged her on and she finally reached out, heaving a sigh of gratitude when the plank above her head moved freely.

With one final effort she pushed herself out into the

welcome freshness of daylight, falling to the ground only a couple of feet below like a boneless rag doll.

She looked around anxiously. But no one was there to see her escape. After only a brief respite to regain her breath and ease the trembling in her tortured limbs, she was on her feet.

Keeping low, she crept along the back of the villa. She could hear voices and the splashing of water coming from the swimming-pool, which was on the far side of the villa and well out of the way of where Rhea wanted to go.

As she moved stealthily through a cluster of lemon-trees she listened carefully. Unless her ears were deceiving her, the voices she could hear were all male. Rhea hoped that indicated the Fonts were out and that only a few of his men, whom she had previously thought to be Sebastian Font's employees but now realized to be his bodyguards, were the only people around. She knew from past experience that when the men were left alone they usually took the opportunity to enjoy the comforts, the swimming-pool being the main comfort, and would not be over-zealous in the guarding of the rest of the villa.

At the corner Rhea knew her luck really was in. The garage came into view and she could see that only two cars stood inside: *Señora* Font's BMW and a vintage Mercedes Sebastian Font had found in a field and had restored. The large black Mercedes belonging to Sebastian Font, and only Sebastian Font, was missing.

Rhea thanked the heavens that her ex-employer was so possessive about his precious car that he never allowed anyone else to drive it; a fact which now told Rhea that if the car was out, so was its owner. She prayed she was right to assume *Señora* Font and the children were with him.

Feeling a little easier in her mind, if not in body, Rhea pushed her way through the grasping branches of a magenta-pink azalea bush. The branches spiked her skin, but a few more scratches were of no account. There was far more at stake than her own skin.

After the protection of the bush the ground sloped steeply away over a barren rockery which afforded no protective cover. Rhea dropped on to her bottom and slid and hitched her way over the stones and soil. She could see the window now and her heart began beating double time once more, ever quickening as her goal came nearer and nearer.

Rhea fell on to all fours and covered the last few yards in a frantic scramble for the fateful window which had allowed Eduardo through and caused all her problems in the first place. Now she sent up a prayer that the window was again open, and she squeezed herself through without hesitation, or thought to what might be on the other side.

The thought came after, when she fell on to the stone stairway and rolled down to land in an ungainly and painful heap at the bottom.

It took a few moments for Rhea to recover. As she did she listened carefully. But the only sound was the tom-tom in her chest and the blood pounding in her ears. Realizing it was too late to worry whether the basement was deserted, she got to her feet and hurried through the wine cellars, seeing nothing of the lines of corks like pistols aimed across her path.

Her chest heaving from both exertion and fear, Rhea looked at the two enormous rusty bolts holding the door fast. The lower one was well within reach and slid back without much trouble. The second was above Rhea's fingertips and she had to push a heavy crate over to stand on before the second bolt was disengaged. Then she needed all her weight to swing the heavy creaking door open just wide enough to walk through.

At first they did not speak. Rhea was too breathless, Jay too stunned.

'Rhea!' Jay uttered in total disbelief, finding his voice first. 'What are you doing back here?'

'You didn't really expect me to leave you here!' she returned, the incredulity of the suggestion high in her voice as she rushed across to his side. 'Now come on. We don't have time to stand chatting.'

Jay looked steadily into her face, disbelief frowning in his eyes. 'Come on where?' he questioned drily. 'Where do you think you are taking me?'

'Out of here! Where else?' she rebuked with equal dryness, taking hold of his arm to help him to his feet.

'Rhea!' The hopeless despair of her name echoed from the cold stone walls, stopping Rhea in her tracks. Irony formed a twisted smile on Jay's face. 'My ankle is broken,' he pointed out.

'Jay,' Rhea returned without the slightest hesitation to give away how much the problem of his ankle worried her, 'I know!'

Jay groaned laughingly. 'Baby, you're priceless. What

do you intend to do? Carry me out?'

'If I have to,' Rhea's reply was quietly confident, ignoring his supposition that she could not do it.

'You've got to be crazy,' Jay's gaze hardened at Rhea's look of determination. 'Now get out of here!'

'No way,' she insisted, rounding on him. 'If you think I have gone to all this trouble to turn round and walk out on you, you can think again. You don't hold the monopoly on chivalry. So get up and get moving.'

It took a moment before Jay could do anything, so stunned was he by the unexpected determination of Rhea. 'You are going to get us both killed,' he remarked with total confidence, reluctantly allowing her to help him struggle to his feet. Then he draped his arm around her shoulder and Rhea wrapped her arm around his waist and helped him out of their ancient prison cell.

It was not easy. Jay used the walls, the endless rows of wine shelves stacked with dusty bottles, anything they happened to pass to ease himself along and take his weight off Rhea's slender shoulders, as he hobbled and hopped along at her side.

Though it was slow and laborious, getting through the old stone cellars and up the ancient stairway was the easy bit. Once they had reached the top of the stairs they were in the living quarters of the villa and in more danger of meeting company.

At the top of the stairs Rhea looked up nervously into Jay's face, the unspoken question 'Can you make it?' in her eyes. For a moment she doubted the reply. He leaned heavily against the wall for support, beads of perspiration stood out on his forehead and top lip and his skin looked grey, drained of all colour. She considered taking him back to the cellar where he could at least rest. But what was the point of rest? she asked herself, pulling her weakened mind back under control. If they were going to go, they might as well go down fighting!

Rhea bit her lip. 'Think you can make it ... ? Or do you want a rest first?'

'Sure. Let's go,' Jay grinned lopsidedly. 'Just don't ask me to jump any fences,' he added, grimacing in pain, as he turned to the arm Rhea held out in support.

'I'm not making any promises that might be difficult to keep,' she replied drily. She had no idea what was going to happen when they reached the outside world. One move at a time was all her brain could manage at that moment and the next move was across the hall and out of the front door. Then ... ? If they were lucky enough to get that far, Rhea could only hope the next move would make itself obvious enough for her to grasp.

'Come on,' she urged, but Jay held her back.

Looking like a stork perched on one leg, he lifted her chin and turned her face up to his own. 'If we get caught out there, you must make a run for it.'

Rhea shook her head. 'Not without ... '

But Jay's finger hushed her mouth and she felt the sting of hot tears pressing at her eyes.

'You must,' he ordered. 'If we meet trouble ... and it will be a miracle if we don't ... I'll try to hold them off. But you must run like the wind. And don't look back,' he added, as if getting an insight into the horrific pictures Rhea's mind had conjured up.

She forced her tears back. 'Come on!' she insisted. Jay

was right. She must have been crazy to even think that this might work. 'Let's get this over with.' She took a peep through the door to make sure the coast was clear. It was. She opened it fully, guiding Jay, swiftly as his leg would allow, out into the vast, impressive marble and glass hallway.

They were half-way across the tiled floor when the doorway darkened.

Rhea froze, her heart leaped into her mouth, at the same time feeling Jay's body react in unison.

'Andreas!' Rhea mouthed, the sound barely audible, as her eyes fixed on the man standing in the doorway, the driver of the car which had brought them to the villa.

Rhea did not know what to say and, strangely, Andreas did not speak. He stood staring at the two, who made lifeless statues in the centre of the grand hall.

Rhea's throat contracted; she swallowed hard, painfully. She could feel her own blood crashing through her head like an express train.

She searched for words, knowing that if any action was taken it would be Jay who got hurt first, but when she opened her mouth the only words to come out were a plaintive, 'Andreas, please!' even though she did not know what she was pleading for.

Andreas' dark eyes stared into Rhea's face for a long, electrifying moment. Then he looked at Jay; then back to Rhea, the intensity of his dark gaze terrifying her. But it was nothing to the terror she experienced the next moment.

Slowly Andreas reached into his pocket. Every muscle in Rhea's body tensed and she felt the same effect in Jay's body.

But, instead of the gun they had both been expecting, when Andreas withdrew his hand, *Señora* Font's car keys dangled in his fingers, the silver fob with her name engraved on it glistening in the sunlight slanting through the windows.

Rhea almost gasped out loud. Her body visibly shrank in relief, and for a moment she was not sure if she was holding Jay up or Jay holding her.

Without speaking a word, Andreas dropped the keys down on the table by the door. For a moment he looked into Rhea's confused face, then turned and walked out.

Rhea could not move. She looked from the now empty doorway to the keys lying on the table, unable to believe Andreas had actually placed the keys down to help them escape.

She recalled the moment in the car, when Carlo would have hit her. It had been Andreas who had stopped him.

It took Jay's insistent voice to break through Rhea's stupor.

'Come on,' he was urging. 'Never look a gift-horse in the mouth.' Seeming to have forgotten his ankle, he pulled Rhea to the door.

'Wait,' she pleaded, still unsure. 'How do we know it isn't a trap?'

'We don't,' Jay pointed out baldly. 'But there is only one way to find out.'

'Yes,' Rhea could only agree, wishing she could feel the renewed enthusiasm Jay was feeling. What did it matter if it was a trap? Their only other choice was to return to the cellar and await their fate.

Goaded into action once more, she tightened her hold around Jay's waist and half carried, half dragged him across the lawn.

Out in the open, without anything for Jay to lean on, his full weight pressed down on Rhea's slender shoulders. She felt her legs beginning to buckle and called up on all her strength to carry on. The garage was not far away. She could make it, she willed herself, fixing her eyes on her goal, ordering her strength to remain for the few more minutes needed, at the same time begging they would not be seen now they were so close to success.

They made it. Jay dropped into the passenger seat of the BMW with a groan that echoed both pain and relief. Rhea closed the door on him as quietly as she could. Then she raced round to the driver's door, flung herself into the seat, grabbed the keys which Jay held dangling from his fingers, started the engine and gunned the car away down the drive and out between the large white pillars of the gateway.

They were well clear of the villa and heading down the road when Rhea's tension exploded.

On a burst of high-pitched relief, she squealed, 'We made it!' The incredulity in her statement spilled from the wide, disbelieving eyes she turned glancingly on Jay.

Rhea's laughter came to an abrupt end. Jay looked worse. Beads of sweat peppered his grey skin and, from the glazed look of his eyes, she feared he was on the verge of unconsciousness.

'Are you all right?' she questioned anxiously. She wondered how much more damage had been done to his injured body by the necessity of having had to make him walk from the cellar to the garage.

'Never felt better,' Jay lied openly, attempting a smile which looked nothing like a smile.

'Just hang on,' Rhea begged, her foot pressing down hard on the accelerator, her fists turning white on the steering-wheel.

Six

The automatic glass doors glided open and Rhea rushed through. There were people everywhere, crying children, harassed parents, people in pain, some quietly waiting.

She looked round anxiously for help, then hurried over to the busy hospital reception desk, pushing her way through the gathered crowd, all seeking attention, causing many an annoyed retort for her rudeness. But Rhea was past caring what anyone thought of her. Jay was all that mattered.

Their hasty flight from the Villa Romano had gone undetected and the car journey to the hospital had been without event. But the effort of the escape with Jay's injuries had taken its toll. He looked terrible and Rhea was frantic for his safety.

'I need help!' she flung in quick-fire Spanish at the already flustered reception nurse. 'My friend has had an accident. I need someone to help me get him out of the car.' Rhea had left Jay in the car, fearing that any further movement would be too much for him. She dared not contemplate what extra damage had already been caused to him.

The nurse gave Rhea a cursory glance and carried on sorting through a box of record cards.

'Now!' Rhea demanded, raising her voice in angry insistence which brought the nurse's attention sharply back to her and silenced the babble of the surrounding crowd. 'He can't walk. He needs a chair or something to carry him in,' Rhea continued with equal urgency, ignoring the staring faces all around her. '*Rapido! Rapido!*' she blazed, when the nurse merely stared at her dumbly. '*Rapido!*' she banged her fists on the desk in true Spanish gesticulating fashion to emphasize her point. She was past caring about causing too much attention to be drawn her way. Jay was all that concerned her and if Sebastian Font or any of his men were around ... it was just too bad! Jay was sitting outside the hospital and nothing was going to stop Rhea getting him inside and getting the attention he needed so badly.

It worked. The nurse suddenly grasped the urgency of the situation. She called a colleague and they hurried after Rhea with a wheelchair.

With the assistance of the two nurses Jay was soon in the wheelchair and being rushed through the hospital doors to a small treatment room.

Rhea would have followed, but as she reached the door it was closed firmly in her face, along with the order to 'Wait outside!'

For a time Rhea could do nothing but stare helplessly at the crooked number three on the grey paintwork only inches from her nose. They had no right to shut her out. She wanted, needed to know the extent of Jay's injuries; had to know that he was going to be all right.

With a sigh she turned around. If Jay was going to be all right, then she had to leave them to put him right.

A row of chairs stretched along the wall opposite and Rhea sank down wearily on to one. Then she fixed her gaze on the door of Jay's room, willing strength into him, willing the door to open and someone to come out whom she could question about his condition.

It was after what seemed like an eternity that a white-coated doctor entered Jay's room, but on checking her watch for around the tenth time, she realized it had been only ten minutes.

There should have been a doctor in there at the beginning, Rhea fumed. Then, knowing she was over-reacting because of her guilty feeling that she was the cause of all Jay's problems, she told herself she was being unreasonable and tried some deep breathing to calm herself down.

The breathing worked on her body. The erratic pulse-throb no longer echoed in her ears. But her mind would not, could not stop worrying about Jay. If he was permanently damaged ... ? Oh stop it, she ordered, but failed to obey.

It was almost forty minutes later that the door opened again. The nurse who had helped get Jay out of the car came over to where Rhea was sitting. Rhea looked uncertainly into the young woman's dark eyes, afraid to ask, afraid of what the reply might be.

'He will be all right,' the nurse assured her, and smiled as Rhea's body relaxed in open relief. 'His ankle is broken and we think he might have some broken ribs.'

'How bad is the ankle?' Rhea asked, momentarily reliving the difficult walk over the uneven stone flags of the cellar floor and up the old worn steps.

'We won't know that until he has been X-rayed,' the nurse explained, her eyes dropping to Rhea's grazed legs and hands. 'Do you want those treated?'

Rhea followed the nurse's gaze. In her anxiety over Jay she had forgotten her own cuts and bruises from the climb up the wine chute.

'Oh, no,' she quickly replied. 'It's nothing. I'm fine.'

'Why don't you let someone check you over?' the nurse suggested.

'I'm fine,' Rhea repeated. Then, realizing the nurse was under the impression that she had been the pillion passenger on Jay's motorcycle when he had crashed, she hurriedly explained that she had not been. 'These are just cuts. Nothing to worry about.' She hoped the nurse would be satisfied with the explanation. She had no idea how she could explain her condition away; the truth was right out of the question.

Thankfully the nurse got the message. 'It will be a while before you can see him,' she continued, returning the conversation to Jay. 'Do you have anywhere to go?'

Rhea looked stunned. How could they expect her to leave Jay here alone?

'It would be better for you to go away and do something,' the nurse pointed out. 'Better than just sitting waiting.' She paused, obviously expecting some response. Rhea remained silent and the nurse continued: 'It will possibly be a few hours before you can see him.'

'I ... ' Rhea began, then changed her mind. She could not say she had nowhere to go. It would sound odd, suspicious. 'I would rather wait,' she finished, feeling she had to stay as close to Jay as possible.

The nurse did not argue and turned away and went back into Jay's room.

But Rhea had not been waiting long, when the car leaped back into her mind. *Señora* Font's BMW was still standing in front of the hospital. It could not stay there. It was an open invitation to tell Sebastian Font and his men exactly where Jay and Rhea had gone to.

Even knowing it was a job she had to do, Rhea did not want to leave the hospital, and it was with reluctance that she pulled her gaze away from the treatment room door and walked outside.

She could not have been so lucky, she told herself, her eyes falling on the gleaming BMW, standing with its door wide open and the keys in the ignition. On any other occasion a car such as *Señora* Font's would have been whisked away within seconds. Pondering on the irony of finding the car still intact, Rhea climbed into the driver's seat. Then she drove away, reminding herself that she had been blessed with a few years' worth of luck already today ... how much more did she expect?

Rhea drove the car to the other side of town and left it there, the keys in the ignition and all the doors securely locked. The car had served its purpose, enabling Rhea to get Jay away from the villa. Without it, she now realized, they would have had no chance. But she would prefer *Señora* Font to get it back in one piece.

Then Rhea hurried to the shopping area. She recalled Andreas' unexpected action. Without his help she would never have managed to get Jay away from the villa and she would never be able to thank Andreas enough for what he had done for them. She felt sad that she would never be able to express her thanks. She doubted she would ever see Andreas again.

Reaching the shops, Rhea quickly purchased a blue cotton sundress, a pair of canvas pumps, a new handbag to replace the one left behind in the wine cellar, and a comb and a tablet of soap. She needed to do something about her appearance. She had to try to make herself look like any other tourist, and at the moment she looked more like a refugee from a dogfight.

She got a taxi back to the hospital to find the door to Jay's room open. Jay was nowhere to be seen and, when she asked after him, she was only told to wait. So she went into the toilets and made the transformation from backstreet waif to respectable human being once more, though she found no pleasure in the mirror. All Rhea could see was the image of someone whose stupidity had caused Jay's injuries.

Looking calm and composed, Rhea returned to the chair she had previously been sitting on. But the people crowding the waiting-room could not see the turmoil going on inside. Could not hear the silent prayers for Jay. Had no notion of the heart that leaped when the low-powered electric whisper heralded the opening of the automatic doors.

Although Rhea tried to dispel her morbid thoughts, she was not very successful, and it seemed like several lifetimes before the nurse finally returned.

The nurse made a quick scrutiny of Rhea's changed appearance, but made no comment. She merely informed Rhea that Jay had been taken to ward sixteen and gave her instructions on how to get there. Then she went about her business, leaving Rhea to quickly make her way along the hospital corridors.

But the joy of reunion, so high on Rhea's mind, was soon doused.

'You little fool!' Jay remonstrated, the moment Rhea appeared through the door. 'You should not have stayed here!'

'You didn't really expect me to leave without knowing you were all right!' she returned bitingly, feeling her earlier enthusiasm sinking fast beneath his cool stare. Then she wondered why she had expected his reaction to be anything more, and cast her eyes disconsolately around the room, looking at anything but Jay.

The small ward contained only two beds, the other one empty. It was decorated in sunshine yellow, light and airy. Very bright. Very cheerful. Which was more than could be said for the face looking up from the pillow when she finally brought her gaze back to him.

'How do you feel?' she asked. He looked much better than the last time she had seen him, and for that she was thankful.

'Fine,' he confirmed tightly, careful not to move his lips too much. 'But you must go, Rhea.'

Thank you, Rhea thought bitterly. Even though she had not wanted any thanks for getting him out of their prison cellar, she was still far more in his debt than he hers, he could at least have shown a little appreciation ... and have looked pleased to see her.

'Where am I supposed to go?' she asked. The idea of returning to Jay's boat alone was not very appealing. It was too lonely, too isolated. At the moment she needed the company of other people.

'Home,' Jay replied.

'Home!' Rhea was amazed, disturbed, confused, and all three emotions traversed her face simultaneously.

'Do you mean England?' she asked, knowing the answer. She wanted to be close to Jay, but Jay just wanted her gone, out of the way.

'Of course I do. You can't stay here alone. They will find you in no time at all now they know you are still here. And I can't look after you ... Not from a hospital bed.'

'Who's going to look after *you?*' Rhea asked pointedly. Jay would be in hospital for some time, but he would need some help when he came out.

'I am perfectly capable of looking after myself,' he insisted.

And I am not, Rhea deduced, staring resignedly at his obstinate features for a long moment, feeling the insistence that he should be obeyed like a tangible flame leaping across the distance between them.

'Have they worked out the full extent of the damage?' she enquired, changing the subject, hoping to find something that would make him change his mind, even though she realized it was a vain hope.

'One broken ankle. Two cracked ribs. The head needed three stitches. Otherwise it is all superficial.'

'Good.' Rhea could not contain her smile of relief. She looked at the black line at his temple, punctuated by three small tufts of stitching. The wound looked nothing now it had been closed up. The bruising had spread further, reaching down the side of his cheek. There was also a new patch of greyish yellow bruising under his chin and up the side of his mouth. He looked battered but well, far more well than Rhea could ever have imagined he would look.

Jay watched her as she studied every inch of his battered flesh. He smiled. 'How do I look?'

'Like Frank Bruno's sparring partner,' she replied, emotion filling her smile.

'Exactly how I feel.' He attempted a self-mocking grin, but failed in a grimace of pain.

Rhea forced a laugh, even though she felt more like crying. He could so easily have been killed, so easily have been maimed for life ... and she would have been to blame.

'Thank you ... for what you did back there,' Jay suddenly said.

It had been so totally unexpected and for a moment Rhea was dumb. Then she shook her head in denial. 'There is no need to thank me. I was paying a debt and I think I am still on the owing side.' It was a lie. Rhea had not really thought of any debts when she had helped Jay. But how could she tell him that? How could she tell him she had been saving the man she loved? Jay did not want to hear about her feelings for him, they would only make him angry.

'You owe me nothing,' Jay assured, and Rhea smiled in the knowledge that he had been content to believe her little white lie.

'What you did took a lot of courage,' Jay continued. 'I don't think there are many women around with the guts to attempt what you did ... never mind pull it off.'

Rhea looked up sharply. Had she heard right? Had he really called her a woman?

'I ...' she began with a self-conscious shrug. 'I just knew I could not leave you there.' Her eyes clouded as she imagined what could have happened back there. 'I could not have left you, Jay,' she added, emotion cracking her voice, all the good intentions of keeping her feelings under control being thrown to the wind.

'Don't say any more ... No, Rhea,' Jay insisted, stopping her in her tracks.

'But ... !' she implored. 'You don't understand.' How could she explain that to return to England and have no contact with him would drive her to distraction?

'Yes I do,' Jay put in knowledgeably. 'You have grown attached to me, fond of me. I think you even believe you have fallen in love with me.'

Rhea stared at him in silence. That was not the only reason she needed to stay. But was she so transparent?

'And,' she began slowly, 'you don't think anything of me?'

'You don't know me, Rhea. We are ...'

Rhea cut him short. 'Oh, don't give me that age bit,' she bit out angrily. 'You are only twelve years older than I am. It's just an excuse. I wish you would be honest with me and tell me the truth.'

'You're upset, Rhea,' Jay explained unnecessarily. She knew very well how she felt herself. 'You're not thinking straight. If I allowed you to fall into my arms you would regret it later.'

If he allowed her! 'Yes, of course, you're probably right!' She bit her tongue against adding a sarcastic retort as usual, as she fought to conceal the tremor of anger his arrogant words had sent through her limbs. She was acting like the kid he had called her, she realized with embarrassment. She did not know what she was doing, it was totally out of character. Before Jay, she had been timid and ill at ease with men, had only had a few boyfriends and nothing very serious. No one had ever affected her the way Jay had done. It *must* be the situation, she slowly acknowledged; all the fear and worry she had gone through would naturally have an affect on her. She should be grateful Jay was a man of principles and had not taken advantage of her.

'You really must go home,' Jay prompted Rhea's silent despair. 'You'll find a nice young chap of your own type and ...'

'Don't patronize me!' Rhea snapped. She did not want to hear about any 'nice young chap'. Jay's delicate condition made her think twice before embarking on the full-scale row she felt like rushing into, her anger fuelled by her own humiliation.

'Have you still got the money and the air ticket?' Jay asked, seeming to sense Rhea's mood and trying to keep her mind on more important matters.

'Yes,' She lifted the handbag. 'It's all in here.'

The despondency of her voice caused Jay to look at her for a long moment. 'You have to go,' he said firmly, brooking no refusal.

'I know,' Rhea replied, resigned to her fate.

She was leaving Jay. She was afraid of being without

him. She knew that for some time to come she would be anxious of walking around corners. But that was something she would come to terms with. What she doubted she would ever come to terms with was the knowledge that she had fallen in love with someone who did not reciprocate the feeling. She had always thought that when it happened it would be a mutual feeling, a special treasure shared by both parties. How wrong could she have been? Jay did not love her. He no longer wanted her there!

She gave a small self-mocking smile. 'I'm not sure you'll survive without me,' she joked, though the sound came out flat, in no way humorous.

The comment put a smile on Jay's face which lighted a fuse deep inside Rhea. Her heart sank in cold regret, and she wished she had not spoken.

'Come here,' Jay patted the bed by his side and Rhea went to him. He took her hand, kindly, fondly, but with enough restraint to stop the action being possessive or loving. 'I just happened to be around at a time when you needed someone ... anyone!' he said, as Rhea looked uncertainly into his eyes, wishing she had the power to pull away from both his gaze and his physical touch. 'It did not matter who they were or what they were, just so long as they were there.'

Rhea did not object, even though she wanted to. Jay was wrong. She knew he was wrong. Had Jay not been Jay, she would not have stayed with him, would not have allowed him to take her to his boat.

'I was that someone, Rhea,' Jay continued, for once not picking up on Rhea's thoughts.' There is nothing more to your feeling for me than a sense of dependency on a safe port in a storm.'

Jay let her hand slip out of his and Rhea pulled back, feeling the cold sense of loss creeping up her arm. But she could not pull her eyes away from his gaze. This might be the last time she looked at him and she wanted to remember the feeling for the rest of her life.

'But I can't do much for you from this bed,' Jay added, a note of regret entering his voice which pleased Rhea a little. 'So you must go back to England. You have no choice,' he concluded with a finality in his voice that sent a shiver down Rhea's spine.

'I'll never forget you,' she vowed, wishing she could read the emotions lingering behind his gaze. There were times when he seemed to have the ability to close his eyes while still keeping them open; to see, yet not to be seen too clearly.

'Yes you will,' Jay replied with laughter in his voice that sounded odd to Rhea, forced and unnatural. 'You will meet that nice young chap and you will want him for himself, not need him for yourself.'

Rhea grimaced. She was not sure she understood. Surely wanting and needing were one and the same when you loved someone?

'Will you answer me one question?' she asked. She was not sure she really wanted to know the answer, was afraid the reply might point the finger of accusation at Jay. But it was something she had put off asking for too long already.

'What exactly does Sebastian Font do?'

Jay hesitated for only a moment, a crooked smile

breaking out on his face that stretched the bruised side a little too far and ended in a grimace. 'I didn't think you would ever get around to asking,' he replied, his eyes looking at her with pride. 'I'm glad you did. Wanting to know means you are accepting the situation ... not trying to pretend it isn't really happening,' he added, as Rhea frowned.

'Wanting to know the truth proves you have come a long way from the frightened kid I grabbed out of the street.'

For once Rhea smiled at the title, though she was not totally convinced she had come as far as Jay considered, and wondered if she had only been over-reacting to the fact that she knew he had been right; that, in her fear and confusion, she had been acting like the kid he called her.

But then Jay continued, and Rhea was too stunned to ponder the whys and wherefores of her own reactions.

'Sebastian Font is one of the top men in a large syndicate of so-called businessmen who have a very profitable line in drug trafficking.'

'Drugs!' Rhea breathed, not entirely aware she was uttering any sound. No! It was not possible. *Señor* Font ... his wife ... the children ... living off money earned by such despicable means ... And herself!

Rhea had indulged in the extravagant lifestyle without a thought for where the money came from. She had just assumed the Fonts' wine-producing company was very profitable.

Rhea wrapped her arms about herself to combat the chill running through her body. She stood up, unable to look Jay in the face and walked to the window, staring unseeingly at the tarmac below.

But she saw none of the ambulances, none of the people walking by. Her mind's eye was filled with the past months of her own life: the lavish parties; expensive holidays; nothing had been lacking, nothing spared ... and all paid for by drugs!

Bank-robbery, suspicious business dealing, fraud; since the fateful morning of finding that he was not as respectable as he seemed, Rhea had considered all those in relation to her ex-employer. Those were bad enough. But never drugs! It was too dirty. Too despicable. They had all lived in the lap of luxury afforded by the degradation of hundreds, maybe thousands of other human beings. Most of them would be young ... like herself!

A shudder of revulsion raced down her spine and she tightened her arms around herself. Then another thought struck, far worse than any of the previous. Oh no! her mind screamed, as she spun round, faced Jay's calmly unmoving features ... Jay was also involved.

Suddenly everything clicked into place. Where had Jay first suggested he take her to catch a plane home? Morocco! Where was there a thriving drugs trade? Morocco.

'Shipments of heroin are brought across from North Africa,' Jay said then, almost as if he had read her mind. 'Then distributed around Europe.'

'No!' Rhea mouthed, almost silently. She did not want to hear anymore.

'So now you see just how much is at stake,' Jay said, his expression serious. 'You have to leave Spain now, for your own safety. You have to take responsibility for yourself. I know you are capable of that,' he encouraged her, when Rhea looked uncertain.

'What about you?' Rhea asked, fear for his safety expanding inside her chest. 'They could find you here.' If only he would return to England with her and have done with all this. But, as her mind put forth the suggestion, she knew it was hopeless. Jay would not return home with her. His life was here.

'Go straight to the airport and get a plane, any plane,' Jay instructed, the old Jay, cool, calm, calculated. 'You can get a taxi right outside the door. And if anyone stops you at the airport, keep walking. Don't stop until you are at the reservations desk and someone is with you.'

'But ... ?' Rhea began.

'No,' Jay quieted her objections. 'Just listen. You will have to go to your aunt's house first. But get another job somewhere else, another part of the country, as soon as you can. Tell everyone you got fed up with the job, with the Spanish weather. Tell them anything. Just make something up. But don't tell the truth.'

Rhea nodded like an obedient child. 'All right,' she agreed flatly. She wondered how she was going to be able to sleep at night. But she had no choice. If she spoke out she would not only be risking her own life, but also Jay's. Nowhere would be safe for them to go. *If* anywhere was safe now. They now knew that Jay had helped her and she realized only too well just how much peril that fact put Jay in.

'If you don't say anything to anyone,' Jay continued, 'they will eventually realize you have kept quiet and, with any luck, will forget you.'

Rhea could see Jay was just trying to reassure her. He was grasping at straws to give her courage. 'You can't be sure,' she said; she felt all her luck had already been used up.

'Trust me, sweetheart,' Jay replied, the intensity of his gaze leaping across the space between them, almost as if his arms had reached out to her.

'Oh Jay!' Rhea gasped, hurrying across the room and wrapping her arms gently around his neck. 'What an awful, awful business this has turned out to be.'

'Hey, come on now!' He held her away, looked fondly, encouragingly into her eyes. 'Is this the lady who saved my life? Who dragged me away from right under their noses?'

Rhea tried to smile, but failed. 'Don't forget Andreas,' she pointed out. 'You will have neither of us around to look after you.'

Jay laughed carefully. 'I think I am big enough to look after myself,' he assured her.

Rhea looked into his eyes for a long moment, praying he was right.

'Will you be able to get a job without much trouble?' Jay asked.

'I got the post with the Fonts through the Safe and Sound Nanny Agency,' Rhea grimaced, seeing the irony of the name. 'I'll go back to them. But next time I'll make sure I know what profession my employer follows.'

'You do that,' Jay agreed. 'You have still got the money with you?' he double-checked.

Rhea nodded.

'On your way then,' he ordered, making it clear that everything was happening far more quickly than Rhea wanted it to happen.

'All right,' she unwillingly agreed. She stood up, taking a last look around the small, neat room, dragging the moment out as long as possible.

'Good girl. You'll be fine,' Jay reassured her with a smile that came over as stiffly exaggerated.

For a long moment Rhea could only remain standing there, looking at him. She did not want to leave. At that moment she would have done anything to stay with Jay. How or why she could feel the way she did about him, she did not know. She took one last look at the eagle's head peering over the top of the white sheet, the long blond hair lying on the pillow. Her perfect pirate, she thought, recalling her first impression of him, still finding it absurd that she could have feelings for such a man.

'Take care of yourself,' Rhea spoke suddenly, knowing it was far past time to leave.

'And you, kid.' He attempted a crooked, lopsided grin, for once with pain-free success.

It made Rhea laugh, although it was a small, sad sound that made her cry inside.

'I will,' she confirmed, and bending forward, placed a gentle kiss on the safe, uninjured side of his mouth.

Then she turned and walked out. No goodbye. No turning back.

Seven

Rhea pulled back the curtains and drank in the early morning sunlight. Freedom! Before Spain it had been nothing more than a word. Now Rhea knew the true meaning had texture, smell, sight and taste. It was everything she held dear.

Billy Millward, the local postman, came through the gate, whistling a merry, if out of tune, version of 'Puppet on a String'. Billy saw Rhea standing at the window, stopped and gave a hearty wolf-whistle followed by a cheeky grin.

'Good-morning Billy,' Rhea called, opening the window for him to pass the mail through to her.

'How come no one writes to the most beautiful girl in the village?' Billy asked, holding the pile of envelopes tight as Rhea tried to pull them from his hand.

'I haven't been here long enough for anyone to miss me,' she pointed out good-naturedly.

Rhea had only been with the Parsons family for twelve weeks. But every morning of those twelve weeks she had held her breath as she scanned through the regular pile of letters Mr Parsons received, hoping by some miracle there might be one for herself.

This morning she was saved the task. Billy had obviously done it for her. Just as he must have looked through the mail every other morning ... if he knew no one was bothering to write to her.

'If there's no one to run after you, I'm always ready, willing and able,' Billy offered, flashing an outrageous grin.

'Get off with you, Billy Millward. Back to that wife and lovely baby of yours. I don't know how she puts up with you.' Rhea laughed as she spoke, taking Billy's suggestions all in good part.

'Course, I'm terrific,' Billy threw over his shoulder, as he bounced jauntily away down the drive.

Rhea shook her head at the retreating figure. Then, just to make sure Billy had not been mistaken, she shuffled through the mail. Two for Mrs Parsons, the other five for Mr Parsons. There was nothing for Rhea. Billy had been correct. No one wanted to write to her.

What did you expect? she asked herself, gazing down the privet-lined lane leading into the centre of the village. Jay Rutherford was not going to come galloping down the road on a white charger. Neither was he going to come walking down the road ... or write to her! Jay did not know where she was ... so how could he?

Rhea had left a message with Aunt Maeve in the nursing-home before coming to work for Mr and Mrs Parsons, even though she was not sure how he was supposed to find Aunt Maeve in the first place. He didn't even know which part of England she lived in and besides, if Aunt Maeve saw Jay with her own eyes, Rhea was not sure her aunt would pass any information to him. Aunt Maeve would take one look at his appearance and judge him no fit company for her niece.

So with Aunt Maeve to get past, and the more than likely possibility that Jay would not be taking the trouble to look for her, Rhea felt her chances of ever seeing him again to be very remote. It was a painful realization, but one she had to accept.

'Rhea! Come and see ... Come and see!'

Rhea smiled, for the moment her sadness forgotten. She hurried through to the kitchen, where the two small voices rose in bubbling excitement.

'Oh, look, Rhea!' Rosie, the younger of the two sisters, turned as Rhea popped her head around the laundry-room door. 'Four!' she exclaimed in childlike wonder. 'Minky has had four kittens.'

'Oh, you clever girl!' Rhea knelt by the converted picnic hamper, praising the new 'Mum' who lay purring contentedly and keeping a watchful eye on the tiny unseeing babies, as they were each in turn picked up and inspected.

'Gently,' Rhea urged, helping Rosie to return the last baby to Minky's side.

'Aren't they beautiful?' Rosie's big blue eyes looked about to pop out of her head.

'The most beautiful kittens in the world,' Amanda chirped in, having found her tongue, previously lost in the amazement of it all.

'Yes,' Rhea confirmed to the little girls' joy. 'The most beautiful kittens I have ever seen.' She hugged both Rosie and Amanda to her, enjoying their pleasure.

'Enough now,' Rhea said, giving both girls a gentle push towards the door. 'The kittens need rest and you need to wash hands before breakfast.'

The two small red-heads skipped away and Rhea took a last look at the new family. The blanket at one end of the basket had come loose and got all crinkled up, uncovering the newspaper which lay beneath.

Careful not to disturb the kittens or Minky, Rhea pulled the blanket straight. She was smoothing out the creases when something caught her eye.

Rhea was not sure why she noticed the brief passage, or quite how she had. It was only five lines long, squeezed in at the bottom of the page at the last moment, she guessed.

'Rumour is rife in Spain that prominent businessman Sebastian Font has been arrested under suspicion of illegal drugs-dealing. Spanish police refuse to comment.'

Rhea's heart did a somersault. She read the words again and again and again, unable to take them in. What had happened? she wondered anxiously. What had made the police pounce on Sebastian Font?

Rhea sat back on her heels, the colour draining from her face. If the police had taken Sebastian Font into custody, who else had they taken? Her mind raced down a long line of names, beginning with Carlo ... ending with Jay!

Oh, Jay! If he was guilty then he deserved to be punished. Yet Rhea could not want to see him punished, even though she knew it was wrong of her to think that way. It had been three long months since she had walked out of the hospital, leaving Jay behind. But her feelings for him were just as strong; time had not dimmed the memories or dulled the emotions that rose within her each time she thought of Jay.

'We washed our hands. Can we have our breakfast?'

'Uh!' Rhea looked round to see the two little faces in the doorway, watching curiously, as if they had been there for some time. 'Oh ... yes. Give me a minute.' She quickly lifted the blanket at the opposite end of the basket and looked at the date of the newspaper. It was the day before.

'Is something wrong?' Amanda enquired, looking anxious.

'Nothing,' Rhea assured her, straightening the basket out again. 'Just reading something I missed.' Jumping to her feet she swept the two girls through to the breakfast bar, plonked them down on the high bar chairs with indecent haste and almost threw Weetabix and toast at them. She needed to get a morning's newspaper to see if the brief report had been followed up.

The day's newspapers were spread on a rack displayed in front of Rhea's eyes as she walked through the newsagent's door. She stopped short. Caught her breath. The front pages leaped out at her.

'Drugs Swoop!' 'Drugs Ring Smashed!' 'Heroin Shipment Seized!'

Was this real? Could it be true? Rhea closed her eyes, counted silently to three, then opened them again. Sebastian Font was still looking back at her from beneath the headlines. The *Express* portrayed *Señor* Font as Rhea had known him: a dark-eyed, sleek-haired Spaniard, sophisticated, upper class. In the *Mail* he was more sombre, brooding as he walked between two policemen ... being escorted! Rhea had the feeling of icy water trickling down her spine, all the bad memories flooding back.

Wherever she looked, Sebastian Font was looking back at her, along with the other man, the Englishman. Greg Thorpe! The papers gave him a name. Rhea had known his face, his voice, but not his name.

Realizing she must be looking rather silly, standing clutching a little girl in each hand, displaying her shock and amazement for all to see, Rhea quickly grabbed a copy of each newspaper carrying the front-page story, paid Mr Wiggins and, before she could be drawn into any lengthy discussions on the weather or the latest bit of local gossip, grabbed the children once more and hurried out of the shop.

There was nothing. Rhea searched and searched the newspaper print, but it told her nothing. A lot of supposition. A great deal of elaboration on the single fact that Sebastian Font had been arrested in Spain, and Greg Thorpe in England, but nothing to tell Rhea if anyone else had been involved ... anyone such as a long-haired buccaneer of an Englishman.

The children began to get fractious at being left unattended and Rhea was forced to put the newspapers aside and go about her rightful business of being a nanny. But even though she outwardly seemed to lose herself in the busy daily schedule of attending to her lively three - and four-year-old charges, Jay Rutherford was never far away.

'Happy birthday dear Rosie. Happy birthday to you!'

There were squeals of delight as Rosie huffed and

puffed at the four pink and white candles on top of the Care Bear birthday cake, until there was not one flicker of flame left.

'I want to cut it! It is my cake!' Rosie protested loudly, as Rhea moved forward, knife in hand.

'I will help you,' Rhea insisted, allowing Rosie to hold the handle while she did the cutting.

'Rhea, there is someone to see you,' Joanna Parsons, Jo to her friends, called, as she came into the room wielding a pitcher of orange squash. 'I've put him in the study,' she announced to Rhea's surprise then turned her attention to the mayhem around the table. 'Who wants more to drink?'

'Someone to see *me*?' Rhea tried to sound calm, but far from felt it. Who could it be ? she wondered worriedly. Her mind could only leap to one conclusion.

'Did he give his name?' Rhea asked, trying to put off the moment of encounter a little longer. But Jo did not hear Rhea's voice above the chorus of 'mes' requesting more orange squash, and continued to fill the paper cups being thrust at her.

'In the study?' Rhea raised her voice so that Jo would hear this time, then hovered over the birthday party until Jo replied. She really did not want to see whoever it was.

Realizing she could put off the day of reckoning no longer, Rhea turned and walked to the study, forcing herself into calmness. Was this the moment she had been dreading for the past six months? she asked herself, anxiety turning to cold dread as she neared the study door. Since the day the papers had been filled with

Sebastian Font's arrest, she had been playing a tense waiting game. Waiting for the knock on the door that would drag her into the case because she had been the Fonts' nanny and lived with them for so long. The barrage of questions that would seek to convict Sebastian Font but, if she was not careful, would also convict Jay Rutherford.

At the door Rhea paused, took a deep breath, straightened her skirt and walked in.

The man stood looking out of the window with his back to her. He was tall; well, policemen always were. His blond hair was short, though not as short as Rhea would have expected; it brushed the collar of his white shirt and the jacket of an extremely well fitting pale-grey suit.

She was grateful to be spared the embarrassment of having someone turn up in uniform, and relief lightened her voice, as she announced, 'I am Rhea Dempster.'

He turned around then. 'Hello, Rhea!'

For a moment all sense and feeling left Rhea. She seemed to be frozen, numbly, speechlessly frozen in the centre of the room, while inside her head her mind spun round and round and round.

It was Jay's face! Jay's voice! But this was not Jay. This man was elegantly attired, business-like, smart, sophisticated. He could not be Jay! Where was all the hair? The tattoo? The scruffy denim cut-offs?

Rhea shook her head in amazement, wonder, disbelief.

'It can't be you!' she uttered, finding her lost voice. 'I thought you were the police.'

Jay smiled at that.

'How did you find me?' she asked, incredulous.

'Through the agency,' he explained, adding, 'The Safe and Sound Nanny Agency,' when Rhea looked puzzled.

'Oh ... Oh yes,' she stammered. She had clean forgotten she had mentioned the name of the agency which had found her the position with the Fonts ... which had also found her present position.

'I need to talk to you, Rhea,' Jay put in, cutting through her hazy mind. 'But it seems I arrived at an inconvenient moment.' He inclined his head towards the dining-room, where the birthday party could be heard in full swing. 'It sounds like you're doing a re-run of "The Charge of the Light Brigade" in there.'

'Something like that.' Rhea gave a smiling shrug. It was so good to see him. She wanted to run to him and throw her arms around him. But Jay had never felt that way about her and she was not sure he was really himself anymore. Her childish behaviour had got on his nerves before, when he was rough and ready. This man looked far too self-possessed to appreciate an open display of her emotions.

'Rhea?' Jo called loudly, before her head came round the door.

Unnecessary tact, Rhea thought.

'Sorry to interrupt.' Jo's contagious smile covered both Jay and Rhea in the same moment. 'I need help,' she pleaded, glancing Jay a look of contrition, before turning her attention to Rhea. 'World War Three will break out if the games don't get under way shortly.'

'I'm coming.' Rhea looked apologetically at Jay.

'I'll be back later,' he said, and Rhea nodded, despondency sinking like a brick inside her stomach. She was afraid that this might be her only chance. That if Jay walked out the door he would never come back. But she could not run out on Jo, leaving her with eighteen under-fives to cope with.

Fortunately, Jo leaped to Rhea's aid. 'There's no need to leave,' she put in. 'Not if you don't have to. We could always use an extra pair of hands ... always assuming you can stand little brats and play a mean game of musical bumps.'

'Well ...' Jay hesitated, looked at Rhea.

Rhea was not sure if he was seeking her permission to stay, or looking for help in escaping. Whichever he wanted, she wanted him to stay. She rested her hand on his arm; holding him back from walking out, or claiming him as her possession in front of Jo; Rhea was not sure. 'Don't go. They'll probably listen to you more than they have been doing to us. And I'll be free later.'

Jay stayed. The children did listen to him. The only problem was, by the time the door-bell rang to herald the first mum to collect her little darling, Rhea had decided they had not gained another assistant in Jay, but another child.

Where Jo and Rhea would have led the games off in a more quiet, gentle direction, Jay had the children shouting their heads off, scrambling over obstacle courses of chairs and cushions, leaping from one newspaper stepping-stone to another and climbing and falling off anything that stood still long enough to be climbed and fallen off.

Fortunately Jo had immediately taken to Jay and, much to Rhea's surprise, did not seem to mind her home being turned into an assault course.

'I could do with a drink,' Jay whispered to Rhea as Jo escorted the last few stragglers out of the door.

'Orange squash, tea or coffee?' she offered. Then she remembered his appreciation for alcoholic beverages. 'Sorry, I don't have anything stronger,' she added. There was a cupboard full across the room, but its contents were not Rhea's to give away.

'Squash will be fine,' he replied, smiling into her eyes for a moment too long. Rhea found the old knot of emotion tightening inside her chest. Jay may not look the same, but she still felt the same way about him. She quickly filled a paper cup and handed it to him.

Just as Jay was placing the cup to his lips, Jo returned. 'Good grief! You're not giving him orange squash? Not after all that!' Her expression remonstrated with Rhea. 'Come on, Jay,' she said, breezing across to the drinks cabinet, beckoning her finger to him to follow. 'I shall imbibe of nothing less than a double GT. I deserve it. We all deserve it!'

Jo poured three large gin-and-tonics. She handed one to Jay, one to Rhea, and took the last herself. 'To the greatest party-games organizer in the world,' she announced, raising her glass to Jay. 'Thank heavens you turned up. Are you free next year?'

'It will take me that long to get my breath back,' Jay

laughed, and took a long swallow of the sparkling liquid.

Rhea took a sip of her own drink, hoping upon hope that he would be around next year.

'Thank you,' Rhea glanced a self-conscious smile at Jay standing by her side, then turned her gaze to a slow-moving barge passing down the canal running close to the bottom of the Parsons' garden. She was alone with Jay, and felt suddenly shy, almost as if she was with a stranger.

'The children loved you.' And so did I. The last was uttered silently, as she snuggled, almost self-protectively, inside her thick woollen coat. This man might not look like the Jay she had known and loved, but he still possessed the same power to swell her emotions.

'I enjoyed it,' Jay replied quietly, then added. 'Have you been all right? I had a devil of a job finding you. The agency was not sure they should be giving out addresses to strange men.'

Rhea was not entirely displeased with that. Anyone could have been trying to find her. 'How did you change their minds?' she asked, hoping it had not been too easy.

Jay gave a laugh. 'I do have certain charms.'

Where? Rhea asked silently. If he could sweet-talk the receptionist at the agency into giving out information that should be kept secret, why couldn't he use a bit on Rhea herself?

'You look different,' she said, after a long silence, not knowing what else to say, having the strange, sad feeling that her dreams were slipping out of reach.

Jay did not speak. He began to walk slowly down the towpath. For a moment Rhea watched his smartly suited figure move away. So very different! She shook her head, trying to cast out the devils from her mind. Was this all really happening? she asked herself, but could not be sure of the answer.

Rhea finally followed, catching up by Jay's side and for a while walking in silence. Jay seemed to be giving something serious consideration, while Rhea was battling with the unexpected feeling of foreboding which she found difficult to explain.

It was Jay who spoke first. 'When you first saw me, you said you thought I was the police ... Why?'

For a moment Rhea was fighting a second battle. If she told the truth she would have to reveal that she felt Jay to be a part of the obnoxious business. But she did not know how not to tell the truth. 'Because I worked for the Fonts,' she began flatly. 'When the arrests were in the headlines I thought the police would want to question me.' She stopped walking, turned to Jay, the pent-up fear that had gnawed away at her for the past months burning brightly in her eyes. 'I was afraid for you.'

'For me?' Jay looked puzzled. 'Why?'

'I didn't know who else the police had arrested. I imagined if they had Sebastian Font it would only be a matter of time before they got to you.'

'To me!' Jay looked amused. 'You thought I was connected!' It was a statement, not a question, one that sent a flood of colour to Rhea's cheeks and made it impossible for her to reply.

'Oh, love,' Jay said, his expression full of remorse for his unthinking attitude. He wrapped his arm around her shoulders and guided her down the towpath. 'There was no reason they should "get to me".' He used Rhea's words with a smile. 'It was I who got to them, love. You see, Rhea, I *am* the police!'

Jay fell silent then, allowing Rhea the time to digest this stunning new information.

For a long moment Rhea stared uncomprehendingly into his face. The face that was the same as the Jay she had known, yet was so very different. Now he was telling her she had been wrong all the time. Jay had not been on the wrong side of the law along with Sebastian Font and his men. Jay had been on the right side of the law ... had been the law!

'You mean ... it was all part of your job? You were on the case?' she finally managed to find voice to ask.

'Sort of,' Jay replied seriously.

Rhea frowned. 'What exactly does that mean?'

'I was not working officially. It was a ... er ... personal matter.' For a moment his gaze wandered far away, out of reach of Rhea's grasp. She watched him silently, wondering just what 'personal matter' had caused him to live like a gypsy. What could have been so important as to make him pursue such dangerous men?

'I traced the line of drug-dealers all the way up from the pushers in the bars and discos, to the top men ... Thorpe in this country, Font in Spain,' Jay explained slowly.

Rhea listened silently, recalling the cool, calculating way Jay had worked out any problem. Just like a criminal, she had thought, never suspecting he worked like a criminal because, in order to catch them, it was his job to know them inside out.

'At first the stuff was delivered to a warehouse Thorpe owned in Bristol,' Jay continued, and a wry smile broke out on his face, as he added, 'Unfortunately the local squad got word of this and planned to raid the place. Somehow Thorpe was tipped off and by the time the boys arrived the place was clean as a whistle.' He gave a bark of ironic laughter. 'And I was left with the prospect of going back to square one to find out where the new warehouse might be.'

'And did you find it?' Rhea asked, all concern that Jay had been thwarted by his own colleagues.

'Yes. I got photographs of the whole procedure. I also had some of Thorpe and Font together. But they were not enough to prove the two were in business together.' He looked down into Rhea's face then, an indulgent smile reaching his eyes. 'But I would not have found it without you.'

'What do you mean?' Rhea was confused. What had she got to do with Thorpe and Font? She did not even know Thorpe.

'The little conversation you overheard,' Jay explained. 'It was worth its weight in gold. Can you remember the comments about the new warehouse being watertight? Being beneath a lake?'

'Yes,' Rhea breathed. Would she ever be able to forget?

'Thorpe lived under the guise of owner of a very respectable country club called the Blue Lagoon. At first

I could not believe he would be so stupid to connect his two businesses.' A group of children came in the opposite direction and Jay stood back to let Rhea go before him on the narrow pathway, though his hand remained on her shoulder, until he returned to her side, once more placing his arm around her shoulders.

'He must have been so smuggly self-assured that his respectable cover was bullet-proof,' Jay spoke with such venom that Rhea looked up sharply, seeing the darkness that briefly shadowed his features. She shivered. This was another Jay Rutherford ... and one she was not sure she liked.

'So you found the supply of heroin beneath Thorpe's club? That was the lake they had spoken about?' she asked, wanting to push the conversation along and rid his face of the hatred that frightened her so much.

'Yes,' Jay's voice was slow and thoughtful. 'They had enough heroin down there to flood every city in England in the same night.' He paused and looked down into her face, as if suddenly remembering she was there. 'All packed in wine cartons ... Sebastian Font's wine cartons!'

'Oh ...!' Rhea uttered, all she could manage, as a sudden thought leaped into her head. She did not like the thought and tried to push it away. But it stuck, would not be moved. The evening turned chill and she shivered inside her thick red woollen coat. Feeling the tremor, Jay pulled her closer, seeking to provide the warmth of his own body to keep out the winter cold.

But Rhea hastened her steps, declining the unspoken invitation, putting space between them. The closeness of Jay's body was the very last thing she needed at that moment. Jay's touch would always have special meaning for her, she sadly realized, but she was better off without it ... if he was only using it as a means of bringing her round to his will.

'So you see,' Jay continued, seeming not to notice anything wrong in Rhea's attitude. 'Your little bit of eavesdropping was not quite so unfortunate, after all. It gave me the evidence needed to implicate both men.'

Oh yes, Rhea could see. Could see only too well. She turned her eyes on the now inky-black waters of the canal, dotted here and there with palely dancing reflections of light bulbs strung from the trees of a nearby hotel and restaurant.

'Let's get something to eat,' Jay suggested, so casually, as if they had been discussing nothing more than the weather. Rhea wanted to go home, end this now before the hurt became unbearable. But the refusal, so strong in her mind, would not come from her lips. Silently, she allowed herself to be guided towards the brightly lit black and white door of the old half-timbered manor house that was now The Tudor House Restaurant.

They sat at a table by the window, ate sole and drank white wine. Jay talked of Spain, of how he had needed to look the part to blend with the sea-faring life of the harbour and infiltrate the seamier side of the city life. He told her how he had resigned from the Special Branch in order to concentrate fully on putting all the people connected behind bars.

Rhea found it rather odd that he should take the matter so personally. She also found it upsetting that he spoke of Jay Rutherford the policeman, but did not touch on Jay Rutherford the man.

Rhea did not say much. She listened, and watched the stars glittering frostily in the clear black sky. She watched a barge moving slowly down the canal and the fairy-lights flickering on the large oak tree standing in the centre of the restaurant's large front lawn. She pondered the inconsistency of life. How she had longed for this moment. To be in such a pleasant situation, Jay by her side. All her troubles would be over ... or so she had imagined.

'Are you happy with the Parsons?'

Rhea turned slowly from the window, looked into Jay's concerned face, into his eyes, feeling as if her soul was being dragged from her. She had heard the question, yet at that moment it seemed totally irrelevant.

'You want me to be a witness ... don't you?' she said matter-of-factly. Every night I have fallen asleep praying that tomorrow I would see you again. And now you have come. You have searched me out, found me. And for what ... ? Because I am useful to your cause. Because I can provide the evidence you need to fulfil your taste for revenge!

'Well ... ' Jay hesitated, looked uncertain. 'It might come to that,' he added, reaching out to cover her hand lying on the table.

Rhea pulled her hand away. 'Why is this case so important to you?'

Jay hesitated, only for a moment, but long enough for Rhea to know he was holding something back. Her heart dropped to her stomach with a sickening thud.

'I've seen too many people ruined by dope,' he replied simply. Rhea nodded, understanding far more than was spoken in the words. The sudden, disquieting thought that Jay had come to get her services for the trial that must follow, had come to Rhea as they had walked along the towpath. His conversation had only proved her correct.

Rhea stood up suddenly. 'Shall we go,' she said, not a question, but an instruction that would not be denied.

They walked in silence back along the towpath, past the barge Rhea had watched move down the canal, which had now moored up for the night. She snuggled into her coat, but the thick wool could not keep out the chill of the night that had grown suddenly colder and darker. She was grateful it was only a short journey, for in the darkness she tripped a couple of times on rough stones and Jay reached out to steady her ... and she did not want to feel his touch, it was too painful.

'You'll let me know when you want me in court?' she asked steadily, letting him know she was not inviting him in, that this was goodbye, as they reached his car standing in the Parsons' drive.

'Don't worry about that.' A look of concern shadowed Jay's face. He studied Rhea's features for a long moment, giving her the impression he was considering whether to say something or not. He turned away, heaved a silent sigh, then looked back into her eyes. 'Don't be too disappointed.' He brushed her cheek in a manner of gentle reassurance. 'You will forget the other Jay Rutherford ever existed.' He paused, and Rhea hated the night that threw a veil over his emotions. She wanted to see exactly what he was feeling, not a mere shadow of what he might be experiencing. She wanted to see him suffering at least some of the hurt she was going through.

'He does not exist, Rhea,' Jay continued, seemingly oblivious to Rhea's torment. 'Not the man you fell in love with.'

Rhea's laugh was too high, brittle, strained. 'Don't you think I can see that for myself?' *He* could not see how much he was hurting her, could not see what he was putting her through. Because he did not care enough to want to see, she realized, despondency darkening and closing round her.

A long silence passed between them. Get in the car and go, Rhea inwardly urged, not having the courage or the heart to speak the words out loud.

Yet, when finally Jay did climb into the car and start the engine, her heart took a sickening dive.

'Look after yourself, love,' he said, through the open window, before driving away.

Rhea nodded, her smile tight, her voice lost.

Don't call me love ... you don't mean it, she thought bitterly, as she watched the car's red rear-lights until they were consumed by the night. Then she turned and walked towards the front door, silent tears streaming down her face.

Eight

Rhea had not known the trial was imminent until suddenly the papers were once more filled with the story of drug shipments being carried from North·Africa to the southern coast of Spain, then distributed around Europe, including Britain. Though it was not Europe the newspapers were concerned with: it was Britain and Greg Thorpe.

This was only Greg Thorpe's trial and a trial did not necessarily mean he could be convicted. Rhea shivered at the thought, as she had shivered at it many times since the night Jay had asked her to be a witness. She was extremely nervous of being called to the witness stand.

She could not understand why she had not been informed when the court would be wanting her to attend. It did seem rather odd to leave it so late. Nevertheless, she assumed, they would be sending for her very shortly ... and whenever it was would be too soon for Rhea.

She had also thought Jay would have been in touch again. Not because he had any feelings for her: their last meeting had proved without doubt that she could love him all she liked, but she would get nothing in return. But he needed her as his special witness, to realize his personal vendetta, or whatever name he might choose to put to his thirst for revenge. So Rhea had expected him to turn up again, if only to make sure she was still alive to stand up and testify for him. It was, after all, fifteen months since he had seen her. A lot could happen in fifteen months.

Though not enough could happen to stop Rhea feeling hurt that Jay had not been in touch. She still woke each morning with the feeling that this might be the day she would see him again, even though she was irritated and annoyed with herself for doing so. If she did see him, it would only be because he needed something from her, she told herself continually.

But still Rhea wanted to see Jay, especially now she had saved up the three hundred pounds she had borrowed from him on the boat.

Rhea folded the last small cardigan and put it away in Amanda's wardrobe.

'Read another story!' Rosie demanded grumpily.

Rhea closed the wardrobe door and turned to Rosie's bed. 'No,' she replied, with a fondly amused smile. 'You are too much of a sleepyhead to listen.'

'I am not going to school tomorrow! I don't like Danielle. She spoiled my picture,' Rosie grumbled.

Rhea pulled the quilt up to Rosie's neck and kissed the tousled red-head. 'It is Saturday tomorrow. You do not have to go to school on Saturday.'

For a moment Rosie looked piqued that she had been done out of her argument. Then she turned over, cuddled her large yellow teddy bear and closed her eyes.

Rhea wished her own problems would vanish so

easily, and turned her attention to Amanda's bed, tucking her second charge in for the night. The trial was into its second week and still Rhea had not been summoned to attend, or heard from Jay. The agony of waiting was getting unbearable. All she wanted was to get it over and done with.

Downstairs Rhea curled up in one of the large grey leather armchairs and picked up the daily newspaper. She scoured the print, but could not make out if the trial was going well or not. The evidence seemed to be stacked against Thorpe but, ridiculous though it seemed to Rhea, it was not so easy to prove. Points that were quite obvious to her had to be proved over and over in the court of law.

'Good grief, Rhea!' Jo exclaimed. 'Isn't that Jay?'

Rhea's gaze leaped to the television news report that Jo was watching. The breath caught in her throat. It *was* Jay!

He was hurrying from the courthouse with another man. Another policeman, Rhea guessed from the look of him.

'Sergeant Rutherford!' the television interviewer called, racing to Jay's side and stuffing a microphone half-way up his nose. 'Is the story about your sister true?'

Sister? Rhea froze. What story about what sister?

Jay did not reply. Rhea knew the muscles at the corners of his jaw had stiffened.

'Did your sister take heroin, Sergeant Rutherford?' the television interviewer prompted.

Jay kept on walking. 'Is it true she got the drug from Thorpe's supply?' the interviewer continued, refusing to be put off.

Rhea could tell by the tight line of Jay's mouth, the glassy anger of his eyes, that he was close to the end of his endurance. She gritted her teeth, waiting for the crunch, the sound of the interviewer's chin crumbling beneath Jay's fist.

Fortunately a waiting police car sped down the road, screeching to a halt in front of Jay. Jay jumped quickly into the back, the other man following, and the car roared away, leaving the television interviewer standing.

'What was all that about?' Jo asked, peering at Rhea over the gold-rimmed spectacles she wore for reading and watching television. 'Do tell me? I am intrigued.'

Rhea was also intrigued. 'I don't know,' she voiced in a half-murmur, only now becoming aware she had stopped breathing and beginning to draw breath again. 'I don't know. I was not aware he had a sister.' She looked blankly at Jo, realizing she must sound foolish.

Jo looked puzzled, then concerned. Rhea could see what was on her mind. If Rhea did not know Jay had a sister, did she know if he had a wife?

'I don't know,' Rhea repeated, almost as if Jo had voiced the question. The only thing she knew at that moment was that she was sounding like a record with the needle stuck.

The television was no help. The news-reader had obviously covered the report before the attempted interview of Jay outside the court, for when the camera returned to the studio, another story was begun.

Rhea glanced quickly at her watch. 7.15!

'Does Mr Wiggins' stay open till seven-thirty every evening?' she asked in a rush.

'Mostly,' Jo confirmed, looking more puzzled.

Rhea leaped from the chair. 'I have to find the paper,' she gasped in hurried explanation, as she crossed the room. She was not entirely certain the story was from a newspaper; it had not been in her own that morning. But she had to do something and was unable to stretch her mind further at that moment.

Rhea found exactly what she was looking for. With the newspaper clutched in her hand she raced back to the house. Then she went straight to her own room to read in private. She did not need anyone's eyes watching her as she learned about Jay. Especially Jo, who would insist on knowing everything and so suffocate Rhea with her kind intentions.

The paper fell to the floor. Rhea's head fell back against the tapestry cushion on the tall-backed rocking-chair.

It was worse than Rhea could ever have imagined.

Oh Jay! Poor Jay! Her heart flew to him.

Jay's parents had been killed in a plane crash when he was twenty, leaving him with a six-year-old sister. His sister had gone to live with their father's brother and his wife. But now she was dead. Killed by heroin four and a half years ago, at the tender age of sixteen.

It was all there in black and white. Every personal detail for all the world to see.

And it was an exclusive interview given by Jay's aunt. The woman who had brought up the young girl.

She had been paid to do this to him! Rhea's disgust for the woman almost choked her. What kind of a woman must she be? Rhea asked herself over and over again. Even if she hated Jay that much, surely she should have some feelings for the child she had watched grow up!

Throughout the night Rhea remained sitting in the rocking-chair, unconsciously moving to and fro. Long before dawn she knew what she had to do.

The courtroom was all wood panelling and brass knobs. It smelled of beeswax, leather and dust and put Rhea in mind of a scholar's ancient study room.

She sat on the front row of the public gallery, squashed between two large gentlemen. But Rhea barely noticed. The moment she sat down, her eyes ran rapid circles over the crowded room until she found him. He was wearing a dark grey suit and tie with a white shirt. He looked very serious, very sombre, a far cry from her perfect pirate. Rhea's sympathies tied a tight knot in the pit of her stomach; her heart went out to him.

I'm here, Jay, she cried inwardly. But he did not hear. His hearing was locked on to every word spoken from the witness box and from the defence and prosecution counsel. His vision was fixed on a patch of floor in front of the tall witness stand. He was like a statue. Rhea imagined that the times he looked up from that spot during the entire morning's hearing could have been counted on the fingers of one hand.

Not until the judge called a recess for lunch did Jay move. Along with everyone else in the courtroom he stood up, spoke a few words to the man by his side, then looked around the crowd that was already beginning to disperse.

Rhea held her breath, willed him to look up, to lift his gaze and see her standing there. But his eyes remained at ground-floor level. The gallery above his head was of no concern to him and he turned and walked towards the door.

Rhea's heart sank and she almost called out his name. Then fate took a hand. Her spirits rose, hardly daring to hope. A man came up behind Jay and tapped him on the shoulder. Jay turned. The man spoke and Jay frowned, put his hand behind his neck as if rubbing away an annoying ache and stretched tiredly. The action tilted his head back, lifting his eyes high enough to meet the statuesque Rhea staring right back at him.

Jay's shock was only momentary. Without taking his eyes off Rhea, he bit out something to the other man, then turned and hurried out of the door.

They met at the top of the stairs.

'What in heaven's name are you doing here?' Jay snapped, coming up in front of Rhea like a brick wall about to topple and crush her.

Rhea was too taken aback by his animosity to speak. His anger burst raw and lustrous from his eyes. Silence stretched between them like a wire at full tension, about to snap.

Rhea wished the floor would open up and swallow her.

'I thought I was needed to give evidence?' she retorted coolly.

'You know very well they would have sent for you if

you were needed! So just *why* are you here?' he demanded.

'I thought you might need some moral support,' she returned, her voice diminishing on the last. How could she ever have thought that this man needed anything from her?

'Why?' Jay demanded cruelly, neither the tone of his voice nor the look in his eyes softening. Just then two women came by, late stragglers from the public gallery. As they passed by, they gave curious glances to the two standing at the top of the stairs in obvious discontent.

The next moment, Jay grabbed Rhea's arm. 'We can't talk here,' he growled, and dragged her down the stairs, overtaking the two women, much to their indignation. He did not stop when they reached the outside world, but dragged Rhea away from the front exit and round the corner to a white Ford Granada waiting there.

Jay drove in silence to the edge of the park, pulled up by the high black metal railings and stopped the engine.

'Why, Rhea? Why have you come?' His anger was no less potent for the few minutes passed in driving.

I wanted to be with you. To give you support. To help you through all this. To stand by your side and show you someone cared. Steeling herself against showing how much his attitude hurt, Rhea merely said, 'I thought you might appreciate having someone to talk to.' She could not speak the rest. Besides, Jay did not want to know. 'When I read about your sister I realized just how personal ... '

She got no further. 'You realized!' Jay stormed, his fury filling the car with the pressure of a whirlwind.

'Who are you to realize anything about me?'

Rhea clenched her teeth. The prickle of tears forced its way to her eyes and she stared rigidly at the number plate of the car in front until the feeling had passed.

'I thought you might need ... ' She hesitated, about to say 'a shoulder to cry on', decided against it, but what else? A hand to hold? Someone to lean on? ... someone to talk to,' she repeated, feeling foolish, feeling she was wasting her time, feeling utterly despondent.

'To talk to!' he growled sarcastically. 'Didn't the papers give you enough? What more do you want? A moment-by-moment account of the whole mess?' He glared at Rhea, his face taut with a bitterness that sent shivers down her spine. 'Do you want to hear how my aunt turned my sister against me until seeing me upset the child so much I stopped visiting her? How I cut her out of my life? How I left her alone for six years ... because that is how I thought *she* wanted it!' He paused, his knuckles white and bloodless on the steering-wheel. His eyes, burning with something far deeper than Rhea could find words for, stared sightlessly over the top of the mini car whose number plate had helped hold back Rhea's own emotions.

'My sister was ten years old when I last saw her alive,' Jay continued, his anger dulled, but still rising within him like bile. 'Until one night I was called out to a body in the street and I found my own sister lying dead in a filthy gutter.'

Jay fell silent then, a tense highly-charged silence that filled the car with an atmosphere tangible enough to be cut with a knife.

Rhea did not speak. She could not speak. She stared out of the side window. Across the park children played on brightly coloured swings and climbing-frames. Had Jay ever taken his sister to the playground? she wondered. Had he done any of the brotherly things with her? He had been so good with the children at Rosie's party. A natural!

Or was he? A frown crept onto Rhea's face. Had Jay played with the children because he wanted to play, and enjoyed doing so? Or had he been feeding a sense of remorse for what he had left too late, but which he felt he should have done?

No! Rhea closed her eyes against the next thoughts leaping to her mind. *Kid*!

The name screamed round and round inside her head until she felt the sound must fill the car and Jay must also be able to hear it. She could hear his own voice booming out, calling her the name she had so detested. The natural choice for an older brother to call a younger sibling! After all, she was only two years older than his sister had been.

Rhea turned to him suddenly, realizing she had to get out of the car and away from Jay. 'I'm sorry about your sister,' she said with true sincerity. 'I wish I had known before. I wish you had told me earlier.'

Jay shrugged his shoulders, but did not speak. He looked suddenly older and very weary.

'It would not have altered my feelings for you,' Rhea continued honestly. Nothing could do that. 'But it would have helped if I had known you had put me in the space left empty by her death.'

Jay's head snapped round, his eyes meeting Rhea's in stony denial.

Rhea shook her head. 'Don't try to tell me it isn't true,' she added firmly, before he could speak. 'You probably don't realize it yourself. But looking after me the way you did was a softener to your own guilt.' Tears once more threatened to erupt and she turned quickly from him.

'You don't know what you're talking about.' Jay tried to insist. Rhea had the feeling he had bitten his tongue against adding the name 'kid' on the end.

'Unfortunately I do,' she replied wearily. 'I wish I was wrong. I wish you could have looked at me just once and seen a woman worthy of loving. I know now you never will.' With a deeply felt sigh, she called on all her reserves to give her the strength needed to face him without her emotions getting the better of her. Strength that was badly needed, for their eyes clashed in a violent shock of betrayal and Rhea shivered, remembering Jay's disgust on the occasions when he had kissed and held her as a lover.

Oh, how she wished those embraces had never happened. It was no longer a memory she wished to cling on to. Yet she knew it would remain with her forever.

'I hope I have helped you a little,' she began, knowing she could not endure being so close to him for much longer. 'I hope the trial goes your way.' She swung the door open, climbed out and walked quickly away.

She thought she heard him call after her. But she was not sure, and even if she had been would not have stopped and turned round.

Even the tears, running freely down her face, could not blur the picture of repellence that filled her mind's eye; the self-loathing that kissing her had put on the face of the man she loved.

Nine

'Don't think I'm interfering, Rhea. I know it's none of my business,' Cathy said, leaning across the table on the open-air veranda of the cricket club in a conspiratorial manner. 'But Jonathan is getting a bit miffed with you.'

Rhea smiled. She knew what was coming next. It was none of Cathy's business, but Cathy made it her business ... regularly!

The union between Rhea and Cathy's brother, Jonathan, had become Cathy's number one interest, ever since Cathy and Mark had become engaged; an occasion which had prompted Cathy to believe her twin brother should be sharing her pre-nuptial bliss.

'Jonathan has nothing to be "miffed' about,' Rhea explained, being careful to hold her temper. She hated the thought that Jonathan discussed her freely with his sister, even though Cathy was her best friend. 'There is nothing between Jonathan and me. *He* knows that!' Rhea added firmly.

'But why?' It was almost a wail and Rhea sighed with despair. 'What's wrong with Jonathan?' Cathy demanded.

Rhea sighed again. She had only gone to the dance with Jonathan in the first place because Cathy had told her he had been let down at the last minute. Since then they had only seen each other alone on three occasions. They had seen each other frequently in the company of Cathy and Mark, but that did not count. At least, to Rhea, it did not count.

Rhea could not understand why Jonathan was still so intent on pursuing her. The last time he had taken her out she had made it quite clear that his fumbling attempts at passes were not gratefully received.

Rhea shuddered, remembering the night, the nausea that had risen with the touch of Jonathan's lips. She really could not imagine why he still wanted anything to do with her.

'There is nothing wrong with your brother,' Rhea replied, hoping the smile she gave Cathy looked sincere. 'Your brother is a very nice boy.'

Rhea pulled herself up short, but the word 'boy' had slipped out and, desperate as she was to take it back, it was too late.

Fortunately Cathy did not seem to see any error in the statement. Neither did she notice her friend's sudden lack of attention and continued to stress her brother's virtues, thrusting Rhea into a dark crevice she had been trying to climb out of for the last month. A crevice which made her compare every man she looked at with Jay Rutherford.

Age had nothing to do with it, she told herself despairingly. Jay was not that much older than Jonathan ... only ten years. Jonathan just was not right for her. There was nothing more to it than a lack of chemistry!

'Fancy another coke?' Rhea asked, getting up and vanishing into the club bar to escape Cathy for a moment.

But the subject was not so easy to dismiss, and Rhea walked back to the table with two cans of Coca Cola in her hands, trying desperately to forget all the times she had looked at Jonathan and thought how immature he appeared.

Rhea did not stay at the cricket club much longer. Before Jonathan and Mark came off the pitch for tea, she excused herself on the pretext of a headache and made her way home wishing she had not gone in the first place.

Rhea had the weekend to herself, or she would not have gone to the cricket match. Jo and Robert had gone away, taking the girls with them to look over a preparatory school they were considering sending them to.

'A welcome weekend off,' Jo had called it.

Rhea was not so sure about the 'welcome' bit; not after spending a day and night alone. She could not explain her feelings. Being on her own had never troubled her before. She imagined it must be after the trouble at the Fonts.

Yet Rhea did not feel fear, only a great loneliness. A solitariness that had, against her better judgement, sent her in search of companionship with Cathy and Mark and Jonathan. A big mistake, she realized, feeling far more isolated now than she had in the beginning.

Rhea saw the car, a racy-looking red Toyota, standing close to the Parsons' gate, as she walked down the lane. She did not take much notice. There was a telephone box close by and people often parked there to use the telephone.

She was fumbling in her bag for the house keys, not looking where she was going, when she was brought up short by the sound of her name.

The breath stilled in her lungs at the sound of the voice. She looked up, speechless, unable to make her mind function and admit what her eyes were seeing. Slowly she pulled herself together. 'Hello Jay,' she said with forced lightness, then continued the search for the keys, found them and ducked around the tall, statuesque form blocking her way and hurried towards the house. If she had to meet him again, then she would rather it were not in the middle of the public road, even though it was a quiet one.

'I did not expect to see you again,' she informed him pointedly, pausing in the half-open gateway in a manner that challenged his right to follow. Which he seemed to take for granted he was going to do.

Jay got the message. He stopped on the outside, pushed his hands deep into the pockets of olive-green jeans and sucked thoughtfully on his bottom lip.

Rhea watched him, wishing he would speak, say whatever he had come to say and go so that she could turn around and not look at him. The casualness of his clothing made him more like the Jay she had known in

Spain, not the smartly suited policeman of the court-room.

'Why have you come here?' she asked, realizing she was wasting her time if she expected him to speak first, a betraying tremor running through her voice.

'Once before, you offered me your ear if I wanted to talk,' he said slowly, thoughtfully. 'I've come to take you up on the offer.'

Rhea almost gave an ironic laugh. 'I don't think we have anything to talk about any longer,' she replied coolly. She would not allow him to walk back into her life and upset everything when she had got over him! Just because he had decided she could be of use to him again.

'We do,' Jay responded confidently. 'We have a lot to talk about.' Stepping forward he grasped the gate with both hands. 'And I am not going until you have listened.' He pushed the gate wide open, forcing Rhea back until she was almost standing in the branches of a prickly conifer tree.

'Don't think you can come here pushing your weight around,' Rhea fumed, giving the gate a hefty shove back at him.

Jay held it fast. 'If pushing my weight around is what it takes to get you to listen, then push it I will. And I don't care if it causes you embarrassment,' he added pointedly.

Rhea was furious. 'Fortunately for you the Parsons are away!' She stopped, realizing her mistake too late, far too late, from the jubilant expression that leaped into

Jay's eyes.

'In that case,' Jay walked around the gate, kicking it closed behind him. 'Unless you would like to be carried to the door, I suggest you walk there.'

Rhea hesitated, but only for a moment. Her first instinct had been to refuse. Then she saw the challenging gleam in his eyes and hurriedly ducked past him and strode rapidly to the front door.

'You cannot come in,' she insisted, standing at the door, waving the hand holding the key in agitated circles in the air to emphasize her point. 'It would not be right,' she added, hating herself for sounding like a coy teenager.

Jay gave a bark of laughter. 'You trusted me on the boat ... I'm sure you could extend that trust for a few more minutes,' he asserted and, though Rhea had no idea how he managed it, got the keys out of her hand and was unlocking the door in the space of the same moment.

'I am not one of your criminals!' Rhea threw angrily over her shoulder, as she marched through the door he held open. She did not invite him in. She knew he needed no invitation. 'Or am I?' she questioned, spinning round on him as he closed the door behind him. 'Am I under house arrest?'

Jay stood directly before her. He smiled slowly. 'Don't put ideas into my head,' he replied.

'And don't you look at me that way!' Rhea warned meaningfully. 'I'm a kid! Remember? Or have you conveniently forgotten I was your substitute sister?'

Heat ran wild in her veins and glowed from her cheeks, firing her anger. She could feel his presence overtaking her reason. She would not let it, she ordered herself.

Like a lion pouncing on its prey, Jay was across the space between them before Rhea knew he had moved. He grasped her by the arms, forcing her to face him. 'You're wrong, Rhea. Very wrong. I'll admit I felt responsible for you in Spain. I did feel I needed to keep you where I could see you because you needed protection and, yes, I needed to protect you. You can relate that to a latent desire to purge myself of my guilty feelings towards my sister if you like. I see it as a normal reaction from any man worth his salt. Never once did I place you where my sister should have been. I never thought of you as a child.'

'You treated me like a child!' Rhea retaliated. 'You called me kid. Do you expect me to believe you were seeing a woman when you looked at me?'

Jay shook his head in slow regret. His face softened. 'I *was* seeing a woman. A beautiful woman. And I wanted her. But I was not me. I was acting a part. It would not have been right of me to lead you on, and I had to keep reminding myself of that fact. Calling you kid was for my benefit, Rhea, not yours.'

Confusion puckered Rhea's brow. 'Why?' she asked, her eyes narrowing with uncertainty. 'You knew how I felt about you. Why couldn't you have told me the truth?'

'The truth would have been too big a burden for you

to carry. The less you knew the safer you were.'

'But I knew everything at the trial and you still seemed to hate me.'

'I had already messed up the life of one young girl,' Jay began quietly, letting Rhea go and walking across to the window, staring out at the privet-lined lane. 'I did not think I had the right to do it to another.'

'Oh Jay,' Rhea whispered, her sympathies rising.

She wanted to go to him, touch him, offering comfort. She remained where she stood, feeling shy of this new Jay Rutherford ... the real Jay Rutherford. 'Don't take the blame for your sister's death. It was not your fault.'

Jay glanced round, his expression unconvinced.

'You were too young to know your own mind ... or so I felt. I thought you would find someone else, soon forget me.' Apology spilled from Jay as he turned to Rhea.

Rhea's emotions whirled round and round inside her head, like a child's playground roundabout, faster and faster, threatening to fling her off into the unknown. She did not know what to make of this complete volte-face. She wanted to believe him. But her own wanting was too strong, and she feared its power over her.

'I'm sorry, Jay,' she said, a breezy smile fixed on her face. 'You are too late. I *have* found someone else.'

A spasm of darkness caught Jay's features for the briefest of moments.

'I have forgotten you,' Rhea added just for good measure, hearing the shaky high pitch of her own voice like a warning bell inside her head.

Jay walked across to her. Rhea turned away frightened more of herself than of Jay, But a large hand reached out, pulling her back.

'I don't believe you,' he said simply. 'You want me as much as I want you.'

'As much as you needed me before,' Rhea replied bitterly. 'When you came crawling back because you needed me in court. I don't need that kind of need.' She felt her strength ebbing into an intense sadness. She would not let him hurt her again. She would not!

Jay's face darkened. 'Did I call you into court?' he demanded.

'No ... Well no,' she had to admit. But that did not change anything. She had not been needed or, she felt sure, he would have had no reservations about calling her.

'I had no intention of dragging you into court,' Jay began, as if reading Rhea's mind. 'Didn't you realize that?'

Rhea looked up into his face, confusion deepening, overwhelming her. 'How could I have realized it? All I knew was that you only turned up because you wanted me to do something for you.'

'Oh love,' Jay pulled her into his arms, regret darkening his features as he lowered his face into her hair.

Rhea did not object, did not push away. The feeling was too nice.

'The man you had fallen in love with was not me,' Jay began, emotion cracking his voice. 'I thought you were disappointed with the new Jay Rutherford you were seeing for the first time. I was so different.' He gave a short ironic laugh. 'I lied about wanting you for a witness because I wanted to make it easy for you. I felt I could walk away from you more easily if you did not realize I had come to find out if you still cared for me. I didn't want to put you under any pressure. But I had to come and find out.' He held his head back and looked down into her face. 'Do you understand?'

'Oh Jay,' Rhea breathed, bathing in the expression she had longed to see yet feared she never would. 'I was not disappointed in you! It had been weeks since I had seen you and all you could talk about was your case ... I thought it was all you cared about. I thought it was more important to you than anything.'

'Not more important than you, sweetheart. I would not have dragged you into the witness box for anything. Not even if Thorpe had looked like getting off. I did not want you involved. I did not want you anywhere near that courthouse where Thorpe and his friends might have seen you.'

'Oh!' Rhea mouthed. She had not thought about the possibilities of being spotted by anyone other than Jay. Her only concern had been that Jay should not feel alone in the world.

'That is why I wanted to strangle you when I saw you standing there.' Jay looked reproving, and shook his head, trying to cast away the awful memory.

'You were so angry,' Rhea said, apology in her voice. Then she was overtaken by a sharp burst of unexpected laughter, as the totally irrelevant image of the two incensed women on the stairs leaped to her mind. 'You almost sent those women flying,' she said, reliving the moment when Jay had dragged her hurriedly down the stairs and away from the court-house.

Jay looked sheepish. 'With luck I will never see either of them again.' He lifted his hand, cupped Rhea's chin, gently, lovingly. 'Will I see you again?' The expression in his eyes echoed the plea in his voice; a glow inside Rhea burst into flame.

She nodded her head. 'Yes,' she replied, her heart and soul in the one simple word, a moment before Jay's mouth touched her own in a gently seeking kiss.

It seemed like an eternity before Jay pulled away. His smile was deep and warm, though a flicker of doubt touched his eyes and, as he took Rhea's hand and led her through to the drawing-room and sat her down on the couch by his side, she frowned.

'I am back on the force, Rhea. Do you realize that?'

'Yes, I know you are,' she replied. Or rather she had assumed, from the trial, that Jay was once more a fully working policeman.

'It is not a nine-to-five occupation. It can get in the way of normal life.'

Suddenly Rhea sat erect. 'What is this?' she demanded laughingly. 'A full confession? Or a proposal?'

Jay smiled, the corners of his eyes crinkling into tiny sun rays. 'A proposal. I might not be the best catch around ... but I do love you, Rhea Dempster.' He brushed her cheek with an action that was almost reverent. 'More than words can tell you,' he added lovingly. 'Do you think you could put up with the old Bill?' he asked jokingly.

A lump swelled in Rhea's chest. 'Oh yes! I could put up with him,' she said, sinking into his arms as they folded around her like a strong, protective fence. She pressed her head against his chest, enjoying the steady thump, thump of his heartbeat beneath her ear.

Jay's hand brushed her cheek once more and Rhea turned her face into his palm, kissed the warm skin, tasted the slightly salty taste of him on her tongue and suddenly her memory was stirred.

She sat upright. A smile of triumph filled her face. 'The tattoo,' she said. The one thing that he could not change. The one thing that would prove her perfect pirate really had existed.

'It was not real,' Jay replied, looking apologetic. 'It is no longer there ... just like the hair.'

Rhea's mouth fell open. 'Where has it gone?' she asked dumbly. 'You can't lose a tattoo!'

'It was not a tattoo,' Jay explained, laughing fondly at Rhea's reaction. 'It was henna. Painted on.'

'What's henna?' Rhea asked, not sure if she was disappointed. The tattoo would have proved that the sailor and the policeman were one and the same.

'A dye,' Jay replied, his laughter dying. 'Asian women use it to paint their bodies. It does not wash off. It wears off after a few weeks. I just had to touch it up now and again.' He looked concerned.

'Does it matter?' he questioned seriously.

'No, it does not matter,' Rhea assured him. Nothing mattered so long as Jay wanted her. Her perfect pirate had come home and, sinking into his arms once more, she was filled with the conviction that she would never lose him again.

Summerland Affair

One

Rain hammered on Alison's sage-green anorak and bounced off her slim, now slightly stooping shoulders. She hoisted up the metal framework of her heavy back-pack.

She glanced up at the ominous, grey sky. 'Summerland!' she muttered. 'Humph!' But then an impish grin spread across her face. 'OK, Summerland. Rain or no rain, I'm here and I'm here to stay whether...'

She stopped chatting to herself and held out her thumb as a car came her way. She knew it was risky – and Simon wouldn't like it a bit. A white Volvo sped past, splashing her jeans.

She was striding along the lane again, still not sure if she wasn't a little relieved the car hadn't stopped, when a maroon Range-Rover hurtled past. Then she realized it had stopped some way ahead of her.

Her heart beat a little faster. She had not flagged him down, but he seemed to be waiting for her. A crack of thunder sent her hurrying towards the vehicle. She felt like an overloaded camel with all the stuff rattling on her back.

Later, she tried to remember what she'd felt when she first saw the man's face. The first lurching in her stomach. The surge like an electric current through her body making her nerve-endings tingle.

And it had nothing to do with the colour of his eyes. She couldn't make them out. Steely-blue? Indigo? It didn't matter. It was the expression under his heavy lids that collided with her senses.

She stared at him, the rain running down her face.

'D'you want a lift, then?' he said.

He tossed her rucksack into the back.

'Me next?' she laughed nervously.

As she untied the strings of her hood she saw hin glance at her thick raven hair as it cascaded over he shoulders. She was about to unzip her anorak bu thought better of it and slid her hand into her pocke instead.

His eyelids unfolded lazily. 'Sure you don't want t change your mind?'

She wasn't sure.

He held out his hand. 'I'm Guy Kington – fron Cliff's Hotel in Summerland.' His grip was tight.

'I thought this *was* Summerland. That's where I'n heading for. I'm Alison Lacie.'

'Well, Miss Lacie, whatever it is you've got in you pocket... you can relax. I stopped to pick you u because I felt sorry for you. I wouldn't put my dog ou in weather like this.' He stroked the gear-lever out o neutral.

Alison reddened. 'It's only my hanky.' She blew he nose delicately.

One corner of his well-formed lips curved upward as if he was thinking a whole lot of things and n letting on what they were. In her estimation, those so of people usually oozed self-esteem. She wondere how old he was. Thirty? Could be older with thos spidery lines at the corners of his eyes. He wa weather-beaten, as if he'd been around. Handsom though. She had to admit it.

Sitting straight-backed, he allowed the drivin

wheel to slide loosely through his long tanned fingers. The cord collar of his toffee-coloured waxed jacket was turned up. He probably thought it made him appear rakish. He was the type her friends at Polytechnic had as a pin-up. All that tousled black hair.

She looked away quickly as he glanced back at her.

'Hardly saw you in that jacket. Thought you were a tree.'

Feeble attempt at humour, she told herself. Ever since she'd climbed in the Range-Rover she'd had a feeling he was having a laugh at her. Not a good old belly-laugh. He wasn't that type. His type was all irony and clever-clogs remarks.

She stared gloomily at the bleak landscape.

'Cheer up. You'll feel better when the sun comes out.'

'Does it?'

'Uh-huh.' He nodded.

She supposed he was right. Unless he lived half his life abroad, where else would he get such a magnificent tan that made her feel she'd been shut up in a dungeon? Well, she had one day off a week in this new job and she vowed to spend some time on the beach sunbathing.

He interrupted her thoughts. 'In fact, this part of the country is reputed to have a very low rainfall. Wonderful landscape, magnificent skies, wide open beaches – and where else would you find so much wildlife scuttering about?'

The words were no sooner out of his mouth than a huge bronze cock-pheasant ran across the lane in front of them. He cursed roundly and, clamping his hands on the wheel, managed to avoid it as it floated into the air and over a hedge at the last minute.

Afterwards when she heard him exhale, Alison threw back her head and laughed, her lips stretching away from her even white teeth. The gaiety spread to her rich brown eyes, wide apart and framed by a fine-boned oval face. It was his turn to study her.

'So where are you from?' he asked her.

'Near Newcastle.'

'Wouldn't have guessed from the accent.'

'It's not my home-town.'

'And you're down here on holiday?'

He was sounding pleasant and interested now. And almost smiling properly. She noticed his features weren't at all even. There was a ruggedness about his square face and a strong jawline that defied anyone to disagree with him.

'I should be so lucky! No, I've got a job here.'

'Where exactly?'

'The holiday camp in Summerland.'

She didn't need to look at him to sense the change in him. She could almost feel him stiffen; see the bloodless knots in his knuckles.

'You know it?' she asked.

'I know it,' he answered woodenly.

'I hope it's a good place to work. I'm going to be a waitress there.'

'Oh, I've no doubt you'll find it suits you perfectly – except you don't strike me as being the type who runs to everyone's beck and call.'

'Don't you like holiday camps?'

'Don't know anything about them.' His lips made a tight line.

'I think they're great, especially for families. When I

was little I was taken to a camp near Lowestoft and we had super fun.'

He jerked to a stop outside some white gates with a gravel drive beyond. 'So why didn't you apply for a job in that area if you already knew it?' he asked drily.

'Because I like the one here, that's why.'

He glanced towards a car coming out of the drive, its roof-rack loaded with cases. 'They're making a quick get-away,' he said and hauled out her rucksack.

'Have super fun,' he drawled before driving away.

Children in the overloaded car waved to her and she waved back. Their week was over. It reminded her she had arrived after the season had started.

She eyed a flag flapping wetly in the wind on a pole, squared her shoulders and headed for the reception area. It was to set the seal on her life.

Alison handed over her letter of acceptance to a woman wearing a striped blazer with a glittering S emblazoned on each lapel.

'Got you medical card, love?' she asked Alison.

A wiry man in his early fifties exploded into the room. He was wearing a gold-flecked, open-necked shirt, with cream jacket and trousers.

The man's sharp, grey-green eyes focused on Alison. 'Good afternoon, young lady.'

'This is Alison, the new waitress, Archie.'

'How d'ya do?' He popped a sweet in his mouth. 'Haven't I seen you before somewhere?'

'I don't think so.'

'I know! You was hitch-hiking in Coulson's Lane, wasn't you? Damn stupid, that. I didn't stop did I? Wouldn't let my little girl go picking up lifts with strange blokes, I'll tell you that.' He crunched on his sweet.

Alison tilted her chin. What she did had nothing to do with him.

'This is a very respectable camp, Alison. I'd like to make that clear.'

Before she could answer him he looked beyond her towards the open door and called. 'Honey, this is the girl who's sharing with you. Can you show her your chalet?'

A blonde girl enveloped in a shiny orange plastic raincoat nodded to Alison. As Alison followed her she heard the receptionist say, 'I've got me fancy dress all fixed up for Friday night. I'm going as traffic lights, Archie.'

'Well, I hope you won't be on red all night!'

The woman burst into giggles.

'Was that the proprietor?' Alison asked the blonde girl.

'Archie? Archie's the boss.'

Through the windows of a building they passed, Alison saw tables laid for a meal. Cooking smells drifting towards them reminded her she was hungry.

'What time is the next meal?'

'Six o'clock. For the holiday crowd that is. We have ours after.'

'My name is Alison. Alison Lacie.'

After a long pause, the other girl responded with an almost inaudible, 'Mine's Honey.'

When they reached the chalet she said sulkily, 'We aren't in with the other waitresses. Their block is full. I didn't know I was going to have to share.'

'Which bed is yours, Honey?'

Honey pointed. Alison scooped up a load of clothes from the other bed, a man's vest among them, and handed them to Honey. 'So this one must be mine, eh?'

Honey scowled, opened the wardrobe door and dropped everything in a heap in there. Then she walked out leaving Alison alone.

That night Alison went to bed early. She wondered why she was so tired. It wasn't as if she'd had to start work yet. Archie's wife, Rita, a timid little woman, had explained what she'd have to do the next morning, telling her not to worry if she forgot because someone would remind her.

She was woken from sleep by a loud whisper outside the door.

'I can't you fool! *She's* in there!'

'I'll see to her as well, then,' a man's voice proclaimed loudly.

Honey spoke with a shrill laugh. 'I can give you what you want!'

There was a long pause then the man said hoarsley, 'Well, that's better. There's a good girl.'

There was a shuffling, followed by a silence, punctuated by groans. This time it came from the back of the chalet. Alison stuck her head under the pillow and tried to sleep again.

Honey finally stumbled in and crashed on to her bed.

Thoughts tumbled in Alison's head. She told herself severely she was going to stick this job out whether she liked it or not. Heavens above, she was lucky to get it at all. But she remembered how Simon had wanted her to spend the summer at his house.

'Your mum's got enough on her plate without extra people around,' she'd told him. It was true. Simon had brothers and sisters galore, all rushing in and out at odd hours. The last time he had taken her there she'd been utterly charmed by their happy togetherness.

She remembered too, the tiny thought that surfaced inside her. If you marry Simon you can be part of all this.

It was the sort of family she'd dreamed about.

Her father left them when she was seven. Later, she heard from kids at school that he'd run off with Dot Green who lived opposite their house on the council estate.

Her mum had grown more acid with the years. Alison never knew where she stood. Sometimes she was treated like a little princess, but at other times her mum would lay into her with a fist like a cricket ball. However much she cried, it was nothing like the sobbing that came from her mother's room.

Her mum was unlucky with men. When she did eventually fall for another one – a road engineer – he turned out to be married. Alison lay awake as Honey snored softly. Thinking was depressing in the middle of the night.

The next morning in the dining-room, Alison tried to appear bright and energetic as she copied the others and carried tea and coffee-pots to the tables. Twice she went through the wrong swing-doors into the kitchen and collided with people coming out.

She was trying to remember who wanted cornflakes, when the supervisor stopped her.

'Where's Honey? You share with her, don't you?'

Alison reddened. As she'd left the chalet, Honey had moaned, 'Oh, my God, I feel terrible. If anybody asks, tell them I'm sick.' Then she'd rolled over and gone back to sleep.

'She – she's not well,' Alison stammered.

'Oh, I see.' The supervisor saw Archie beckoning her from the other side of the dining-room and hurried across to him. Alison breathed a sigh of relief.

'Sick again is she?' a waiter murmured in her ear. 'Mm – tell her to give up the evening job!'

He glided away holding his tray in the air, his legs in their black trousers moving so rapidly he might have been on casters.

The room filled up quickly after that with everyone chattering and laughing and nodding to new acquaintances. As the clatter of cutlery and clamour of voices reached a crescendo, Alison twisted in and out between tables, giving a cheery, 'Good-morning,' to those she had to serve.

Some of the campers teased her when she muddled up orders, taking slimmers' breakfasts to those who wanted fried, and vice-versa, and forgetting who wanted more milk. Then, to her absolute horror, a heap of plates and their contents cascaded through her nervous fingers to the floor.

'Cheer up, cocky. You only die once,' piped the gliding waiter. But it seemed to Alison that everyone, including Archie, was watching her.

When she returned to the chalet, Honey was not there. Her bedding had been left in a tangled pyramid. There were cigarette-butts in the washbasin and talcum powder all over the mat.

Alison sat limply on the edge of her own bed and remembered the neat room she'd left behind at Northside Polytechnic.

Simon's words came back to her. 'OK, Miss Independent, go and earn yourself some holiday money, but promise you'll let me know straight away if it doesn't work out. I can be there the same day to collect you.'

Dear, kind Simon. When she'd first arrived at Northside Poly, he'd taken her under his wing. Later, he'd said she'd looked like a waif. She grinned ruefully. She'd felt as lost then as she did now in this new job. But she hadn't been so clumsy!

Her large brown eyes clouded. Her troubles had been inside her then. Just before she'd left home for Poly, her mother had decided right out of the blue that she didn't want her to leave after all. Alison spent months writing long letters to cheer her up and listening to her tirades on the phone. If it hadn't been for Simon persuading her to carry on with the course, she'd have packed up and gone home.

If only she had!

She stood up quickly and wiped her cheeks, then she changed into pale blue jeans and white sweater. With a determined stride she marched outside past chalets and empty tennis courts and across fields to the beach.

'It'll bring roses to your cheeks down there. It's blowing a gale,' joked a camper with cheerful familiarity. The man's wife added, 'And the path is really soggy farther along. I'd use the path up there if I were you.' She pointed towards the perimeter of the field.

Alison thanked them, smiled and walked towards the next field where the path was on higher ground. She stood on the clifftop with the wind teasing her long dark hair into unruly streamers.

Below her, the North Sea smashed steely-grey rollers on to the shore, sucking them back noisily, dragging in pebbles and debris and leaving shingle in steeper banks dotted with yeast-like froth.

With her pale cheeks whipped pink, she made her way down to the beach where some steps had been carved out. Was it heavy rain that had caused the edges of the path to crumble?

Without warning, her feet slid from under her and even though she was holding on to the rope-railing she slipped down. Some loose pieces of rocks rattled down to the beach. Shaken, she stood up and beat sand and mud from her jeans.

The beach was practically deserted, except for someone walking a dog. She recognized who it was and thought of turning back. No, you don't she told herself, you came out for a walk and that's what you'll do.

Guy Kington had looked large sitting at the wheel of the Range-Rover but she hadn't realized he was this tall. He came striding towards her, wearing jeans and a black, leather jacket with the collar turned up.

'You didn't take long to make an escape. What's it like? "Wakey-wakey" and "Goodnight, campers"?'

'I don't know where you got your quaint ideas, but it isn't like that at all,' she said coldly, patting the Alsation which gazed up at her wagging its tail.

'So you've settled in nicely?' There was wry amusement in his face.

'I... I take a long time to settle in new places – but if there's anything wrong around here, it's that path.' She glanced over her shoulder and inclined her head.

'Oh?'

'It isn't safe.'

'Well, it is not meant for sliding down, skipping down, or running down!'

'There ought to be warning notices.'

'There are. They say Private. It happens to be for the use of hotel residents only.'

She followed his gaze towards a large Victorian building farther along, on top of the cliff.

'That?'

'Yes. Cliff's Hotel. It belongs to my father.'

His tone, and the obstinate line of his jaw began to irritate her. She tilted her head. 'You mean to say you don't even bend your precious rules on a filthy day like this when rain has made the other path so soggy?'

'I think you'll find an alternative path over the far side of that field.'

'Oh well! Then I'll make very sure that's the one I'll use next time!' She assumed a sweet smile. 'I assume the beach doesn't belong to you?'

'Hi!'

They both looked up. A man with a slighter figure than Guy ran nimbly down the path towards them. The Alsation bounded across to him and he ruffled its coat energetically.

He looked at Guy expectantly. 'Introduce me then, big brother.'

'This is my brother, Neil... Alison Lacie. She's a waitress at the camp. She didn't know about the path belonging to us. I was just telling her.'

'Hell, Guy... we don't have to go to those extremes. We've not bothered about that for ages.'

'So I gathered,' responded Guy drily. 'There's a distinct gap in the hedge between them and us.'

'Well, you needn't worry that I shall be using the path again,' interjected Alison. 'I've slipped on it once already.'

'You didn't say,' Guy said quickly.

'You didn't ask.'

'Did you hurt yourself?'

She fancied he was genuinely concerned, but his 'them and us' remarks still rankled. The man was a downright snob. She wondered what his position was at the hotel. Neil grinned at her. 'Well, I give you permission to use our path whenever you want, Alison.'

As she smiled at him she heard Guy murmur something about opening the floodgates. He called the dog and remarked to Alison, 'If you did any damage to your clothes, the hotel will reimburse you.'

Alison noted how Neil glanced sharply at his brother. Guy looked at him meaningfully and raised his well-formed eyebrows. 'OK?'

'I was about to suggest it myself,' said Neil tightly. 'Oh, and if you can spare the time, father would like to see you.' He turned round. 'I'll look forward to seeing you again, Alison. Sorry I can't stay, but I've a hotel to run.' He smiled at her before running back up the steps.

There was no mistaking the two were brothers... the same long legs and slim waists, but Neil's features were more even, without Guy's toughness. Neil's hair was a shorter style, too. But although he was the younger, he appeared to have the upper hand in running the hotel, although Guy seemed the more dominant.

Guy was watching Neil as he flew up the steps. 'He doesn't look as if he has any bother with the path, and I haven't heard anyone else complaining. Hotel guests seem perfectly satisfied.'

Alison noted the way he said 'hotel', making it sound very grand.

'You run the hotel, too?'

He scrutinized her through half-closed eyes as if somewhat amused by her remark, and said lazily, 'You could say I was general dogsbody. I've been away from Summerland for some time. My father has been ill. I came home to see him. And now, like you, Miss Lacie, I'm finding my feet.' His eyelids lifted to reveal piercing blue eyes. 'Just like you,' he continued softly.

In that instant, his eyes held hers. Then momentarily, his glance shifted to the gentle swell of her breasts under her sweater. For the second time since they had met, she felt her chest tighten, almost like a missed heartbeat. Such feelings over which she'd no power, made her uneasy – especially in this case – but she was not sure why.

He clicked his fingers and the dog charged to be with him. Turning away from her, Guy lifted his arm in a casual gesture of farewell and sauntered in the direction of the hotel.

Alison started walking briskly the other way.

Soon her feet crunched the shingle-bank and then on to wet sand where the tide was ebbing. Just as she had as a child, she started searching for stones and pebbles, promising herself she'd come again when she had more time. This was a treasure trove. She might find anything: semi-precious stones – even a fossilized sea-urchin many millions of years old. Wasn't it this very coastline that had prompted her to look for a job here in the first place?

Then there were the famous Summerland cliffs. Not in the pages of some text-book but right here before her eyes.

She gazed into the distance beyond groynes with waves crashing round them, out to a small island she'd seen from the clifftop. An island with a lighthouse on it. Gulls screamed plaintively around her. It was a haunting, doleful sound.

She made her way to where the cliffs were no longer a sheer suicidal drop to the beach below. Soon, she was clambering over dunes seemingly held together with marram grass. There was no way she intended to return via the path meant for *Hotel* residents only!

When she got back to the chalet, she stepped inside and stared. It was perfectly tidy; no clutter at all. Honey had even made her bed and was sitting at the dressing-table in a tiny, lacy uplift bra and mini-bikini briefs with a leopard-skin pattern on them. She paused in the process of stretching the wet strands of her blonde hair into a huge roller. She turned to look at Alison. She smiled.

'Thanks a lot.'

Alison was puzzled. Did she imagine that beam of gratitude lighting up Honey's face?

Honey continued, 'I was coming from the toilet block and saw the dining-room supervisor. I thought, Oh, my God, I'm in for it now, but all she did was ask me if I was feeling better. You told her I was in bed, then?'

Alison was about to say it was the last time she lied for Honey, but then she checked herself. What she said now could put paid to a happy relationship between them and she, probably more than Honey needed a friend.

'That's OK.' Alison shrugged casually and returned the smile.

Honey spoke with the comb between her teeth. 'Is this the first time you've worked in a place like this?'

'Yes.'

'Bet you aren't on the dole all winter, like me. Bumming around till May. You're a student aren't you? Need the bread?'

Alison nodded. 'Vacation job. I'm at a polytechnic.'

'What's it like there?'

'Pretty good. Emphasis on practical work as well...'

'Bit different from here, eh? What d'you think of Summerland so far?... Rubbish!' She laughed.

'Well... I made a complete fool of myself this morning.'

'Don't worry. When I started I was always putting the rings between the plates upside down. Had to be a juggler to balance the damn things. You'll soon get the hang of it.'

'I expect so. What's Archie like to work for?'

'OK. Doesn't pay much but it's better than being on Income Support. Mind, I don't know how he makes a tiny little camp like this pay year after year.' She inclined her head to one side, screwed up her eyes and scrutinized Alison. 'Have you ever thought of dyeing your hair? You've got a good figure and ever such sparkling eyes, haven't you? But that hair! Men like blondes you know.' She turned away to look in her mirror again. 'What you studying at polytechnic?'

'Geology.'

'Yeah?'

'Probably sounds boring, but it's not.'

'Got a boyfriend?'

'Yes. He was at poly, but he's got a job this year.'

'Geology too?'

'Yes – and he knows a lot more about it than I do.' Alison grinned on a nod.

'I bet he's got letters after his name. Will you get

letters after your name?'

Alison hesitated before murmuring, 'If I carry on with the course.' Simon's voice came back to her as if he was standing right there beside her. 'You've *got* to go on, Ali. You worked hard to get that grant. Don't chuck it all away. I know you were knocked out when your mum died but you must rid yourself of this guilt. Her illness had nothing to do with you leaving for poly. Finish the course and then, when we're married...' He'd taken it for granted they were a permanent couple. Everyone had taken it for granted.

She owed Simon so much. She doubted she'd have got through those awful months after the funeral without him. But now she was right away from him and from poly she was surprised to discover she was not very enthusiastic about returning to finish the course. Odd thoughts had been drifting through her mind. Like, was her mum right? Where did all this learning really get you? Hadn't it taken her away from her roots? From the people and places with which she was familiar?

When she did return home, people treated her in a different way – as if she were a stranger. And she felt as if she *was* slowly changing. That was all very well, she thought, but you weren't quite sure where you belonged any more.

The only certainty was that she hadn't been at home when her mum needed her most.

'It – it involves so much work, you see. I mean, this summer I'm supposed to be working on a thesis about the environment, the coastline and that sort of thing.'

Honey rolled up another section of hair. 'Rather have a bit of fun myself, personally.'

'I enjoy walking on the beach. I always have done.'

'Is that where you've just been? God, it must have been cold and empty down there this morning.' She switched on the hairdryer.

Alison finished changing, ready to be in the dining-room half an hour before the guests.

'True. There weren't many people down there. I did meet a couple of men from the hotel.'

Honey lowered the dryer and looked up with renewed interest. 'What were they like?'

Alison shrugged. 'Tall. I suppose you'd say they were good-looking. Brothers.'

Honey's jaw dropped open. 'The Kingtons? The older one...' She lifted her hands in a cupping movement to the sides of her shoulders. 'Big shoulders, athletic, hair blacker than yours.'

'Yes – yes, like that.'

'That's it. The Kington brothers. Aw!'

'So?' Alison gave a short laugh.

'The older one – he looks sulky, but I wouldn't mind...' She shivered. 'Ever since he came back a couple of weeks ago we've been nipping down to the beach in the hope of bumping into him. He sends prickles up your spine, doesn't he?'

'I think he's arrogant.'

'I've heard he can be snooty, but I know somebody who works at the hotel and he says he's a real good bloke.' She added after a pause, 'Which is surprising when you think about it.'

'What do you mean?'

'Well, after what he did.'

'What?'

Honey shrugged, as if suddenly thinking better of it. 'Could be rumours of course. They've been circulating ever since he got here. But what I say is, Archie's done all right by me – gives me a job here every summer. So what's his business is his business. See?'

Alison didn't see, but she nodded. If she and Honey were to share this chalet all summer, she was going to keep the peace. She liked the friendly way Honey was treating her now. Even if it was because she'd lied for her.

'Well, I've bumped into him twice now and...'

'Where've you met him before?'

'He gave me a lift yesterday,' said Alison, still wondering what Guy Kington had to do with Archie.

Honey studied her closely. She was about Alison's age, twenty-three, but her next remark made her sound years older.

'Look, I know I made out I wouldn't mind having a bit of a fling with him. What woman wouldn't? You've only got to look at the bloke to know that. But I reckon my life and yours are poles apart. After what I've been through, I can look after myself.

'But from what I've heard,' Honey went on, 'well, put it this way. Don't ever tangle with him, Alison. Don't *ever*. He's big trouble!'

Two

Honey gazed earnestly at Alison from under raised eyebrows. 'Know what I mean?'

'He's not my type, Honey, so don't give it a thought.'

Janet, another waitress, popped her head round the door. 'You the girl who dropped the plates this morning?'

Alison nodded.

'Archie wants you.'

Honey switched off the dryer and adjusted her ample breasts back into their half-cups. 'Go on Alison, get going. When Archie says "Jump" we jump – if we want to keep our jobs.'

Alison was irritated to find herself running after Janet along paths and lawns to Archie's house on the edge of camp.

The house was made from Norfolk red bricks and L-shaped with picture windows. Janet rang the bell and chimes played 'Oranges and Lemons'.

A thin barefoot girl in skin-tight jeans and denim jacket opened the door. Her auburn hair was piled into a top-knot and tied with a wide pink organdie ribbon; corkscrew curls dangled against her ears. Her sultry green eyes questioned their presence as if she wanted to know why they were there but couldn't be bothered to ask.

Janet tipped her head towards Alison and said to the girl, 'Archie wants to see her.'

'Dad's in the garden. Go round the side and you'll find him.'

The door was shut abruptly.

Janet mimicked, '"Go round the side and you'll find him". Miserable kid. She could easily have told him we were here.'

'Don't worry – I'll find him,' Alison said.

Archie was bending over one of the immaculate flower-beds. He pulled out a small weed, stood up and shouted, 'If he can't look after this garden properly I'll get somebody else!'

His wife Rita, a tiny woman about ten years younger than him materialized from a nearby shrubbery. 'He does very well dear. You know how quickly weeds...' She stopped when she saw Alison. 'Oh – did you...?'

Archie swung round. Alison was standing with her shoulders squared thinking there was no way he was going to bellow at *her*.

'Oh. It's you,' he said then looked towards Rita. 'This is the girl who dropped the plates. Didn't you show her how to hold them properly?'

'Yes she did,' blurted Alison. 'I just happen to be clumsy.'

'You can say that again.' Archie scowled at her.

'I'm sorry,' said Alison in a voice that indicated she wasn't going down on her knees. 'And I'm prepared to pay for the breakages.'

'I'm not bothered about the money! It's not the money bothering me. It's your face!'

Alison's eyes widened. She knew she wasn't pretty but this was a bit much! Even Rita seemed taken aback. She was hovering near him fluttering her small hands as if she was hoping to catch hold of his words before they reached Alison.

'What's wrong with it?' Alison spoke with quiet icy politeness.

'It's your expression girlie. If you have another accident don't look so bloody terrified. This is a fun place. People come here to enjoy themselves. They don't want to see long faces, especially first thing in the morning.' He poked his face closer to her and emphasized his words. 'Everybody *smiles* here! I bet they all thought you was going to get the sack the way you looked. That's not good for morale see?'

'I'll remember next time.'

'There'd better not be a next time! Plates is money!'

'Dad!' The girl who had opened the door was leaning out of a bedroom window. Archie beamed. 'Yes, Tracy?'

'I'm off to see Mary now.'

'You said after dinner.'

'I've changed my mind.'

'Well you can unchange it pet. You're to have a proper dinner with us before you go.'

'Dad!'

'No argument.'

The window slammed and Tracy's petulant face disappeared. Red now, Archie turned to his wife. 'She's always going out – and look at her – thin as a flag-pole. She doesn't eat enough. You never saw our Debbie...' He stopped quite suddenly as if it hurt him to carry on.

Rita placed her hand gently on his shoulder. 'All young girls watch out for their figures.' She glanced towards Alison with a hint of an appeal in her eyes. 'I expect you were just the same at seventeen weren't you?' she said, looking at Alison's slim but nicely developed figure and nodding rapidly as if encouraging her to agree.

Alison gave a mumbled 'Yes,' but told herself all she could remember about being seventeen was a diet of work.

She'd wanted to stay on at school. Teachers had tried to pursuade her mother to let her do so but her mum's boyfriend said he could get Alison a job in a civil engineer's office. Her mum insisted it was an opportunity that wouldn't come twice, saying, 'If you do stay on to the sixth form, our Alison, there's still no knowing if you'll get a job at the end of it, then think of all that time wasted an' all.'

It had been hard work with little time for either lads – or food-ads.

'Which one is Mary?' Archie said.

'One of her friends,' Rita reported. 'She told you she was seeing her today.'

Archie grunted and then turned to Alison. 'So no more breakages eh?'

'No sir.'

'Call me Archie. Everybody calls me Archie. We're one big happy family here.'

The window upstairs opened again. Tracy shouted, 'Mary's mum has gone and got dinner ready for me Dad.'

Archie shook is head. 'Tsk!' Then he called, 'Just this once then...' He put his hand over his eyes for a moment. 'When is she supposed to be working on her A-level stuff?' He looked at Alison. 'You're at college aren't you? How much work did you have to...'

To Alison's surprise, Rita broke in. 'Young people have marvellous opportunities these days. I wish I'd had the chance to go to college.'

Archie twined her arm in his. 'You're all right as you are. You'll do for me. Being educated doesn't mean you can cook any better or look after your man any better.' He patted her hand and looked at Alison, saying proudly, 'There's no better wife than this one.'

Rita gave Alison a secret wry grin, pressing her lips together and giving her chin a little jerk as if to say, 'Listen to him'. And if it hadn't been for the odd expression in her eyes, Alison would have put them down as the perfect married couple.

That afternoon Alison went for a walk along the coast road. A watery sun was doing its best to shine.

Her mind skittered round the subject of her thesis. She was as bad as Tracy. She was making all sorts of excuses to herself as to why she couldn't get on with it. She knew full well nothing would stop her if she was really keen.

She looked to where the tide was battling in. She'd read about the devastating floods in the area years before. So many people killed. So many buildings wiped out.

Her astute brown eyes scanned the coastline. Parts of the cliff were crumbling, especially where coast defences were inadequate. As she gazed at the arc of cliffs sweeping into the distance, words like chalk-seam, sand, gravels, jumped into her brain.

A man was walking his dog on the beach. A girl was running to catch up with him. She was dressed in denim jeans and jacket. Surely it was Tracy? And was it Guy with her? He put his arm around her.

Alison turned away and shrugged. Whoever it was, it was no business of hers, she thought. But before she started walking back to the road she found her gaze dragged sideways again to the couple. This time she realized the girl *was* Tracy but the man was Neil.

She was barely conscious of a new lightness in her mind.

Before long, she was passing Cliff's Hotel. Honey had said it was named after Clifford Kington, Guy's father.

Alison was not keen on rambling Victorian buildings. She preferred Georgian houses or something really modern, where sunshine could get in and lick the corners. I bet it's dark and gloomy in there, she thought.

The hotel had sharply pointed gables and steps that led up to a wooden-panelled door with stained-glass windows either side, and a veranda in front. There wasn't much she liked about the place, except perhaps the ornate red chimney, and that had a nasty crack.

She had to admit the hotel would have the most fabulous sea-views, positioned as it was on top of the cliffs. She had a bet with herself that one could even feel vibrations from the waves when there was a storm.

Then, for some odd reason, she experienced an uncanny sensation she could not explain – like the instinct of an animal when it senses danger. Frightening thoughts hovered in her mind. She gave herself a mental shake. She had to learn to keep a check on her too-vivid imagination.

As she walked on, she saw a stretch of grassland next to the hotel. She passed it and fancied she could hear a cry. She stood still, but could only hear the intermittent thump of waves on the shore and smell the tangy salt air.

But then she heard the cry again.

She hurried through the grass where hawthorn bushes straggled the cliff-edge. She gazed through them and down to the beach. Nothing unusual down there.

'Can somebody come?' shouted a voice. It was all too clear this time.

She ran towards the fence that doubtless surrounded the grounds at the back of the hotel and scrambled up it, scraping the toes of her trainers. As she balanced herself she saw an elderly man sitting at an awkward angle in a wheel-chair that had one of its wheels jammed between a rockery and the path. A red-checked rug had fallen to the ground and the man, who looked as if he'd been trying to pick it up, was hopelessly stuck.

'Hold on. I'm coming,' she shouted and sprang down then ran back to the road and round to the hotel. Guests in the front vestibule stared at her as she flew past them into the hall.

'Man stuck out there!' she called as she hurried through one of the open doors to where she'd spotted a conservatory beyond, leading into the garden. She dodged between white basket chairs and tall potted palms to reach the man outside.

'Can you get me out of this confounded mess?' he snapped.

She tried to free the chair.

'I'm not totally helpless! I can walk if somebody gives me a hand you know,' he said.

'Right. Lean on me then and I'll ease you out.'

He stared at her slender figure. Her eyes were merry. 'Don't worry. I'm stronger than I look.' But the weight of him made her stagger.

'Let me do that,' intoned a deep voice behind her

and the next minute Guy Kington's strong arms were wrapped round his father.

'Spoilsport,' muttered Clifford Kington and a grin that was half-reproving, half-amused, spread across Guy's face as he almost carried his father towards the conservatory. He murmured, 'Thank you, Alison.'

Clifford glanced at him and then at Alison, 'Yes – thank you, Alison.' He looked up at his son and muttered again, 'Home barely a fortnight and you know 'em all. Are you starting over where you left off?'

Alison wheeled the chair to the conservatory after releasing it from the rockery and Guy eased his father back into it and leaned forward his well-shaped hands on its arms. 'Now Dad – what possessed you to wheel yourself out there on a changeable day like this eh?' he said gently.

Clifford twisted himself irritably in the chair. 'If I want to go into *my* garden and look at *my* roses I'll go whether it's a storm or a heatwave.'

Both men had the same lean features but age and illness had made Clifford's chiselled jaw-line sag and become less pronounced and his rangy shoulders were now stooping. His paleness made Guy's skin look even more swarthy at the side of him – and there was not the same luminosity in Clifford's blue eyes – but the fire of battle was still there and both men were obviously a law unto themselves.

Several guests hovered with curious concerned eyes beyond the spacious rectangular conservatory. From the centre of them stepped a tall willowy woman in jodphurs. She bent towards Clifford, her long fair hair falling to one side of her beautiful flawless face.

'Oh Mr Kington; are you all right?'

'I'm fine Kedrun; fine.' He patted her hand. She turned her head from side to side with a worried expression. 'We had no idea you were out there. It's dreadful no one heard you. I asked Guy to show me his wordprocessor and we were tucked in his room...'

'Stop worrying.' Clifford tipped his head towards Alison, who was about to slip away. 'That little elfin face popped itself over the fence when I shouted. She helped me.' He slewed his gaze between the three of them. 'This is Alison – she's a friend of Guy's.'

Alison couldn't be absolutely sure there wasn't the slightest gleam of malevolence in the old man's eyes.

'I happened to be passing, that's all.'

'Very fortunate.' Alison saw Kedrun's eyes flicker towards her bright waitress's uniform and then towards Guy. 'I'm sorry darling. I have to go now.'

'I'll come with you,' said Guy and turned to wheel his father.

'Where's Neil?' barked Clifford.

'Neil isn't here so you'll have to put up with me instead,' said Guy with what Alison thought was a good-humoured manner – for him.

Clifford wrenched at the big wheels of his chair and began to propel himself, 'And what good is that? I'll just be getting used to you when you'll leave me again. Won't you?'

As Alison followed Clifford she saw Guy talking to Kedrun, her face uptilted and close to his.

'Edna!' called Clifford to the receptionist.'Please give this young woman some tea.' He nodded towards Alison.

'Oh no, I really can't stay...' she began.

'Too late – she's gone now,' he said and indicated she should go into the drawing-room.

Alison found herself alone in there. If she'd thought the outside of the hotel was dreary she'd to think again about the inside. It was decorated with great taste and flair, with the Victorian atmosphere retained. There were deep rich colours – crimsons and golds – and the wallpaper was highly patterned with one wall covered in lovely miniature paintings and other small pictures with fancy gilt frames. At the windows were exquisite lace drapes. She bent to smell the perfect scent from a bowl of yellow roses on a small round table.

'So this is where you are?' Guy strode into the room.

Now they were alone together, Alison noticed everything about him: the peat-coloured roll-neck sweater and that, like Kedrun, he wore jodphurs; his expensive gold wrist-watch and top quality riding-boots. Here was a man who didn't stint himself – who had probably never known a day's worry about money in his life.

'Like the roses?' He came to stand beside her and she caught the tang of his spicy aftershave.

'They're lovely. Marvellous arrangement,' Alison said.

'Neil did it. He's the artistic one in the family.'

She felt suddenly dwarfed by him, looked up and smiled shyly. 'We – seem to have frightened your guests away.'

'They are probably enjoying this bit of sunshine. Sit down, Alison.'

She liked the sound of her name on his lips. He held out his arms to take her anorak and she wished she'd changed out of her waitress's outfit before leaving the camp.

Guy lounged on a deep, floral, chintz armchair, stretching out his long, loose legs. She thought, this was where a man like him belonged – in sumptuous rooms, lolling idly and letting the world roll by.

'So, how's the waitressing going?' he asked.

She grinned. 'You wouldn't believe it if I told you – heavens!' She stopped and gazed at the trolley being wheeled in by a waiter. It held a large, silver teapot and fine bone-china crockery together with enough food for about six people.

'I – I thought just a cup of tea...'

The chef will be tight-lipped all day if we don't demolish it. Come on.'

As Guy leaned towards her holding a silver dish of hot toasted tea-cakes she took in the delicious aroma of home baking. She was hungrier than she'd realized and enjoyed the food. Between eating she told him about the incident with the plates. To her surprise he threw back his head and laughed.

'It's not your forte is it?'

'It's my holiday job – but I'm getting better at it.'

'So what do you do the rest of the time?'

'I'm a geology student.'

He couldn't have been more astonished if she'd shovelled all the cakes in her mouth at once. She admitted to a tiny thrill of satisfaction that she'd made him sit up and take notice.

'Good Lord!' There was no laughter now. His deep blue eyes were fixed on her. She'd noticed some people looked at you when they listened but not when they talked. Guy Kington was a man who looked all the time. Almost as if he could see right through a person. It could be... uncomfortable.

'How on earth did you take up a subject like geology?' he added, curiosity wrinkling his wide brow.

She asked herself, how much is a man with his well-to-do background going to understand about someone with mine? I didn't follow in a family tradition of going straight from school to university as I expect he did.

She levelled her gaze at him. 'From the time I was sixteen I worked in an engineer's office. Very boring! At first that is. I made coffee, ran errands – answered phones and then...'

'Then?' He'd put down his plate and nodded encouragingly.

'Well then they began to give me real jobs. I thought so anyway. Like printing plans from negatives and plotting bore-hole drawings.' Alison paused and then added, 'I loved going on site. Oh, I only did beginner's things, like holding the tape and that sort of thing, but when I'd been going to day-release classes I was able to do soil investigations and suchlike.

'Fortunately, I managed to get enough qualifications to go to the polytechnic.' She stopped as she remembered her mum's reaction to that.

'Well, I could certainly have done with a grounding like yours.'

Her eyes widened. She hadn't expected that reaction. Perhaps it had not been all private schools and college for him, after all.

'Oh, anyone can do what I did!' she enthused, spurred on now by his obvious interest. She went on to talk about her course more enthusiastically than she had for a long time.

'I probably inherited a natural leaning towards geology from my father. He was very interested in rock formations.'

'Was he a scientist?'

'Well... no,' she said aloud, but added to herself, but he might have been in another time, another place. She could remember trotting after him on holiday as he collected stones and pebbles from the beach. He'd told her all he knew about quartz and granite and limestone.

After her father left home, her mother threw out his shoe-boxes of stones. Even now, Alison recalled her own feelings of desolation. It was as if nothing remained of him after that. As if he'd died.

As Guy continued to ask questions, his sensuous mouth formed a smile, but she knew it was in friendship rather than amusement now. Was he being so nice because she'd helped his father? Or something else? Perhaps he just admired people who could do things?

She wondered again why Honey had warned her off him. But then Honey was inclined to exaggerate when it came to the subject of men.

Gradually the idea formed in her mind she'd like to invite him to the camp as her guest. Honey said staff often had visitors. It would a way of returning his hospitality.

'I... I wonder...?' He looked at her enquiringly. She swallowed. 'Have you ever actually been inside Summerland camp?'

As he frowned she went on quickly. 'I'm sure you'd be pleasantly surprised – there's a lovely atmosphere – perhaps you'd like to come for a drink...?'

His curt 'No thanks!' came like a slap on the cheek. His deep voice sounded more aloof than she would have believed. She was furious with herself. After only a short time in his presence she'd been seduced into thinking he liked her after all.

He cleared his throat. 'Alison there's something I think you should...'

'Mr Kington. There you are!' Two small silver-haired ladies hurried into the room. 'We've just heard your father had an accident in his wheelchair. Is he all right?'

'Nothing to worry about, Mrs Bennet. His wheel jammed and he couldn't get out of the chair without assistance. Fortunately Miss Lacie here heard him shouting and came to help. He's fine now.' He smiled at them.

'Oh that's good.'

Guy had stood up and Mrs Bennet leaned towards him smiling archly. 'Saw you out riding with your young lady – wish I was a hundred years younger!' She giggled as he gently squeezed her hand.

Her companion nudged her and mouthed, 'Ask him.'

'Er... Mr Kington...'

'Mrs Bennet?'

She ran her tongue over her lips. 'Now I don't want you to answer this if you don't want to – but there's a rumour going round that you – that you're...' He bent low when she indicated she wanted to whisper to him. When he straightened up Alison noticed a slight frown on his face. He pressed his lips together and nodded.

'And you wrote all those bestsellers?' she gasped.

He placed his hands lightly on her forearms, saying softly, 'I was hoping to keep it a secret. You understand?'

'Of course I do, my dear. You don't want the press pestering you on holiday.'

'Dad needs peace and quiet...'

'And you can count on me.' She held up her fingers

then turned to her companion. 'Come on, Miriam. And *you* can keep your mouth shut too.' She turned at the door and looked at Guy. 'But you will give me your autograph before you go home to Greece, won't you?'

'As many as you like.'

While the two had been talking, Alison had been feeling a mixture of astonishment – and embarrassment as well. What was it she'd gabbled out? 'Oh anyone can do what I did'! She groaned to herself. And he, a well-known writer, pretending he wished he'd had her grounding. Had he been laughing at her after all? Oh she wished she'd not put on such airs when she'd been talking about herself!

She swallowed. 'Congratulations,' she said with a sincere smile. 'I had no idea you were a famous author.'

'Thanks, but I was hoping no one in Summerland would recognize me. I've been away for a long time – even shaved off my beard.' He stroked his chin. 'And I do use a pseudonym.'

'Which is?'

Her jaw dropped open when he told her. *'The Falkland Sound? Temple to Bacchus?* You wrote them? she whispered. *'Monument to...?'*

'Uh-huh.' He sighed. 'It doesn't matter how long one's away from a place, news leaks out; Dad and Neil won't appreciate it.'

'I would have thought the publicity would be good for the hotel.'

'No!' He barked out the word.

She was already stinging from his sharp refusal to her invitation and thought, I'm not staying around while he uses that tone. She snatched up her anorak.

'Alison...'

'I don't appear to be on your wavelength at all, do I?'

'Look, I'm sorry if I lost my cool.'

'Perhaps if I knew as much about you as you've found out about me in the last few minutes I might understand!'

'I apologized!' he said stiffly.

'And *I* accepted!' At the door she turned unsmiling. 'Oh, by the way, my dad worked on the railway from when he was fourteen. And we didn't have any scientists in our family and probably never will, unless of course I come up with something spectacular for my thesis – that's if I decide to finish this never-ending course for which I'm having to slog every inch of the way!' She stopped to catch her breath.

He was beside her in a moment, glaring at her. 'What is all this? What's really the matter?'

'Nothing's the matter.' She shook his hand from her arm.

He took a deep breath. 'Alison, I was very grateful indeed you came to my dad's assistance but you must understand I cannot ever visit Summerland camp – if that's what's getting under your skin.'

'I'm not in the least concerned whether you come or not!' It was the tail-end of his remark that incensed her and she added over-sweetly, 'I only thought you might enjoy seeing how the rest of us live. Thank you for the tea Mr Kington.' She stalked away from him.

Two days later the sun came out in full force. Alison spent any spare time sunbathing and swimming. Sometimes she and Honey played around in the pool with Maurice, the waiter, and Jack, who played the guitar and sang folk-songs and helped to organize the entertainment. He was stockily built and flirted with all the lady guests.

Maurice was bandy-legged and looked quite different from when he was gliding around the dining-room. But she liked him a lot.

It was after Jack dragged her with him to help judge the Mr Knobbly-Knees contest and she finished up with tears of laughter running down her face, that she found the holiday magic of the camp was working its spell on her. It was a place where people could forget their worries.

She forgot about poly. She forgot about her thesis, until Simon's letters came to remind her. She told herself there just wasn't time to study – and to a certain extent it was true.

She always seemed to be rushing to get to the dining-room to serve the meals; to stand in queues. As the weather became hotter her feet began to ache and her clothes stuck to her body.

But there was always the smile; the big happy smile. Even when campers, cool in sun-tops and shorts, complained about the jelly and ice-cream that melted together into rivulets of white and crimson, she smiled understandingly and carried the dishes away to join more queues.

She started having horrific dreams. She'd been carrying too many plates full of sausages, eggs, bacon, kippers, ham, chips – runny jelly. And she always dropped them.

One night she woke perspiring. There was an airless musty smell in the chalet. She knew she wouldn't be able to go back to sleep and climbed softly out of bed.

It was bright moonlight outside and, wearing a sleeveless yellow dress, she strolled across the camp grounds. The only sound was of a baby crying in one of the chalets.

She crossed the field and was soon climbing over the dunes to the beach. The sea was like wrinkled silk, swishing hypnotically at her feet. She took off her shoes and paddled in the deliciously cool water in the direction of the hotel.

Suddenly she heard a muffled thump. She looked quickly towards the cliffs. A great lump from the cliff-face had fallen to the beach. She padded over the sand to look closer, almost tripping over the prow of an old boat protruding from the sand like a broken tooth.

Even as she inspected the cliff, more of it disintegrated and slid away like putty. She knew it was an area eroded by underground streams and high tides. Tidal surges could wreak havoc on this east coast.

All the time there was an uneasy feeling in the back of her mind. She tried in vain to remember the study sessions she'd had on landslips – on a similar set of circumstances to these. She shook her head impatiently. 'Why don't I learn to listen properly!'

The worried frown stayed on her face as she made her way back to the camp. Then she saw a figure hurrying towards the hotel.

'Tracy?' she called.

The girl glanced round and pulled the small blue sun-hat over her face as if hoping that Alison would think she'd been mistaken. Alison shrugged. Tracy was no business of hers. But those cliffs were a different matter! She couldn't be certain until she'd spoken to Simon – and how she suddenly missed him – but she suspected something awful concerning the hotel. She ought to tell *someone* in Summerland. And she didn't intend to push herself at Guy Kington again! Perhaps she should speak to Archie?

It was a move she was to regret bitterly.

Three

After thinking hard Alison decided Archie was definitely the one to speak to. It was true he [illegible] was in no danger, but he [illegible] [illegible] was sure to feel responsible for strangers who used the coast road.

She never guessed it would be so hard to get hold of Archie. She'd no sooner seen him in one place than he vanished again.

'Ha ha! Nobody catches Archie,' laughed Maurice. 'Unless of course he has got a mind to speak to you. Come on – talk to me instead!'

He grasped her wrist and led her to where people were running races. They sat on the grass licking ice creams. Alison nodded towards the stripped shirts. 'They're [illegible]'

'My mother got them from [illegible] catalogue.'

'Does she live [illegible]?'

'Suffolk.' [illegible] ice cream [illegible] down [illegible]

'Maurice – do you remember the [illegible] the coast? [illegible]'

'Do you mind? I'm not that old!' [illegible] shoulder [illegible] to be [illegible]

'Sorry.'

'Huh!' he said [illegible] 'Anyway [illegible] want to know?'

'I was only [illegible]

Three

After thinking hard Alison decided Archie was definitely the one to speak to. It was true the camp was in no danger, being well back from the beach, but he was sure to feel responsible for campers who used the coast road.

She never guessed it would be so hard to get hold of Archie. She'd no sooner seen him in one spot than he vanished again.

'Ha ha! Nobody catches Archie,' laughed Maurice. 'Unless of course he has it in mind to speak to *you!* Come on – talk to me instead!'

He grasped her wrist and led her to where people were running races. They sat on the grass licking ice-creams. Alison nodded towards his stripped shorts. 'They're natty.'

My mother got them from her mail-order catalogue.'

'Does she live near here?'

'Suffolk.' His pink tongue curled round dribbles of ice-cream as they melted down the sides of his cone.

'Maurice – do you remember the awful floods on this coast? 1953 I think.'

'Do you mind? I'm not that old!' He jerked his shoulder and pretended to be offended.

'Sorry.'

'Huh!' he said on a grin. 'Anyway, why do you want to know?'

'I was only thinking how vulnerable this coastline is.'

'Sure. The sea has been known to break through the dunes.'

'It doesn't help when folk wear paths across them – or drag boats.'

'Well I don't drag my boat across there.'

'Didn't know you had one Maurice.'

'I keep it in Archie's hut near the beach. You can use it any time you like – but be warned – there are some nasty currents round here.'

She smiled widely and thanked him. He crunched into his cone. 'I – er – do happen to know a little bit about the 1953 floods. But only because I read about them! They devastated this coast; smashed concrete walls – and killed people. Mind you, we are partly protected by the cliffs.'

'From what I can see Maurice, they're made up of material that can easily be worn away. Still, we're well back from the shore here so I suppose...'

Maurice rolled on his stomach.

My mother tells all sorts of tales – true ones too. Like the complete village that vanished in a terrible storm hundreds of years ago. Then much later, when the tide washed the sand away, you could see the outline of the whole village and...' his voice grew menacingly softer, 'skeletons unearthed from their graves.'

'Will you come in the two-legged race with me Alison?' Honey appeared wearing tight white shorts and equally tight T-shirt.'

'Ooh, *I* will!' Maurice bounced upright.

Honey's mouth turned down at the corners.

'Oh blimey no. I don't want anybody with bandy legs.'

'At least I wouldn't be running just to show

off all I've got,' pouted Maurice.

'Hah!'

Alison intervened when she saw Maurice scowling. 'Maurice has just been telling me stories...'

'He tells everybody stories,' groaned Honey 'about the Roman soldier...'

'I was coming to the Roman soldier,' interrupted Maurice tetchily. He looked at Alison. 'There was once a Roman camp over the road where the pinewoods are now. There's a legend – whatever she says – that when there's an impending disaster, the soldier appears...'

'I've never seen one!' retorted Honey. She giggled. 'And it's not for want of looking.'

'I can believe that,' snorted Maurice. 'And if you look behind you now, you'll see the current boyfriend. I expect he'll be only too keen to tie his ankle to yours. Come on Alison – I'll show you how to win a three-legged race.'

Alison was jogging back towards the chalet afterwards when to her surprise Archie called to her from outside the snack-bar. 'I'm glad to see you settling in now. How about a cold drink?'

She sat opposite him at one of the outside tables, sipped pineapple juice and eyed Archie warily. What did he want?

'You ever done any coaching Alison?' He unwrapped a sweet.

She shook her head.

'Our Tracy could do with some coaching if she's to get through A-levels and go on to college. I want her to have a better education than me – not as though I'm ashamed of what I am. Oh no.' He moved his head slowly from side to side.

'Made my way from being a butcher's boy to owning a shop and then...' he looked around him and opened his arms wide, 'I started all of this. And I'm not finished yet either. I've got plans that will put everybody round her out of business. I'm going to turn this into a massive holiday-centre – won't be called a camp then. And I'll succeed too. Know why? Because I can use this!' He tapped the side of his head. 'And so could our Tracy if she'd only settle down.'

'Of course I'll help her with her A-level work if she wants me to. I know how she feels about putting off studying. I'm supposed to be getting down to some myself.'

'Oh?'

'I should be writing a thesis on the changing coastline.'

'Well I don't see how you'll fit that in with waitressing!'

Or with three-legged racing, she thought drily. Aloud she said, 'I will. I have to, because...'

Archie had turned away from her to wave to campers on their way to the beach with sun-beds and balls. 'Mm?' he murmured.

She raised her voice slightly. 'Because I believe the cliffs in this area are dangerous.'

He swung round, his eyebrows raised. 'What are you talking about? Dangerous? You'll start a flaming panic! Put folk off coming here for holidays! For God's sake! You ain't even qualified!'

She nodded. 'I know. And I realize I could be wrong – but I still want to look into it...'

'You just keep your thoughts to yourself!'

'Surely it's better to be warned about these things? I

was only reading the other day about a terrible storm that caused a hundred metres of cliff to...'

'Reading!' He sprang to his feet. 'We aren't likely to get conditions bad enough to wipe away great lumps of cliff.'

'They're very soft. And I certainly don't think Cliff's hotel on the headland is particularly safe...' she began but he was talking at the same time exclaiming, 'Before you start making damn-fool...' He stopped and narrowed his eyes. 'What did you say?'

'The cliffs are soft.'

'No – about the hotel.'

'It might not be safe. The cliffs there are badly eroded. If there was a severe storm – a really bad one, the coast defences might not prove adequate. But as you say – I'm not qualified.'

Archie sat down slowly. Another group of campers passed but this time he hardly looked at them. Alison continued. 'Obviously I'd have to study them a lot more. My boyfriend Simon is very busy but he might come down.'

'Boyfriend?'

'He's a geologist.' She couldn't help adding, with a mischievous twinkle in her brown eyes, 'A qualified one.'

Archie ran the back of his hand across his mouth. 'I dunno. Perhaps I haven't given this enough thought. I mean, if you think people's lives could be in danger that's a different thing altogether isn't it? And if you say you might be able to get this Simon down here to give an expert opinion, I'd be lacking in responsibility if I didn't go half-way to meet you.'

She studied him closely. What was he up to? Why

had he suddenly changed his tune? She didn't trust him one bit.

'What about your worry that visitors might be put off coming to this part of the coast?'

'I told you – I'm having second thoughts. I just realized, when this place is transformed into a magnificent complex with every top-class facility, people aren't going to be bothered about trekking down to the beach.

'Now, I'll tell you what I'm prepared to do to help you. You've already got one day off a week when you can get on with your studying; what if I let you off serving at some of the meals? That would help wouldn't it?

'After all, everything that happens to this coast should concern us all, especially when it comes to looking after holiday makers. I'm giving you carte-blanche to get on with your study of the environment!' He leaned back chewing his sweet, his arms folded.

She thought, this is much too easy. But Archie isn't a person to make life easy. For anyone.

She pushed her hands deep in the large patch pockets of her pink cotton sun-dress. 'Why are you really doing all this?'

His hands dropped to his thighs. 'You've got a very suspicious nature!' He looked at her intently for a moment before pointing his finger and saying, '*You* can do with my co-operation in this business – and *I* want to be the person you bring your findings to. See, I'd like to be the one who starts any campaign for better sea-walls and, er...'

'Stronger coastal defences?' Alison suggested.

'Yeah. Stronger coastal defences. And *I* know who to see on the district council. As a matter of fact, I wouldn't mind being a councillor myself, one day.'

'And if *you* start the ball rolling, you'll get the publicity for yourself and the camp as well?' Alison tapped her fingers on the table as she spoke.

'Centre. That's what it will be, or complex. Not camp. Anyway, I'll decide when it's time to see the council, and in the meantime, we keep all this strictly between ourselves.'

'But, when...?'

He leaned across and put his hand over hers. 'We don't want to start a panic, do we? Not till we're a hundred per cent sure about this cliff business.' He tapped his head again. 'We got to use our noddles. You just bring me all your findings. Oh, and get that boyfriend of yours down here. I'm not saying I haven't got confidence in a woman, but I'd like to hear what he's got to say... him being qualified an' all.'

What was wrong in him seeking publicity? Alison asked herself, as long as something was being done about the situation.

'I – er, don't mind if you tell the others I'm giving you time off to study,' Archie said nonchalantly. 'They all know I'm a great believer in education. I'll just go and see Lorna about it.'

After he'd left, Alison cupped her chin in her hands, as her thoughts began to weave unfamiliar patterns.

With the extra time she'd have, anything was possible. I could produce a really valuable piece of work if I'm right about the cliffs, she thought. Valuable to everybody, not only me. It wouldn't just be your average sort of student's thesis. It would be special. Who knows, there might be reports about Archie and me in the local paper – even the national papers – for bringing this to everyone's attention. I'd really be on the way to becoming a geologist then. Perhaps even a famous one! The idea excited her.

She smiled to herself. She had never considered anything like it before. She gave her head a little tap and grinned to herself. She couldn't wait to get cracking.

In her ice-blue jeans and yellow T-shirt, Alison carefully picked her way along the cliff incline in front of the hotel. She knocked a small wooden peg into the thick sand and gravel surface. Then she moved farther along and did the same thing again.

When there was a row of pegs, she bent down and made sure they were in a straight line. She stood up and scrambled towards a path that led to the top of the incline. She was brushing down her jeans when a deep, amused voice, asked, 'Been exploring?'

She jerked herself upright and felt colour stream into her cheeks when she saw Guy leaning his long body languidly against a white gate at the end of the hotel grounds. She felt guilty.

'I – I was having a look at the cliffs.'

'Find anything interesting?'

'T... too soon to say.'

'Let me know if you do find anything dramatic. It's all grist to my mill.'

'Of course – for your books. I'll tell you if I find anything really gruesome.' She lowered the pitch of her voice. 'Like the skeleton of someone who died in mysterious...'

She stopped. The expression on his handsome face had changed and now he was staring out to sea, his eyes bleak.

'Although I don't know if you write mysteries...' Her voice trailed off weakly.

He looked quickly in her direction. 'Oh – yes – sometimes. But if I were you I'd be careful it's not your body anyone finds. Ridiculous to go scrambling around down there. Leaving the path.'

'They aren't safe then? These cliffs?'

'Are you an experienced climber?'

'No.'

'Then of course they aren't damn-well safe.'

He opened the gate and went out to the pathway to stand beside her. Buttons on his cream linen shirt were undone as if he'd thrown it on after sun-bathing and she could see the sable-coloured hairs glistening on his expansive chest. His skin-tight jeans followed every contour of his body.

Alison had never been so close to a man with such a figure. She'd seen men like him on films and television of course. That was the best way. This way gave her a feeling of wanting to rush away from her own-heartbeat.

His skin was richly tanned as if he'd been born brown. With his physique he could have stretched out his long arms, picked her up and tossed her to land on the shore.

She began to chatter self-consciously. 'Did you know the sea level is rising?'

'Is your mind always on work?'

She blushed and fingered the rest of the pegs and string in her pocket.

He folded his arms. 'I think we had a silly misunderstanding the last time we met. These things happen and...'

'Don't give it another thought,' she said brightly.

'You obviously had reasons for not wanting to visit Summerland camp. Let's leave it at that.'

She turned to walk away.

'No, let's not. I'd like to talk to you about it. How about coming for supper on Friday? Or would that mean you'd miss end-of-week jollies?'

He had to get in a dig didn't he? she thought. 'I would miss Friday-night fun as a matter of fact. There's usually a fancy-dress party. Thank you all the same. Some other time perhaps?' She gave him a cool smile.

'Is it Alison?' said a voice she recognized as Clifford's. Neil was wheeling his father towards them. They'd come across the patch of ground beside the hotel where a wide path had been worn by holidaymakers when they took a short cut to the cliff top.

'Hello Mr Kington. Are you well?' Alison said.

'Enjoy you outing Dad?' said Guy.

Clifford's face was impassive. He looked at Alison. 'Has my son invited you for supper on Friday?'

She thought, so it wasn't Guy's idea. She ignored a small stab of disappointment. Guy opened the gate saying, 'She can't make it Dad.'

'Surely you can make one evening?' Clifford was frowning. He jerked at the big wheels of his chair to turn it towards her. Neil had been day-dreaming but now started visibly as the chair moved. Clifford repeated the offer and Neil added, 'We'd like to repay you for coming to Dad's help.'

'Oh but there's no need...' she began.

'It's nothing to do with repayment! Don't be tactless Neil,' snapped Clifford. Alison felt acutely uncomfortable to see Neil flush but Guy quickly intervened and remarked quietly, 'It's both gratitude and a desire for your company.'

Pretty words she thought. Did he really mean them or was he simply coming to the rescue? Clifford gave a quick nod of agreement but Neil pushed the wheelchair towards the gate, then stared stonily at Guy and muttered, 'You want to take it?'

'While you're both deciding what to do with me I still want to know from Alison when she's coming for supper?' Clifford announced. Alison saw where Guy got his brusque manner. She smiled evenly. 'I could make a Saturday night – say a week on Saturday.'

'We'll expect you.' Clifford frowned and looked suddenly uncomfortable as Guy stepped forward to push him. 'Neil can take me.'

'Sure.' Guy shrugged and stepped to one side. He gave the impression of being unconcerned but Alison noticed a moment when his clear blue eyes dulled. From an outsider's point of view it seemed Clifford Kington enjoyed lording it over his younger son but ignored his elder. Almost as if he was in awe of him – or was angry with him? She wasn't sure which.

As Neil pushed his father towards the conservatory at the back of the house Guy turned towards her. 'On Saturdays we join our guests in a supperdance. You'll enjoy that.'

'Yes,' she said, wondering if she would.

'Will – will Kedrun be there?' she said casually.

It was an absolute shock to her system when he suddenly tilted her small chin with his finger.

'No, Kedrun won't be there,' he said softly.

She realized she had given him *entirely* the wrong impression! He obviously thought she was attracted to him. Wanted him to herself even. She felt mortified!

Except for her well-shaped breasts, she had a slim, almost coltish figure, but now, under his long exploring gaze, her weight felt too much for her legs to carry.

The whole way back to the camp she tried, unsuccessfully, to rid herself of the feel of his touch on her skin.

'You're bloody well what?' bawled Honey.

'It's not such a big deal! I'm only going for supper with them.' Alison tossed aside the letter she'd been writing to Simon.

'Well, I wouldn't tell Archie what you're about!'

'What on earth has it got to do with Archie?'

'You'll find out!'

Honey leaned out of the chalet window and hung a pair of freshly washed briefs on the small plastic clothes drier attached to the frame. She dropped back on to her bed.

Alison had a job to stop herself yelling, too. Every time she mentioned Guy, Honey hinted at some mysterious happening she was not at liberty to talk about.

But now, she looked hard at Alison and exclaimed, 'OK. I suppose I'd better tell you, being as you haven't taken a blind bit of notice of a single thing I've said. I only know what I've been told. You understand?' Honey tucked her bare feet under her. 'There have been rumours flying for years, all to do with Archie's daughter.'

'Tracy?'

'No. Debbie, his eldest. It seems Guy Kington was a bit of a lad when he was younger. That was before

Archie started this place. He had a shop near here at the time it all happened. Debbie and Guy were crazy about each other. But Guy must have done something awful because... she was found dead.'

'Oh, no!'

'Killed herself... they say. There were enquiries of course, because he was with her at the time! Terrible scandal. That's why he left Summerland. Joined the marines. I think he went to the Falklands.

'He didn't come back until his dad was taken bad. Archie never got over what happened. He hates them all – the Kingtons – especially that Guy.'

'I can't believe it would be Guy's fault!'

'There you are. Hooked! That's how it happened to Debbie – and you were so sure...'

'I'm certainly not hooked! That's a wild assumption.'

'She was crazy about him, she didn't want to live any more after he spurned her.' Honey's voice lowered as she whispered hoarsely, 'He was her sole reason for living.'

Alison frowned. 'Are you quite sure about all this?'

'You don't have to believe it if you don't want! That's your privilege – just as it's your funeral if you carry on seeing Guy Kington.'

'How do the Kingtons feel about Archie and his family?' asked Alison, wondering at the same time what Archie would say if he knew Tracy was seeing Neil.

'Well none of them speak to one another. After Debbie died Archie was shattered. Later on he sold the shop and started up the camp. I suppose it took trade away from the hotel. Perhaps that's what he wanted. Mind, it seems to be doing all right now doesn't it?

Neil Kington's been running the place since his father's been...' She stopped and looked hard at Alison. 'What's up?'

Alison had been staring at the ground, her teeth nipping her lower lip, thinking, had Archie been telling her a pack of lies after all? Had he latched on to her remarks about the cliffs because he wanted to see the hotel closed down? The Kingtons getting their just desserts?

If it was the case should it make any difference to her?

'N–nothing's wrong. I – I was only thinking about a conversation I had with Archie.' She fingered the letter she'd been writing and said nonchalantly,'I didn't tell you did I that he's giving me some time off from work to do my thesis?'

She knew the minute she'd spoken she'd made a mistake. Honey cocked her head pertly to one side. 'Well isn't that nice for you? That'll go down ever so well with the other girls!' she answered sarcastically.

Alison wanted to tell her why – and she almost did until she told herself it was the daftest thing she could do – to let it be known she thought the area was in for a major landslip. That would be downright irresponsible, especially before Simon had seen it. And even if he agreed with her, there was still a lot of work to be done in the way of detailed studies.

Honey began to dress. 'So why has the old devil given you time off, eh? He's never done that before. Not to anybody. Especially not to me – and I've been working for him for years. Fat lot of good it's done me.'

'But I've told you...'

'Archie's got a motto. He says it's one of his dad's.

"If the' does owt for nowt, do it for the 'self.' So, you tell me, what's in it for Archie?'

'He's interested in...'

'Geology?' Honey pulled a face.

'No.'

'Or should I say *who* is he interested in? I may as well tell you, it hasn't gone unnoticed that you and Archie were seen having a drink together at Willy's bar – and at one point Archie held your hand!

'Janet says you were ages with him in his back garden, too. By God, you're a dark horse. You look as if butter wouldn't melt...' Honey snapped up her skirt zip.

Alison couldn't believe what she was hearing. She couldn't make up her mind whether to laugh or not.

'How about telling us what the secret is, then perhaps some of us old hands might get time off, too?'

'Honey!' exclaimed Alison.

Honey snapped, 'Even *I* don't throw myself at married men – or those suspected of killing schoolgirls!'

Later that day Alison noticed Honey whispering with other waitresses in the dining-room and knew she was in for a bleak time.

One evening Archie stopped to speak to her when she was vacuuming the floor after the meal.

'I told you you could have tonight off. What's happening about the project we spoke about? Why aren't you getting on with it?'

She switched off the cleaner and said awkwardly, 'There's not a lot I can do at this stage.'

'Well there won't be. Not while you're here!'

'I've got to go and look at the reference books in the library sometime,' she mumbled.

'Well go then! Take the day off girlie.'

Honey and Janet were passing and exchanged glances. Alison groaned inside.

After they'd gone she drew in her breath and said, 'This is going to lead to a lot of ill-feeling Archie – me disappearing when I should be working in here.'

'I run this place. I decide what happens here. Now put down that damn cleaner and let somebody else take over.' He turned round and crooked his finger, calling, 'Honey – come here. I've got a little job for you.'

It was Saturday. Changeover day. Holidaymakers she'd got to know and like were going home. The van with clean linen was being driven around. Cleaners were changing beds and leaving chalets pine-fresh.

Alison felt curiously lonely. And then, to her astonishment, she saw Simon.

'It's only a flying-visit – a surprise,' he said as she flung her arms round him. 'I'm on my way to a conference... oh Ali... I miss you like hell.'

In the security of his arms, his kind familiar face close to hers, she felt warm and safe and closed her eyes, allowing his kiss to linger. His lips were cool. And comforting.

She took him into her chalet and he clasped her to him again, tighter this time. 'Missed me?'

She nodded and stroked the back of his neck, her finger-tips touching his short sandy hair.

He murmured, 'If you do that again I'll have you down on that silly little bed before...'

That was when Honey burst in.

Later the two of them walked together on the beach

near the cliffs. Alison told him about the conversation she'd had with Archie. 'I feel he's using me to wreak his revenge on the Kington family.'

'What does it matter what his motives are? If a building is unsafe then it *should* be closed. There's no need for you to concern yourself in any sort of feud between these two families. Just keep personalities out of it. Do what you've got to do and keep the boss informed. He's the one you're working for after all. The one who's paying you.'

All the time he'd been speaking he'd been looking about him at the cliffs. 'You've got the chance of a lifetime here Ali. You could turn in one hell of a thesis.' He seemed to drift into a world of his own, muttering about glacial deposits.

'What d'you think Simon?'

'Any exposure of strata?'

'Yes – where they put in a pipe-line.'

He stopped walking and stood looking at her. 'Why are we wasting precious time? I've got to go soon. Come here!'

He pulled her with him into a crevice and kissed her again. The sun was on her back. In the distance she could hear sea-gulls crying.

She could almost imagine she and Simon were on holiday together. It was a lovely relaxing feeling.

'Hold me close Si' she whispered, wondering why she was being unusually clingy.

'Will I?' His lips came down again on hers. Harder this time.

She murmured, 'You're always the same aren't you? Always dependable.'

'I wish I could stay longer...'

She glanced up at the cliff where they were

standing. 'There's subaerial denudation...'

'Eh?' He blinked.

'What?'

'Hell Ali – I was about to kiss you again!'

'I'm sorry. I've got these damn cliffs on the brain.'

He sighed. 'Come on then! Let's go and see if any of those pegs have moved.'

It seemed to her in no time at all Simon had to leave. Archie insisted they had coffee with him and Rita first. He listened intently to everything Simon had to say, not understanding some technical terms but glued to his words, especially when the hotel was mentioned.

The next day he said to Alison, 'That was a clever young bloke, that Simon. Pity he couldn't stop to do a bit more investigating on the beach. But he doesn't like the look of things at all does he? I heard him tell you to keep in touch by phone. When is he coming again?'

'As soon as he can, but he's so tied up at the moment. He's just started a new job.'

Rita was hovering near Archie and said, 'I do hope we don't have any of those dreadful storms he was telling us about. I'll be keeping a close eye on my barometer from now on, especially when there're high winds and spring tides.'

Archie gaped. 'What do you know about it?'

'I was listening to what he said Arch. I never knew groynes in one part of the beach could sometimes make it worse in another...'

Archie ignored her. 'If I'm going to take this matter of the cliffs further, Alison, I want confirmation of the situation from a qualified bloke, so you remind Simon of that when you write to him. In the meantime I suppose I'll have to wait for your findings.'

'I suppose you will,' she said drily. She turned to go.

Archie added as an afterthought, 'And tell that Honey not to go hanging her knickers from the chalet window.'

Suddenly Alison was fed up with him telling her what she could or could not do. 'No. *You* tell her.'

'She's your mate isn't she?' he snapped.

'I'm not exactly flavour of the month with the other girls. Not with skipping my duties.'

'We all have to make sacrifices for the common good.'

'Well I'm not taking any more time off Archie – and if it means I can't get as much done – it can't be helped.' As she began to march away she caught a glimpse of Rita staring at her with her mouth open.

The next day when she had some free time after leaving the dining-room Alison chose to ignore all thoughts of studying. It had even crossed her mind not to bother at all with the thesis. Never mind what Simon had said – personalities couldn't be ignored. Archie was too interfering – and she was already involved with the Kingtons.

She'd thought a lot about Guy Kington since Honey had told her about him and Debbie. She couldn't help it. What dreadful thing had happened to cause such a tragedy?

Wearing a pale-blue bikini she joined campers on the beach. She was splashing in the sea when she saw Neil. He was an enigma to her. Sometimes he seemed dreamy and withdrawn but other times he was full of life.

Now he was running and cavorting with the dog.

He spotted her and shouted, 'Hi Alison!'

The next minute he was racing into the water towards her in his plimsolls and shorts. She laughed and then squealed as he rushed at her. Swimming away from him she suddenly spotted Tracy watching them. Alison beckoned her to join them but Tracy stormed away.

That evening Alison stood alone on the edge of the cliffs gazing at the stars. She thought she saw a light in the disused lighthouse on the island but it vanished. I've been listening to too many of Maurice's stories – I'll be seeing a Roman soldier next! she told herself.

There was a sound behind her. She turned quickly. Her heart pounded as Guy's tall figure loomed. But his voice was ice-cold.

'And what the hell do you think you've been playing at?'

Four

'What on earth...?' she began.

'Don't pretend you don't know what I'm talking about.' He was glowering.

'Get out of my way please!' She stepped to one side but he still blocked her way.

'Sure – when you tell me what sort of underhand game you're playing here.'

'Even if I knew what you're talking about – which I don't – I'm not prepared to explain...'

'I've known hundreds of women in my time but never one like you. You had me fooled all right. All that stuff about coming to Summerland to be a waitress...!' He clamped his knuckles against his hips and glared down at her. 'Why couldn't you be honest at least? Say you'd come at Archie's request?'

'What?' she squeaked and screwed up her face. Who had fed him this false information?

'Although I can see it might have been difficult,' he conceded sarcastically. 'He probably told you to keep your mouth shut. Investigating a rival concern is hardly something to shout your mouth off about. Archie never gives up does he? Won't be happy until he's seen a closure notice slapped on us. Well he's on to a loser this time. As for you!'

His tone threatened her. He stepped closer. She realized now they were quite alone as they stood near the cliff-edge. She remembered how Honey had hinted at Guy's involvement in Debbie's death. Her mind catapulted. What did she really know about this man? Only that he came from a peculiar family where his brother's behaviour was erratic and his father's vindictive.

One shove from him would send me crashing to the beach, she thought. I've got to get away from him. The turmoil inside her made her jabber. 'I didn't come to Summerland because Archie asked me. I'd never seen him before I came here. But if you must know, I'm the one who brought the state of these cliffs to his notice – and I presume it's what all this is about...' She'd been talking faster and faster and now she suddenly punched out at him.

It was like hitting a brick wall as her fists banged against his chest to push him out of her way. He snatched at her wrists and clamped his long fingers round them. At the same time the edge of the cliff gave way beneath her. Sand and gravel avalanched.

She screamed.

The way he snatched her towards him hurt her neck and shoulders. They both overbalanced. They rolled over and over, limbs locked. At last they came to a halt. Gasping she gazed up at him.

'Are you OK?' he said, breathing heavily against her, his long legs still entwined around hers.

'You – you saved my life.' Her voice was weak and shaky like the rest of her.

'If you'd gone over the edge you'd have taken us both. What in God's name made you punch out like that?'

She hesitated. A moment later she saw realization dawn in his eyes. They glittered diamond-bright and his voice came deeply, 'Nil out of ten for judgement. You don't choose the right moments to be scared.'

There was an odd expression on his face. She felt his body pressure increase on hers and winced as his hard muscles dug into her.

'L-let me up!'

For a moment she thought he was going to refuse and her heart hammered but then he sprang to his feet. She stood up unsteadily and tried to regain her composure.

'Perhaps you can see now why I've been investigating these cliffs.' Her voice betrayed her by shaking.

'You shouldn't have stood so close to the edge in the first place, should you?'

'Doesn't it bother you at all that your father's hotel could be sited on dangerous ground?'

'Doesn't it bother you that you could cause a great deal of worry to an old man, if he gets to hear about all this?

'I know you said you wanted to come up with something spectacular for your thesis but I'd say you were going over the top. There must be other ways you can distinguish yourself,' he added contemptuously.

She gaped. Surely he didn't believe...? But then he *was* quoting her. What was even worse was knowing there'd been a moment when it had excited her to think she might produce a piece of work that would impress everyone.

'All right then – if you don't believe me – believe the tell-tales!'

'Ah – the neat little row of pegs you hammered in near the hotel,' Guy muttered sarcastically.

'They prove the path there is creeping down the cliff because those pegs were in a perfectly straight line when I put them in but now the middle ones have moved...'

'Oh yes. Meant to tell you about that and apologise. I was slithering about on there with the dog and knocked them out. I put them back – obviously not quite in the same place.' He shrugged.

She fumed inside. She knew he'd known exactly what he was doing. She might as well throw all her calculations away. Without speaking she turned and began to walk back to the camp but he strode beside her.

'There's really no need for all these investigations of yours, you know. Dad had his own done. Unbiased ones.'

She didn't like his emphasis on the "unbiased". He continued 'He had the foundations of the house strengthened and a report on general ground conditions. They were found to be adequate for what was needed. But if there's anything more you or Archie want to know, don't hesitate to ask,' he added acidly.

'I will. Thank you,' she said unsmiling. She was bewildered. Had she been on the wrong tack all along? If Cliff had already had a report...

But I must believe in my own judgement, she thought. I may not be qualified but I can suss out the situation using the knowledge I've got. If I'm wrong I make a fool of myself. So what? But the small frown on her face belied the reasoning.

'I'd be grateful if you didn't bring the subject up when you come for supper. My father's still not well and I don't want him concerned in any way.'

'I'm not stupid,' she murmured.

'I know.'

She looked up quickly, surprised by the change in his tone. He nodded towards the chalets. 'This is as far as I go.'

'Who told you what I was doing?'

'Tracy told Neil.'

'Tracy?'

'Didn't you know she's chasing my brother? Silly little girl doesn't know the first thing about him. For some reason she doesn't like you – seemed to think we should know what you were up to. She heard you and the boyfriend talking to her parents and told my brother.'

'Neil was bothered about Dad finding out, and for once he took me into his confidence.'

'And – and she told Neil Archie employed me simply to investigate the cliffs?' Her eyes were round with astonishment?

'Simple enough deduction. Archie's been waiting for years to...' He stopped and they both listened. There was a noise like someone sobbing. A figure came hobbling across the field towards them from the direction of the chalets. Alison thought she recognized Honey and as she came closer she ran towards her.

Honey's blouse was torn and hanging from her shoulder. One pendulous breast swung loose from its brief bra-cup.

'Honey!'

Honey gazed at them from under swollen eyelids. She stood like a child, arms hanging limply by her side as Alison put her own cardigan on her and buttoned it. Honey saw Guy standing behind Alison and turned her face away to try and hide it.

Then she fell to her knees and was sick. Afterwards she put her hands over her face and began to cry again.

'Who did this to you?' said Guy savagely.

'N'body,' she muttered.

He put one hand round her to help her up. She sagged against him. He then slid his other arm under her legs and lifted her.

'Show me her chalet Alison.'

'Not there! He's...' Honey gave up the struggle and rolled her head against Guy's broad chest.

The chalet was empty when they reached it. Whoever Honey was afraid of had left. Guy laid her on the bed while Alison squeezed a face-cloth under cold water and gently wiped the cut on Honey's face.

'Oh Hon. You've got to tell us who did it,' she said.

'No no no...'

'OK,' soothed Alison, stroking her hair.

'And tell *him* not to do anything either.' Honey slid her gaze towards Guy, who seemed to fill the chalet.

'I'm only going to look outside.' He opened the door. 'If he's done it once he'll do it again.' Honey sat up. 'You'll cost me my bloody job.'

'He punched you; that's obvious – tore your clothes and Gods knows what else. He...'

'I got away didn't I?' Honey was talking as if she'd got a plum in her mouth now. Her lip was swelling.

Alison said quietly, 'The man's got to be found, Honey.'

'Oh yes. And then what happens eh? He shops me.' She glowered. 'You know Archie. This place is advertized for families...' Tears filled her eyes and she held the cloth against her mouth. Suddenly she swung her legs to the ground. 'Put the kettle on, eh, Ali? You might as well because I'm not leaving this chalet, not to go to the police and give statements or go to hospital or anything else.

'And you needn't worry. I got the bastard. I reckon I broke his little finger. Grabbed it and bent it back hard.'

'I think you should get some rest,' Guy said.

'You *are* going to do something, aren't you? I know your sort. You're the type who doesn't take any notice of what people say,' gabbled Honey.

'No he won't. Not if you don't want him to. Will you?' Alison stared at Guy.

'Wanna bet?' Honey sounded cynical but anxious too.

Alison frowned. She knew Honey was right. He'd go straight to the police. She could see it in his eyes. She sat on the bed beside Honey. 'Go on. Tell him.'

After a pause, Honey mumbled, 'My chalet number is one of the first that blokes get to know when they arrive. It's passed on, see. They know it before they get to know where the Arcade is, or the Games room – or anything.'

'I see. Popular lady.' His eyes were unblinking.

'You could say that. But... I don't take on marrieds!' She looked up. 'I got my principles in spite of everything. I – I was married myself once.'

'I didn't know that.' Alison was surprised.

'Lot you don't know – like he beat me up regular.' She brought up her hand and stroked her cheek lightly. 'Got one like him tonight didn't I? But this is nothing, I can tell you. I got worse than this from my husband.'

'Where is he now?' said Alison softly.

'God knows. I don't, and I don't care either. I got a baby you know? He's with my mum. Nearly two he is.

Brent's his name.' She eyed them both. 'I like to send extra money home. My mum's a widow. She hasn't got much.'

Guy nodded and said softly, 'It isn't worth getting it this way. You're at risk in too many ways.'

'Yeah I know. But you see – if Archie finds out what I've been doing, that's me without a job. He's always on about what a respectable place this is.'

There was a pause. 'OK. If you really insist on nothing being done about this then I'll respect your wishes. But you're wrong! No woman should tolerate being abused by any man ether mentally or physically. She's the same rights to consideration as he has.'

His voice rose. 'Look in the mirror, Honey. Say to yourself, NO ONE has the right to do this to my body and what's more I'm not going to let him do it to anyone else.'

Honey said nothing but lowered her head. Guy left the chalet and Alison followed him.

'It sickens me!' he fumed. 'He shouldn't get away with it.'

'She must decide,' she said quietly.

She'd seen a different side to him that night. She added softly, 'I'm glad you were with me when she needed help.'

'She's got problems and she'll have even more if she goes on like this, whatever the reason.'

'She's right about Archie. He wouldn't let her stay on if he knew.'

'Highly moralistic is he? So what happened to morals when he sneaked you in to look for ways to have Dad's hotel closed down?'

'You refuse to believe me, don't you? I really did come here as a waitress! When I told him I was studying geology and thought the place could be due for a landslip he gave me time off to investigate further.'

'And you honestly don't believe he snapped up that information to use it to his own ends?'

'Yes.'

'Yes you do, or yes you don't?'

'I believe he did. But that doesn't alter facts. It doesn't alter what I think about the cliffs.'

'We talk about Archie being rigid – what about you? You could be wrong. Those cliffs have been like that for years. The buildings near them have stood the test of time. I told you Dad had his own engineer's report.'

'I know, and that does make a difference.' She frowned.

'And after all you aren't...'

'Qualified? I know!'

'I was going to say, you aren't a woman who'll jump to conclusions until you've considered *all* aspects – without being influenced by Archie's dubious motives.'

Her instincts told her he was a man she could trust – more than she could ever trust Archie. She could believe him when he said the hotel had been studied for safety aspects. He would never take risks with guests' lives. He was too compassionate. She'd seen that in the chalet just now.

She looked up as his hands touched her shoulders. Stars glimmered above him on a velvet sky. From a distance the disco slammed its vibrancy into the night air.

'You're ambitious Alison. You want to prove yourself don't you?'

His fingers moved against the back of her neck and she felt a prickling in the fine hairs there. She knew he was about to kiss her. Her back arched and her heart beat harder.

'Goodnight Alison,' he whispered. And he walked away.

She stood alone trembling. Perhaps he didn't find her attractive after all? And yet she was certain...

You fool! said her brain. Don't you know he *wants* you to swoon over him just like Debbie did? Then you might abandon the project rather than displease him. You've just experienced an expert little seduction scene.

As Alison climbed into bed that night, Honey said, 'I heard you two talking. Is it true Archie wants you to find out if the cliffs are dangerous? Why didn't you say that's why he gave you time off? Archie would be dead pleased if the hotel had to close.'

'Please forget what you heard. Nothing's certain any more. I thought I was right about the movement of some pegs I knocked in but... oh, let's not talk about it!' She leaned on her elbow. 'Are you sure you're OK Honey?'

'I wish I could forget how the swine went for me. Trouble is he's bust off a lump of my tooth. It feels like a dagger.'

Alison sat bolt upright.

'What's up?' said Honey.

'I just remembered something! An old boat on the beach.' She lay back again. 'Tomorrow. I'll look tomorrow,' she said wearily and closed her eyes.

There was a long silence before Honey murmured, 'That Guy is really something else. I never knew he was so nice.' A moment later she started to snore. But Alison was wide awake again.

The following morning was the start of the heat-wave.

After breakfast Alison sat with Honey in the ballroom.

'Don't you want to go and watch them pick Miss Beautiful Hands?' asked Honey dolefully, her mouth swollen and bruised.

Alison shook her head. She hadn't the least intention of leaving Honey alone.

A small boy ran across the caramel-coloured floor.

'My Brent wears little red shorts like that.' Honey sighed deeply.

'Is there anything you'd like to do today?' Alison breezed.

'I don't want to go where I'll hear any more comments like, "Who've *you* been fighting with Honey?" I want to go where it's quiet. Like the island. That's it – the island! Maurice will let us borrow his boat.'

Alison spotted Tracy at the far end of the room. She excused herself for a minute and hurried across to her.

'Yeah?' said Tracy sulkily.

Alison ordered herself to keep her cool. She wanted to clear the air with her – find out why she'd been making trouble.

Before she could speak, Tracy snapped, 'Dad tells me he's asked you to help me with schoolwork? Well I'd like you to know I don't want any help from you or anybody else.'

'There's no need to be so rude about it.'

'My God, Tracy! What a miserable kid you are! Honey's voice echoed from behind Alison.

Tracy slewed them a black look. 'D'you think I'd be friends with anybody who tried to steal my boyfriend?'

'Heck, I was only swimming near him,' Alison retorted.

'You were flirting. I saw you.'

Honey stepped closer to Tracy. 'If you're talking about who I think you are, then I wouldn't let your old man find out if I were you.'

'And if I were *you*, I wouldn't let him find out about the little business you've got going on the side, because I don't reckon he'd like that, not one little bit.'

'Let's go, Honey,' murmured Alison.

Tracy looked at Alison and sneered, 'I'm not surprised she's been done over. What happened? Did he want more than his money's worth? Her client?'

She'd barely got the words out when Honey hurled herself at Tracy, snatching at her hair. The two of them began kicking and scratching one another with the impact of all-in wrestlers.

'Stop it!' Alison shouted.

A group of startled campers turned and gaped.

Archie appeared from nowhere, his expression like thunder. He seized hold of both Honey and Tracy and yanked them apart. Dishevelled and breathing heavily, they glowered at one another. Archie shook them. 'Marvellous! Bloody marvellous example! My daughter and a waitress fighting like a couple of alley-cats! Now, what the hell do you think you're both playing at?'

He saw the bruise on Honey's mouth and rapped out, 'Did you do that, Trace?'

'No I didn't! It was one of her...' She stopped, still out of breath and caught the look on Honey's face. In that instant both girls knew they depended on one another's silence. Tracy mumbled sulkily, 'No I didn't.'

'Fine state of affairs! Look at the two of you! And here's me and your mum going away for the weekend and thinking we can leave you to help run the place, Trace. Both of you go and get yourselves cleaned up!'

As they both slunk away, Alison saw Honey glance towards her and give a surreptitious grin, opening her hand behind her back. In it was a big clump of ginger-coloured hair.

When Alison went down to the beach it seemed to her the whole of Summerland must be sunbathing, swimming or playing there. She picked her way between tanned bodies and eventually reached the part of the beach in front of the hotel. She knew what she was looking for. She'd seen it the day before but it hadn't registered. Not until Honey spoke about her broken tooth did it occur to her it was an important piece of evidence for her thesis – and she'd missed it.

Fine geologist you're going to make, she told herself cynically.

She stopped when she reached the bow of the old boat, sunk in the sand. Yes, she was certain there was less of it on the surface. The greater part of it was now hidden by sand and gravel – sand and gravel that had not been there the first time she spotted it. Simon had agreed there were springs permeating through the cliff, softening it and causing parts of it to slide down to the beach. Now it was happening more often.

She gazed up the cliff-side with an anxious expression. But this time she told herself she wasn't charging off to report her findings to anyone, not even Simon. She'd use common sense this time; get her results properly tabulated first.

She pressed her lips together and looked up to where the pegs she'd knocked in had been dislodged, then she started to climb up to re-align them.

That afternoon she was poring over books in the chalet when Honey burst in.

'I don't know how you can sit here in all this heat. And anyway I thought we were going over to the island? Maurice'll lend us his boat.'

'Have you been there before?' Alison looked up, pencil poised over her notebook.

"Course. We snuck over once to have a beach-party. You'd like it.'

Honey had just started the boat when they spotted Janet racing towards them.

'Hold it Hon! There's been an accident. Your mum phoned. It's Brent.'

'What's up?'

'It's not serious – but you know what your mum's like. Rita says you can go home.'

'Can I help?' Alison jumped from the boat as well.

'Only if you know how to stop my mum ringing up every time my Brent falls down and scratches himself. I got to go though. You go on to the island. You'll like it.'

After Honey and Janet left, Alison hesitated, but after looking at the crowded beach and then towards the island with its towering lighthouse, she got back in the boat.

At the island she tied it to a jetty and padded over deep sand. On such a beautiful day it was hard to imagine this was a destructive coastline with storms wreaking havoc along its shore. But they didn't build the lighthouse for nothing she told herself, nor the fine modern one further along the coast leaving this one disused.

She clambered over rocks and stones and then began to climb steps to the tall grey building.

The entrance room held a stillness that startled her. It was much cooler in there, and she pulled on her sweater and gazed around the circular chamber. More steps wound upwards.

She guessed the next level must have been the engine room. She rested her arms on a deep window-sill and gazed through the small window. A wide turquoise sea rocked gently for miles. The sight made her feel suddenly small and unimportant.

There was a noise that sounded like someone on the steps. But she hadn't seen a soul when she approached the lighthouse. Perhaps some visitors had arrived in the meantime?

She went to look but could only see a small beam of dusty sunshine dancing through the doorway.

But when she climbed to the next level she saw signs of someone having settled themselves down in there: upturned boxes covered by a rug, empty cans of drink – and there was an oddly sweet smell in there.

She sat on the box. The rug was warm. So she hadn't been mistaken? Someone else had been in the lighthouse with her – and they weren't closetted in there smoking ordinary cigarettes.

She felt apprehensive now. Suppose that person was still lurking in the place? She told herself her best bet was to get out – fast.

She breathed a sigh of relief when she reached the entrance again and saw no one, then she marched forthrightly out to the jetty.

She stood in the sunshine and laughed. No one there at all! Whoever had been in the lighthouse must have wanted to get away as quickly as she did. Then her expression changed. There was no sign of the boat either.

Then to her great dismay she spotted it half-way between the island and the mainland. All she could do now was to hope some holidaymakers would come out there and take her back with them.

She climbed back up the cliff steps. The sun was scorching. She clipped her dark silken hair into a top-knot for coolness and felt her legs starting to burn below her small white shorts. She found a spot near hawthorn bushes that was shady, and where she could look out from the clifftop and wave to any boat she saw.

She rested her elbows on her sweater on the ground and watched sea-birds dunking their beaks in a drifting sea.

I'm really lucky to have the chance to write a thesis about this lovely area and live here at the same time, she told herself. Fancy – I nearly gave up the opportunity when Mum died. Life has to go on... like the sea ebbing and flowing; sun rising and s ... She lay back and closed her eyes.

She didn't know how long she'd been asleep when she woke to hear rustling in the bushes. She blinked and sat up, her pulse racing.

'Well! You're good at camouflaging yourself! I've been looking everywhere for you,' said a deep voice.

She sprang to her feet, exclaimed 'Guy!' and just stopped herself from falling into his arms with relief.

'Some bloke spoke to Neil on the beach – worried

because he'd lent you his boat and you hadn't got back. He said you should have been in the dining-room. Anyway I wasn't doing anything and borrowed Neil's boat to come over here. Nice day for it. Hope it stays that way.' He glanced towards the sea.

'I'm so pleased to see you!' she exclaimed.

'Heh, don't look so worried.' Without warning he drew her towards him and caressed the nape of her neck. Her body seemed to melt against him.

She wondered if he could feel her heartbeat against his broad chest. 'You're hungry?' he said.

'Very!'

'I grabbed a bit of food on the way out.'

She demolished chicken drumsticks, granary bread – and champagne. Bubbles seemed to float into her head and explode. When she looked up he was watching her with an amused smile. It made him look more attractive than ever. He was wearing a scarlet Lacoste T-shirt and cream pants. He sat with one knee crooked, his elbow resting on it as he held a glass of champagne. She noticed the dark hairs on his tanned arms and the Rolex watch round his wrist.

'So are you going to tell me what happened?' he said.

When she told him about her visit to the lighthouse he only shrugged.

'People aren't supposed to come over here but they do. It was probably a tramp – or kids from Summerland. We used...' He stopped as if thinking better of it, then said, 'We'd better get back; looks like a mist coming down.'

'Shall I show you the room with the boxes in it? There's a peculiar sme–'

'No point,' he said quickly, almost abruptly. He

stood up to leave and she followed, her legs feeling hollow. Her head was about clear enough for her to realize she wasn't herself. Guy helped her down the steps to the jetty and into Neil's boat. She knew he thought she hadn't tied up Maurice's securely. She was even beginning to wonder as much herself.

Neil's boat wouldn't start.

'Don't worry – won't take me long to fix it,' he said. 'In the meantime you'd better sit down... The champagne wasn't such a good idea.'

By the time he'd got the boat started the mist had turned into a fog that enveloped the mainland. He looked out to sea, frowning.

'Well *I* think it was a lovely idea!' she piped. When he glanced at her with a puzzled expression she added, smiling, 'The champagne.'

'You haven't a clue what's happening.' The corner of his mouth twitched.

'I have!'

'We're going to have to hang on a bit until this lot clears.'

'I know,' she remarked, ignoring the turmoil growing inside her; a longing... for what? she asked herself. Her stomach twisted when he touched her cheek lightly, his eyes gazing deeply into hers.

'Show me this room in the lighthouse then,' he murmured.

Five

Guy gripped Alison's hand as they walked back together. Her bones felt like egg-shells.

Inside its shroud, the island seemed to be disappearing. Waves slapped it while gulls cried plaintively.

As they approached the lonely lighthouse, she remembered what Honey had said about not getting involved with Guy. But wasn't that before Honey had got to know him better?

Alison stumbled as they climbed the rocky path and Guy caught her. But as soon as they entered the lower chamber of the lighthouse, he released her hand. Suddenly he seemed aloof. He glanced quickly about him. He spoke gruffly without looking at her.

'Put your sweater on.'

'I'm warm enough.'

'You won't be for long. Not in here.'

There was a desolate emptiness about the place. Alison swung her sweater around her shoulders and tied the sleeves under her chin.

Guy's sudden cool and distant manner puzzled her. He had the look of a man who had entered an alien world, and yet he had been to the lighthouse before.

She dragged her feet as she followed him to the next level. Sometimes she wished she'd had more experience with men – enough to be able to sort out dreams from reality.

The only man she'd know really well was Simon,

who had helped and encouraged her when life had been at its most bleak; Simon who had assumed they would marry. She felt a twinge of guilt. She owed Simon.

'Is this the room you were telling me about?' Guy said.

She pointed to the rug spread across the boxes. 'That was still warm when I sat on it.'

'Probably kids messing around,' said Guy.

'If so, they could have let my boat go simply for a laugh.' The place seemed fairly normal to her, now.

'Possibly.' She realized he was still deep in his own thoughts, and had been since entering the lighthouse.

'Shall we go and see the rest of the place?' She tried to sound bright but her head was still woolly.

'I haven't come for a guided tour.'

Alison wanted to ask him why he had come. Instead she said stonily, 'Perhaps it would be a better idea if we tried to make it back to the mainland after all.'

'No way. There are tricky currents round here at the best of times but in this fog we'd be asking for trouble. We may as well make ourselves comfortable.'

He pushed the boxes against the wall, sat at one end and indicated that Alison sat beside him. She ignored him and pretended to examine the chamber. When she looked at him again, his eyes were closed, his arms folded, his long legs stretched out.

'You might as well. We could be here all night,' he murmured.

'I'm not staying all night!' Alison declared.

'What are you going to do? Swim?'

She perched on the end of the boxes. She thought he'd fallen asleep, he was quiet for so long, but then he said, without opening his eyes, 'This boyfriend of yours...'

'Simon?'

'What does he do?'

'He's a geologist.'

'Useful.'

'What does that mean?'

'He can help you write your thesis on how to condemn our home.'

Alison refused to rise to the bait. He continued, 'Is it serious? You and him?'

'I – he –' She couldn't answer. The doubt and confusion concerning Simon which she'd felt for a long time only added to the lightness in her head. Guy opened one eye sleepily. She heard herself gabbling.

'Simon has been wonderful to me. He's helped me a lot. He's a very, very kind person.'

'Sounds like a good guy.' He turned towards her. Now his deep blue eyes were fixed on her with a more gentle expression. 'But gratitude is no substitute for love, is it? Or desire.'

'I want...' she began hotly.

'What? What do you want?' Guy interrupted. 'It's my guess you don't know. Correction – I don't think you'll admit to what you want. You might have done for a second, out there on the boat, but now...'

'It was you who changed! From the minute we came into the lighthouse you were like a different person.'

'There you are – it just proves I'm an unsociable pig of a man.' He narrowed his eyes and grinned disarmingly, mimicking a gangster's drawl. 'Well, we gotta make the best of things, kid, because there's only you and me here now.'

In spite of everything, Alison felt a giggle rise in her throat. She decided she wasn't quite sober. Suddenly she jerked her head and listened. 'What's that?'

'I didn't hear anything.'

'I was sure...'

'Relax.' He laid his large brown hand over her small one.

'But suppose there's someone lurking about?'

'Are you still scared? With me here?' His tone was jocular now. He'd dismissed whatever had been on his mind before.

So, she thought cynically, it was OK now, was it, to be all jolly and friendly again? She tried to draw her fingers away from his, but couldn't. She wondered if he could feel how her pulse was galloping? Her mouth dried as he edged closer to her.

'Shall I tell you why you really wanted to come in here, Alison?'

'No... I...' She didn't finish the sentence. She tried to push him away but as his lips lingered on hers, her body melted.

'You don't love him you know,' he murmured at last.

'How would *you* know how I feel?' she said breathlessly.

'Alison.' His voice was like a caress.

'I shouldn't have come. It was a mistake,' she said weakly.

'No. No mistake.' He was whispering, kissing her cheeks, her hair, her neck.

Dreamlike, she felt his hands slide down her sweater. There were only the two of them in an intimate world of mists and dangerous currents. Only he could extinguish the fires that began to rage inside her.

She felt weightless as he laid her back on the rug. Her body was like a small drifting boat about to be crushed on the rocks. His lips bruised her but the taste of him was exquisite. Her body ached for him.

He suddenly released her, leaned back and put his finger to his lips.

'What's wrong, Guy?'

Alison heard someone call, 'Is anybody there?'

Later, when she tried to think rationally about the interruption, all she could remember was how her body would not stop tingling.

The two tourists, who had got themselves stranded on the island, stayed to keep them company until the mist lifted.

It was in the early hours when Guy helped her out of the boat near the hotel. She saw Maurice's bobbing boat in the distance and ran along the beach. She waded into the sea towards it. Guy followed her.

'I'll teach you how to tie decent knots...' he began, then stopped, frowning, as he examined the rope trailing from the boat. 'This has been cut. If I were you, I'd stay away from the island.'

Alison saw genuine concern in his face. As they walked back together he put his arm around her. She felt warm and protected. Her heart soared.

It was Archie's manager who brought her down to earth.

'Damn silly to go out there on your own. Everyone knows that stretch of water is lethal. It's bad enough Honey wasn't here without you going missing, making us even more short-handed.'

'I'm sorry.'

'You don't look sorry. As it happens, we were all worried about you.'

That subdued Alison and she threw herself into work to make up for the time she'd missed.

She wondered when Guy would contact her again.

Honey returned that evening. 'Mum is so fussy. I knew Brent would be OK. Still – it was smashing to see him again... but Mum kept going on about my face. She didn't believe me when I said I'd walked into a door. She's seen it all before. So... what happened on the island?'

'I told you, those tourists came along and stayed with us.'

'You go a funny colour when you talk about it.'

'Probably because I've got a headache.'

'Hangover. That's what that is!' Honey grinned. 'So, when are you seeing Guy again?'

Alison adopted a casual attitude. 'No idea. Oh... I am going to supper at the hotel next week.' She frowned. 'The trouble is, I've nothing decent to wear.'

'None of my clothes would fit you, but, if you like, I can show you a place where you can buy great stuff. Designer clothes and everythin'.'

'I can't afford designer clothes, Honey!'

'Don't worry. Leave it to me.'

Friday night was balloons and fancy-dress but Alison found it difficult to get into the festive spirit. She'd been so sure Guy would have contacted her.

Honey's fancy-dress was a mask that concealed a developing black eye. She shouted above the thumping disco. 'I'm not staying long. Not with Tracy showing off all night. Anyway, it's too hot for dancing.'

Jack shouted back, 'You know where Archie and Rita have gone?'

'Yeah. They're visiting some fabulous holiday chalet hotel at Hopton-on-Sea – being wined and dined for the weekend, lucky things. I expect Archie's gone to pinch ideas. I reckon there are going to be big changes round here.'

'I hate change. We're all right as we are,' moaned Jack.

'Well, if he smartens up the place and makes it all modern, he won't go for amateur entertainment like you. He'll want the big names then. You and your guitar...'

Honey stopped and leapt from her chair when one of the staff asked her to dance.

Left alone with Jack, Alison felt sorry for him. 'Big names cost money, Jack.'

'Oh, I'm not worried. I won't be losing *my* job! Archie's known me too long. I worked for him when he had a shop. He knows who his friends are.'

Alison found it uncomfortably hot in the room. She wondered what on earth had possessed her to come as Neptune's daughter. Her hair was thick and heavy enough without seaweed twined in it!

She moved towards one of the open doors for some fresh air and spotted a figure she thought she recognized. Her pulse went full gallop – until she realized the tall dark man wearing a mask was not Guy.

Tracy raced past her and spoke excitedly to him. 'I *knew* you'd come! I knew!' Her eyes were shining.

'I've only come to see what goes on here. My God, the place is jumping.'

'I know. Great isn't it? Dance with me, Neil.'

'I'm gasping for a drink.'

'I'll get you one! Don't go away!'

After Tracy had rushed off, Neil flipped up his mask and winked at Alison. 'Her old man *is* away for the weekend, isn't he?'

'You're crazy. Someone is going to recognize you and tell him.'

'Not if I keep this mask on, little mermaid.'

Alison fancied his hands shook slightly as he re-adjusted the mask. He grinned. 'This is the sort of dancing we should have at the hotel. We need a bit more life – bit more fun for the kids. I want to have a good look round this place.'

'Have you just come to pinch ideas?'

'Could be.'

She wondered how much he'd drunk already when he partnered Tracy on the dance floor and began larking around and calling out silly remarks. Some of the older guests looked on disapprovingly, but Tracy laughed hysterically at his antics.

It had been announced earlier that the speciality act had failed to turn up and there was a last minute surprise item. As the dancing finished and everyone sat down, Alison was agog with curiosity.

The first bars of 'One Singular Sensation' brought an attractively dressed woman wearing sequinned midnight-blue on to the floor. She flourished a chiffon scarf and sank into a low curtsey. As the spotlight swept over her the crowd gasped as they recognized Maurice.

There was a burst of applause. With a cheeky grin,

Maurice launched into a raucous rendering of 'There Is Nothing Like A Dame'. He was such a roaring success, Alison wondered later why he hadn't left it at that instead of cavorting between tables flicking his scarf provocatively at the men and finishing up sitting on Neil's lap.

Everyone laughed – except Neil. He jerked his elbows back then thrust his arms forward, giving Maurice a push that propelled the slight figure along the shiny floor. Maurice sat up, pulling a comical face and rubbing his head, as if the whole incident were part of the clowning act.

But Neil wasn't finished. With his face contorted, he marched across to Maurice and dragged him up by his shoulder straps. It was the crowd hissing and booing that made him let go and stride angrily to the door, with Tracy in anxious pursuit.

As Honey and Alison were leaving, Honey said, 'Only a bit of fun, wasn't it? No need for that guy to have a go at Maurice – and I can guess who it was, too!' She wiped her forehead. 'It's so hot. Why don't we go for a swim?'

'At this time of night?'

'I've wanted to have a swim all day,' sighed Honey.

'Why didn't you?'

'And let everybody see my bruises? You must be kiddin'.'

'OK. Let's get our cossies.'

'No need for cossies. No one will see us in the dark.'

Had Alison realized it was such a magical experience swimming in the nude, she would have done it before. Waves slapped silkily against her soft skin as she splashed happily, making fluorescent tracers with her fingers.

'This is marvellous!'

'Told you.' Honey's voice came from the distance.

'Where are you? I can't see you.'

'Over here.'

Alison saw phosphorescent sparks in the direction of her voice. She relaxed and glided lazily on her back in the inky water.

Suddenly she heard a soft splashing near her. The next minute Guy rose from the water beside her like a magnificent Poseidon. She gasped.

'Seems we all had the same idea,' he said softly with wry amusement.

Alison stared. She had never seen such a body. And she had never felt so vulnerable.

'My God, you're beautiful Alison,' he whispered, moving even closer. She was too startled and dumbstruck to get any words out, but she pressed her hands against his massive shoulders to push him away as he circled her with his arms like a steel girdle.

'Don't...' she began, but his mouth was over hers to silence her and she was locked hard against him. She was trembling under the power that grew in his rock-like limbs as they stiffened against her and she became weak and unresisting.

The sea sucked persistently, trying to force a channel between them.

He released her as suddenly as he'd appeared, diving under the water and striking out for the shore. Alison staggered from the impact of him, blood coursing round her body.

'Heh! Why didn't you answer me?' Honey had swam to her side.

'I – I didn't hear you.' Alison felt out of breath.
'You OK?'
'Fine!'
'Ready to get out?'
'Not yet... In a minute.'
A few minutes later as they walked along the beach, Alison asked, 'Has Guy Kington really been around so much?'
'You mean, has he had a lot of women? I'll say. He's not the type to settle down with one. I've told you, don't raise your hopes in that direction... Heh! Listen!'
From the direction of Archie's little boat-shed they heard Tracy's voice followed by Neil's.
'What's the matter, Neil? Aren't I good enough for you or something?'
'Just clear off and leave me alone!'
Honey whispered, 'She don't never learn.'
Alison glanced over her shoulders. In the distance she could see the lights twinkling on the pier at Larborough. So much glitz and glitter. But how many seaside romances would collapse like sand-castles when the summer was over? In spite of what Honey had said about Guy, she was sure theirs would not be one of them.

When Archie and Rita returned from Hopton, he was like a fire-cracker waiting to be lit.
'I got these great ideas! Great ideas!' he enthused at the party he gave for Rita's birthday. He called out, 'I give you all – Summerland Camp! – except it ain't going to be called that any more.' He paused to enjoy the curiosity he'd aroused.
'Are you going to expand, boss?' asked Jack hesitantly.

'Why must everybody talk about expansion? It isn't always the best way, not in today's climate, Jack.'

'But I thought...'

'Look Jack, there's owners of holiday centres who're de-bedding. Do you know that?'

Jack looked perplexed. Archie chewed a sweet. 'It's *quality* I want. Exciting developments – that's the secret. We provide facilities that keep our guests so happy they don't want – or need – to go abroad. There'll be everything here, indoors and outdoors. New exciting facilities. Get it?'

Alison saw doubts on Jack's face.

'Wh-where's that going to leave me, Archie?'

'Exactly where you want to be, Jack. Exactly where you want to be. It's up to you. But we've all got to move with the times.'

Archie's eyes glazed over. He opened his arms wide. 'Summerland Holiday World. I can see it now.'

But he didn't see Rita join the group.

'Is he telling you about the magnificent Chalet-Hotel complex we've just visited? Oh, we had ever such a smashing time. The director there was ever so kind and showed us...'

'I did have a few ideas of my own before we went there,' pronounced Archie.

'Oh, there was everything there, wasn't there, Archie? Snooker, clay-pigeon shooting, badminton, indoor bowls...'

'I shall have all that. And de luxe chalets with tel-'

'And swimming-pools...'

'I shall have an indoor swimming-pool...'

'Fitness studio...'

'I didn't know you were keen on sport,' cut in Archie testily.

'Flexible meal times...'

'Rit!' Archie scowled.

Rita glanced at her husband then drifted off into the room. Alison followed her.

'You really enjoyed the weekend, didn't you, Rita?'

'Oh, I did! I can't wait for Archie to start alterations here.'

'I expect there'll be a lot of new buildings.'

'Oh, there will be – to house all the lovely new facilities.' She added on a whisper of excitement, her eyes dancing, 'I've got a few ideas of my own.'

And I bet Archie knows nothing about those, thought Alison.

Later that week, Alison and Honey took a train to Larborough.

Honey showed her the second-hand charity shop where clothes were packed on free-standing rails.

'You'll find some good stuff in this lot, Ali. Women sometimes bring in frocks they've only worn once. They want to get their hands on some extra bread without the old man knowing. Look for designer labels.'

'If they bring in clothes with designer labels, they can't be short of money.'

'Don't you believe it. Some guys like their wives to be totally dependent on them for everything. Look at Archie. He loves being Mr Big, don't he? Poor old Rita relies on him for everything. He doesn't like her doing anything on her own. He was the same with his first wife.'

'I didn't know Archie had been married before.'

Alison searched through the rails. Then she spotted

a jade dress hanging against the wall. A plump motherly assistant smiled at her.

'That's only just this minute come in. It's really classy.'

Alison slipped into the tiny changing-room behind a curtain. She unzipped the beautiful jade dress and allowed the fine material to float over her head. One glance in the mirror told her she looked good. The cut of the material was superb. It emphasized her slim waist and softly rounded hips. It was dim in the little changing-room and she stepped outside to look in the shop mirror.

'Oh! It looks lovely on you!' the assistant beamed.

'I think it needs to be shortened, but I can soon do that.'

Honey was open-mouthed. 'That colour don't half suit you.'

'Ever done any modelling, dear?' asked the assistant. Alison shook her head. Suddenly the thought of her evening at Cliff's Hotel was becoming more appealing.

Afterwards, while Honey shopped, Alison went to the library. She pored over copies of old newspapers, researching flooding and erosion in the area. She was reading about sea-walls and their need to withstand extreme tidal conditions when her eyes caught the headline – DEATH PLUNGE FROM LIGHTHOUSE.'

She snatched up the paper and read on: – 'Eighteen-year-old Deborah Sheperd crashed to her death on jagged rocks pounded by waves.

"I saw her jump,' said 19-year-old boyfriend Guy Kington, playboy son of Cliff's Hotel owner.

Alison sat motionless, staring at the print. She stood up and walked to the reception desk.

'Could I please see later editions of this newspaper?'

A few moments later, a librarian padded to her table and laid a pile of papers on it.

On the way back to Summerland, Alison was engrossed in her thoughts and scarcely heard Honey chattering about her shopping expedition.

It looked as if the police had been suspicious of Guy's involvement in the affair, but it seemed there had not been enough evidence to accuse him of anything.

Archie's vitriolic rantings had been quoted at length. 'Two spoilt brats of that hotel owner... My Debbie – an innocent young girl who would never have taken to drugs of her own free will, besotted by Guy Kington who used his power over her. No! We didn't know our daughter was pregnant. If it takes for ever, I'll get even with the whole Kington family...'

The phrases swirled in Alison's head. She glanced at Honey and saw she'd nodded off to sleep.

She wondered if Debbie had been racing to get away from Guy when she landed up in the gallery of the lighthouse? If so, why?

She remembered how Guy had been with her in there. What would have happened if she'd resisted his advances? He was a pretty determined character. Suppose *she* had run away? She gave a start as Honey snored.

Alison ran her fingers through her hair. What on earth was she thinking of? Guy would never hurt anyone. Hadn't he saved her from toppling over the cliff?

But one of Archie's remarks rang true. There was no doubt Guy did have a strange power over women. She'd seen how they reacted when he smiled that slow seductive smile... the way she herself had reacted.

But by the time they got back, Alison had devised a dozen alibis for Guy. She'd also managed to convince herself their relationship was nothing like the one he'd had with Debbie.

He loves me. I'm sure he does, she repeated to herself. She frowned and bit her lip. She had read something else in the library that troubled her – about erosion. The facts matched up to a lecture she'd heard at college and had been trying to remember.

A set of circumstances that could lead to a full-scale disaster.

Should she disregard them? Tell herself she could be mistaken? It would make life easier. If she brought them to light she could say goodbye to any relationship between her and Guy... but wasn't it her job to dig out the truth?

'You look worried. And you just bought yourself a lovely new dress, too,' said Honey.

Alison gave a determined nod. 'Yes! And I'm going to enjoy myself in it! And I'm going to forget about my stupid old thesis!'

'I'll tell you this much. When you get to the hotel in that frock, you'll knock 'em sideways.'

But neither of them were to know that fate was about to play one of its dirty tricks on Alison.

Six

Alison tingled with excitement as she approached Cliff's hotel, where she was to be a supper guest. Guy had never seen her dressed up.

She resisted an urge to skip up the steps to the veranda; she wanted to maintain the new sophisticated image. The original owner of the beautiful jade dress she was wearing, would never have skipped up steps.

'Ah. Good evening – Alison.' Cliff hobbled with his stick across the vestibule. She knew he'd nearly forgotten her name.

When Guy suddenly appeared from the lounge, her heart raced.

'Looks as if it's going to be a pleasurable evening, eh, Guy?' Cliff slid his son a foxy glance. Guy's dark dinner jacket lay sleek across his wide shoulders. His white shirt was luminous against his bronze skin.

His cool hands enfolded hers. 'You look nearly as good as the last time we met.'

Colour swamped her cheeks as she remembered the midnight swim and she quickly averted his gaze.

'That's not a very gallant remark,' Cliff said as they went to the bar lounge with its comfortable green leather armchairs. 'There's a world of difference between Alison's waitress's uniform and that expensive-looking dress. I must change my ideas about staff at holiday camps being poorly paid.'

'Not camps any more, Dad. They're called centres now, or holiday parks...'

'Huh! As far as I'm concerned, that place across the road is a camp, and one up from tents.'

'You wouldn't say that if you'd been there.' Guy smiled wryly.

'Good God. Don't tell me *you* have?'

'Sure.'

'Then you must be out of your mind, that's all I can say.'

Cliff fell into a stony silence while Guy ordered drinks.

Alison noted Guy's self-possessed manner. This was not a man who would be afraid of a confrontation with Archie, but he *would* be wary of the publicity such a meeting might provoke, with any subsequent damage to the hotel's business.

As she sipped her Martini, Alison became aware of his sensual gaze sweeping her body.

'That dress,' Cliff said, stroking his chin. 'I'm sure I've seen...'

'I suggest we go on to the dining-room,' interrupted Guy.

They sat at a table set for five, near a window. Outside, lawns and rockeries tumbled towards a shiny wrinkled sea.

I bet Archie would like to see this lot, thought Alison. The room was like a crystal palace with glittering chandeliers and twinkling glass and cutlery that must have been polished for hours!

'This is a beautiful room, Mr Kington,' she enthused.

'I hope you find the menu to your liking too. Big change from that camp, eh? Don't suppose you get much of a choice there?

'As a matter of fact, the meals are pretty good,' she said.

Cliff grunted. He glanced towards one of the doors. 'Where the hell is Neil? Oh... and about time too.'

Alison's jaw dropped when she spotted Neil. With Kedrun.

Kedrun's wide eyes encompassed the men as they stood up. She pouted poppy-moist lips. 'I'm sorry if we're late,' she crooned.

'Not a bit, my dear. You aren't at all. Let me see, you two ladies know one another, don't you?' Cliff's gaze slanted from Kedrun to Alison before realization flooded his eyes. 'Of course! I know where I've seen that colour before!' He stared at Alison's jade dress. Their looks told her all she needed to know.

'Let's order, Dad,' said Guy brusquely.

Alison did not have her usual hearty appetite, although the meal was perfect for a summer evening, from the fresh salmon to the creamy tangerine charlotte. Neil knew how to get the best out of his staff. How different he appeared this evening to the time she had seen him at the dance. He was a man of many moods, she thought.

Tact hung over the table like mist over the island. The conversation had been directed at every topic except clothes.

Kedrun had been too well bred to do more than raise a carefully pencilled eyebrow when she saw Alison's dress. Kedrun herself was wearing a slim black tube of a gown. It showed off her shiny blonde hair to perfection. It glittered as she talked animatedly to Guy.

It's ridiculous to ruin my appetite because of a little

thing like pride, Alison thought. So, what if she was wearing Kedrun's dress? It was simply an unfortunate stroke of fate and she had to make the best of it.

'Did you enjoy the meal?' asked Guy.

'It was delicious. Really lovely.'

'And you – you look really lovely.'

His lingering stare made her blush as he took in the sight of her thick raven hair licking at the snug-fitting bodice.

She said brightly, 'I had to take up the hem. It originally belonged to a taller lady.' Her voice faltered slightly. 'But you know that, of course.'

Alison realized Kedrun was watching them both with a frown playing on her smooth aristocratic forehead. That frown spelt trouble.

Kedrun's voice rang out loud and clear. 'I hear you are investigating the state of the cliffs?' she said to Alison.

'What cliffs?' Cliff was immediately alerted.

'More wine anyone?' Guy beckoned a waiter.

'What part of the cliffs?' His father's steely eyes were pinned on her. Guy threw her a warning look. Kedrun saw it. Although she had wanted to make things awkward for Alison, she had not intended to displease Guy and now tried to make amends by changing the topic of conversation entirely.

'How far have you got with your new book, Guy?'

'I'm working on...'

'Alison?' Cliff now sounded peeved.

'It's a thesis I'm doing for college, Mr Kington. That's all. I'm studying the coastline.'

'The coastline near my hotel?'

She nodded.

'Why the interest? Why this area?'

Alison wet her lips. She glanced around at happy chattering guests; men, women, children who might fall into a deep contented sleep one night after a sandy sun-soaked day, unaware that the weather was about to change for the worst. Unaware of gales that could occur when tides were at spring.

How she had wanted to put all such thoughts behind her, especially that night, but it was useless. Before leaving the chalet she had heard on the news about cliffs crumbling in a coastal town in the south-east. How clay at the foot of the cliffs had eroded, leaving no support for sandstone above. The district council had declared houses within fifty feet of the cliff-edge, unsafe.

Her mind had switched to similar calculations as she worked out the distance between Clifford's hotel and the edge of the cliff.

'Why?' he repeated doggedly.

'It's a very interesting area geologically and... and...' They were staring at her. 'And I believe the cliffs in front of the hotel are on the move.' She had not meant the statement to come out in such a staccato way. The silence that followed it screamed at her.

Cliff's face grew pink and puffy. 'I've never heard such rubbish – if you'll forgive me saying so. Good God!' He laughed, except it did not sound like a laugh. 'Those cliffs have been there for ever. They aren't suddenly going to take off and scuttle down the beach!' He ran his fingers through the air like a spider.

'Not a topic for discussion now,' Guy said, frowning.

Neil stood up and signalled to the band assembled on a dais beside the dance floor.

Cliff leaned towards Alison. 'I'm hardly stupid

enough to have spent hard cash improving the hotel without getting a survey done first, my dear. And my reports from *experts* are sound enough, as for the land...' He stopped his carefully modulated argument to scowl at Neil. 'For heaven's sake, sit down, boy!'

Alison saw the colour rise in Neil's cheeks. In an almost defiant gesture, he dragged his chair away from the table. 'It's about time we livened this place up a bit!' He snaked between couples starting to dance a slow foxtrot. He spoke to the band leader and the music trailed away. Seconds later, a livelier, much noisier rhythm filled the room.

Cliff screwed up his face as if he felt pain, but the dancers, in all their finery, began to jig about, laughing.

Neil returned to the table and held out his palms. 'See, they like it!'

His father rose from his chair unsteadily and spoke through clenched teeth. 'If you think, for one minute, I'm going to see this hotel turned into a cheap low-class...'

Guy said quietly, 'I'd let this one go, Dad. They all seem to be enjoying themselves.'

Cliff glared at Neil. 'How much have you had to drink tonight?'

'I...'

'Don't tell me. I can guess.'

'No one has had too much to drink, Dad. This sort of dancing can be great fun,' said Guy, in a lighter tone.

'Not to me it's not. And one thing is certain. I don't have to stay here and be deafened.'

He limped away, holding tightly on to his stick.

Guy read Alison's thoughts. 'He's best left alone when he's like this.'

Neil rounded on Guy. 'Why do you have to interfere between him and me? We managed to sort out our own problems before you decided to come home on your – extended holiday! And sure as hell, we'll manage when you disappear again!'

'Can't we all go and dance?' said Kedrun nervously.

'I'd like to,' agreed Alison quickly.

'It isn't the first time, is it big brother? In fact I can't remember a time when you didn't try to play God...' As Neil ranted on, Alison watched in astonishment that his father's reprimand could bring about such a swing in Neil's mood.

Guy stood up. 'Leave it, Neil.'

He turned to Alison, but Neil put a claw-like hand on his shoulder. 'You leave it! And leave us. The old man isn't ill any more. That's why you came home, wasn't it? Or was it to make sure he'd forgiven you? Not left you out of his will?' He was shouting. The music beat loudly. Guy remained silent and stony-faced.

'Let's dance.' Guy put out his hand to Alison.

Neil clenched his fists. 'This hotel is *mine!* Why don't you bugger off back to Greece?'

Alison felt Guy almost pushing her towards the dance floor. Neil's outburst was utterly bewildering to her. And why hadn't Guy stood up to him?

After they had been dancing a while, Guy looked down at her. 'What's wrong?'

'Nothing.'

'Don't lie.'

'All right. If you must know – I can't understand why you let Neil talk to you like he did.'

'Forget it,' he said firmly.

'It isn't...'

'I said forget it!'

She did not like his tone. Whatever had been going on in this family, it did not give him cause to speak to her so abruptly. She drew in her breath. 'Sometimes you sound, and behave, like your father.'

'And sometimes you behave like a child.'

'You didn't appear to think there was anything childish about me last night!'

'That was being mature, was it? Plunging naked into the sea where I was bathing and then playing hard to get...'

'And is that what Debbie did? Play hard to get?' The words were out before she could stop herself. Her anger gave way to alarm.

He stood quite still. His hands gripped her upper arms. His eyes splintered. Alison swallowed and felt her stomach tighten under his ferocious expression.

Why didn't he speak? Bawl her out, or something? she thought miserably.

'Guy, I...'

'Don't *ever* mention Debbie's name to me again!' There was stone – cold control in his voice.

'I'm... I'm sorry, Guy.'

'And, while we're at it, there is something else you should know about me. I won't tolerate you, or anyone else, trying to interfere between me and any member of my family. Got it?'

Alison knew now that he regarded her as a rank outsider. She nodded dumbly.

Guy continued, 'Then we understand one another. Now we'll forget it and dance again.'

She blinked in amazement. Sure, she regretted her remark about Debbie – but that didn't mean she was going to dance to order! She glanced towards their table. Kedrun was sitting alone. Kedrun, who Guy had said, would *not* be coming!

'Why don't you ask Kedrun to dance?' she said stiffly.

He looked towards Kedrun then his eyes scanned the room. 'Where the devil has Neil got to, now? Excuse me a moment.'

Alison returned to the table to collect her bag. Kedrun fingered her glass of tequila. 'Well, this has turned out to be a deadly evening. Neil has vanished, Guy looks thunderous and...'

'And I'm wearing your dress.' Alison shrugged and gave a sheepish grin.

'It suits you. I thought so when I passed the shop window.'

'When you...?'

'Shortly after I took the dress in.' She went on smoothly, 'I wasn't to know you would wear it tonight, was I?'

'No Kedrun, you weren't to know that,' Alison agreed quietly.

'Yes, a most peculiar evening. When Neil asked me to come at the last minute, I had an idea he was trying to bring Guy and me together again, but after his little display, I can't imagine him doing anything to please big brother. Poor Guy.'

'"Poor Guy" looks as if he is coming to ask you to dance,' said Alison and went to find Cliff to say goodnight.

Cliff's room was a sumptuous fusion of crimson and leather. He sat in a high-backed chair smoking a cigar.

'I hope Neil has apologized for ...'

'I'm afraid I must go, Mr Kington. But thank you for a lovely evening,' she said politely.

'You aren't letting a family tiff drive you away, are you?'

'Of course not.' Alison had to sound as sincere as possible.

'That's all it was, a family tiff. Not a bad way of clearing the air, really.'

Alison had her doubts about that. His remarks to Neil had acted like a trigger, releasing strange pent-up emotions in his son. Cliff bowed his shoulders and sighed.

'Perhaps he's right and I'm old-fashioned. Perhaps it's time for the old to give way to the new. Let the young ones have the reins.' The corners of his mouth became ragged. 'But it isn't in my hands any longer.' There was a pause before he continued sadly, 'I don't have much more time left for this world.'

'You mustn't say that, Mr Kington!'

'I'm a sick old man, my dear. It's foolish of me to allow myself to get so stressed. One of these days it will kill me.'

'I'm sure Neil and Guy...'

'Neil and I might have our disagreements, but he's a good son. He's stood by me.' He raised his eyes to her. They were red-rimmed. 'He'll miss me when I'm gone.'

Alison crouched at his side. 'They would *both* miss you. But you aren't going to die!'

He patted her hair. 'I didn't mean to upset you. Now – no more talk about me. Tell me more about you. Tell me about your project.'

She stood up. 'I don't think...'

'Go on. I'm very interested in what you said. These

cliffs, now, you really believe they are dangerous, Alison?'

'Well...'

'Suppose I hold myself responsible for putting up more signs telling the public not to go too close; more fences, eh? Areas deemed out of bounds. That is the very least...' he clamped his hand to his chest.

'Mr Kington? What is it?' Alison dropped her bag.

'Tab... tablets – on coffee table...' he gasped.

Her hands were shaking as she handed him the box of tiny tablets. She rushed out to find Guy, who was dancing with Kedrun.

'I'm fine now! I'm fine. Don't fuss. You know how I hate fuss,' she heard Cliff say as she stood outside his room with Kedrun.

'I'll get the doctor, anyway,' said Guy.

'Don't want him. I want Neil.'

Guy left the room and spoke to Alison. 'God knows where Neil is. I'm calling for the GP.'

'Would you like me to stay with your father?'

His look of gratitude gave a sudden lift to her feelings which only a moment before, in his father's room, had become tangled in a cat's cradle of emotions.

How could she present her evidence about the cliffs to the authorities and start something that would stress the old man even further?

The following day, Alison stood behind the hotel, staring down at the tell-tales. They had moved again. Guy would not have touched them this time. She was sure about that.

She walked slowly along the cliffs, looking out

across a shimmering glass-topped sea. A tiny breeze brought the gritty smell of mussels and stringy seaweed. Bare-bottomed toddlers were splashing in glittering pools between the sun bathers.

She wondered how many of these beach-happy holidaymakers were staying at the hotel. She gave a quick shrug. Cliff had had a survey – he'd said so.

But conditions change, and you know it, she told herself.

She reminded herself sharply that she was simply writing a thesis... not putting herself forward as a supreme authority!

When Alison knew Simon was coming to see her, she made up her mind to tell him she could never marry him. She wished with all her heart that she were in love with him. Life without Simon would be an empty place.

She was alone in the chalet when he arrived. He seemed ill at ease. She wasn't feeling so easy herself. They both spoke at the same time. They laughed awkwardly. He kissed her, then Alison sat on Honey's bed with her hands clasped between her knees. He stuffed his hands in his pockets and gazed out of the window.

'I... er... I'm going away, Alison.'

'Oh?'

'The Netherlands.'

'Oh. Not far.' She added brightly, 'Netherlands – Pleistocene sands. Are you...?'

'I won't be going alone.' He turned, his cheeks pink.

'I see.'

'I had to come and tell you. It was only fair.'

She wondered why her stomach knotted. If he meant what she thought, it was a surprise, but surely it solved everything. He continued hesitantly, 'I met Renate on a trip to Germany. I – I think I once mentioned her. She was just a friend, then. We corresponded and, well, somewhere along the line the relationship changed. She came over to this country and I helped to get her a job in the department.'

Alison swallowed. So no explanations were needed on her side after all? Simon loosened his tie.

'I'm sorry. But, you know, I've had the feeling things haven't been the same between us since you came to work in this damned awful place.'

'It's a nice place.' She managed lightness.

'You were hardly responsive the last time I came to see you.'

'Were you seeing Renate, then?'

'Have you ever been truly in love with me? Like I was with you?' He leaned towards her, his forehead creased.

'I don't know, Si. I don't know. I wish I did,' she said dully. She suddenly realized she might never see him again. She touched his arm as he sat opposite her. 'Has it all been my fault, Si?'

He flushed again and started stammering that it hadn't. Of course not. And she knew for certain, he'd been seeing Renate for much longer then he admitted. It was then that her pride took a dive.

'I came for another reason, too,' he said as if happy to change the subject. 'I've been talking to the guys at work about these cliffs. They were all keen to contribute.' He unrolled a large sheet of paper and spread it out. He pointed to the diagrams he had drawn, showing areas of weakness.

'We all reckon you are on to something here. Some of the coastal towns used to be inland years ago, as you know, and the hotel you told me about on the crumbling headland...'

'They had a survey done.'

'Date?'

'I don't know, but...'

'For heaven's sake, Ali!'

'I know; I know! I'll find out.'

'I reckon they're in trouble. During the last war, a hotel near here went over the cliff. Tell them about that.'

'No... I...'

'What's wrong?'

'There's a very sick old man there... I mean, houses, hotels – they've been here for years. Perhaps we're looking for trouble where there isn't any.'

'I've not heard so much unprofessional clap-trap for ages.' He frowned. 'You've got yourself involved with the family who owns it, haven't you? Pity. Everyone I've spoken to thinks you could come up with a brilliant thesis.'

'Damn the thesis! Guy...' she stopped.

He stared at her. There was a long pause before he spoke again. 'And you let me go on about Renate! You are more interested in this Guy what's-his-name, than you ever were about me, aren't you?'

'Simon, when I knew you were coming to see me, I'd decided to tell you I couldn't marry you. But it has nothing to do with Guy Kington. Like you, I've thought for a long time, things haven't been the same between us. But that doesn't mean I'm not going to miss you. Dreadfully.' She gazed about her despondently.

'D'you know what I think? I think you don't *want* us to be right about the cliffs. I warned you not to let relationships get in the way. Does he love you?'

She shook her head.

'Then I suggest you get yourself down to earth again; back to work. Proper work! Or are you hell-bent on giving up what could be a tremendous career? Never mind this Guy person. Or some doddering old man who's got your conscience working overtime.

'You know, it's what I admire most about Renate. She never lets emotions get in the way. She's a scientist to her fingertips... as I once thought you were.'

'I'm sure you'll both be ever so happy.' She couldn't stop the trace of cynicism creeping into her voice. She was not prepared for what Simon did next. He bent low so his face was close to hers and whispered, 'The stupid idiotic thing is that I suddenly want to make love to you.' His hand cupped her breast.

'Si...!'

'Don't worry. I won't. Goodbye, Lissy. Good luck.' He stopped at the door. 'I want to see your boss before I leave. Unless... unless you'd like me to stay here a little longer – for old time's sake? We don't have to part like this.'

'Goodbye Simon,' she breathed.

The nick-name had brought back memories of college days. Of Simon and her. Together. Now he'd gone and a chapter had ended. Her feelings were a tangle of contradiction. She bent her head. She didn't hear Honey come in.

'Cheer up. They aren't bleeping well worth it, Ali.'

'I feel as if I'd lost an arm or something.'

'Last straw, eh?'

'Yup.'

'Haven't seen you so fed up since you came here. You haven't been the same since the supper-do.'

'I don't know what's wrong with me.'

'Men! That's what's wrong with all of us. How about keeping me company in the bar?'

'Not tonight, thanks, Honey.'

'OK, then we'll forget the whole lot of 'em in another way.'

'That would be nice,' Alison said glumly.

Honey glanced at Alison thoughtfully, then she said quietly, 'You and me... we're friends, aren't we? Good friends?'

'Yes,' said Alison, puzzled by her earnest tone.

'Then I can trust you. See, I want to do something for you, for a change. Make you feel better.' She shut the door and turned the key; she closed the window.

Alison wafted the bodice of her blouse, 'It's hot...'

'That won't worry you. Not in a minute.'

'Wh-what are you talking about, Honey?'

'I'm talking about giving ourselves a buzz. OK?'

Alison stared as Honey took a small package out of her shoulder-bag. 'You don't need to inject. Just a sniff. Once won't hurt you, and you'll forget your worries.'

Alison gaped. She couldn't believe what Honey was suggesting.

'Go on!' Honey jerked her wrist with the packet in her hand.

'Do you know what that stuff does to you?' Alison croaked, after a dumbfounded silence.

'You the expert, then?' Honey stiffened.

'I know someone at college who screwed up his life like that.'

'For Gawd's sake! What are you looking at me like

that for? I'm not strung out on the stuff. I only sniffed it once. You won't find marks on me. Look!' She thrust forward arms as smooth as alabaster.

'Where did you get it?' Alison tried not to sound as horrified as she felt.

'You must be joking, asking me that.' Honey folded the packet in sulky silence and shoved it in her skirt pocket. 'I was only trying to help. You looked like a wet dishcloth when I came in here.'

Alison swallowed and said in a hushed voice, 'You could be done for being in possession, Hon.'

Honey yanked back the curtains and opened the window. She lit a cigarette and said from the side of her mouth, 'Its *only* a fag!'

'I don't care what it is. I'm not your keeper.'

'It's so easy for you, isn't it? You roll up here playing at being a waitress, then, at the end of summer, you'll toddle off back to poly where you'll be all nice and cosy. Well, it's not the same for the rest of us. We can't all escape to a comfy life when we've done our time here.'

'I...'

'What do you think happens to me at the end of the summer, eh?'

'I thought you got another job?'

'Just like that!' Honey clicked her finger and thumb. 'Ever thought what it's like looking for a job when you're a one-parent family? My mum don't have Brent in the winter, you know?'

Alison ran her fingers through the thick dark strands of her hair. 'It must be very difficult.'

'It is. And there's times when I think about what's coming and I want to escape from myself.' She sniffed. There was a smudge of mascara on her cheek.

Alison felt sorry, and angry, and sad all at the same time. 'Come on, Hon. Let's go for a walk. We both need it.'

They stood on the beach and watched waves fizzing round their feet. Alison said hesitantly, 'Suppose I could help you get a winter job? What would happen to Brent?'

Honey caught on quickly. 'The hotel! You could ask Guy!'

'Remember, he's very unpredictable. Anyway, Neil manages the place.'

'But you could try! You could try, Ali!' Honey pleaded.

'Yes... yes, I could... but not while you're messing about with that stuff. You are bound to be found out...'

'I swear! I swear I've only tried it once. Oh!... what the hell!' Honey tightened her lips and pulled the package from her pocket. She screwed it up and threw it into the sea. It bobbed about like a tiny crumpled face spewed up with the froth.

'Satisfied? And before you ask, I haven't got any more. I could get some – but I won't.'

'In Summerland?'

'Anywhere. All you need is the bread. But I said, I won't touch it again. *Especially* if you can help me get this job.'

Two joggers in shorts wheezed past them.

Suddenly Alison wanted to be free of this conversation. 'Come on!' she shouted and began to run along the flat stone-coloured sand.

Soon they were both splashing and running about with the exuberance of little kids let out of school. At last, they stopped, breathless, laughing and soaked.

'Look!' Honey hissed.

Alison's pulse bounded even harder as she saw Guy riding a horse towards them along the firm sand near the shore.

'Ask him about the job!' Honey urged.

Alison bit her lip. Was it madness to choose this moment to ask him for a favour? Because she knew, now, she must make a decision that could devastate his father. She had to. Too many people were at risk.

She was going to present her findings about the cliffs to the Council.

She closed her eyes, half hoping Guy would have vanished when she opened them. She wished with all her being she had never heard of Summerland. That she had never allowed Guy Kington to take hold of her heart.

Seven

Sitting astride his magnificent chestnut mare, Guy smiled down at them.

Honey giggled. 'Archie would have a fit if he saw us so wet and bedraggled.'

'How is your father?' asked Alison.

'He appears OK but you can never tell with Dad. We've got a nurse with him.'

He pressed his strong thighs against the horse's quivering flanks to steady her. His long muscled arms glowed under the short-sleeved tawny T-shirt. He looked like a great bronze statue, thought Alison.

Honey glanced towards Alison, then at Guy. 'I'd... er, I'd better be getting back.'

'How are things with you, Honey?' asked Guy.

'Me? Oh, fine, Mr Kington.' She added hastily, 'I've learnt my lesson all right. I won't be getting into any more tangles.' She gave a coy smile.

'Good for you,' he said.

'I've got to go, but *you* stay, Alison. I expect you've got *lots* to talk about.'

As Honey skipped across the beach Guy swung himself down, his expressive blue eyes fixed on Alison. She was suddenly conscious of the white T-shirt clinging wetly to her body.

She decided to broach the subject of a job for Honey, but he interrupted her.

'I'm glad we're alone, Alison. I want to apologize.'

Her mouth hung open, mid-sentence.

He continued, 'I think I was rude to you when you had supper with us. I'm sorry. I hadn't meant to be. It... it was a rather strange sort of evening.'

'Was Neil...?'

'Am I forgiven?' He put his arm lightly across her back as they walked along the shore, leading his horse with the other hand.

Guy glanced towards her. 'Neil's got a point you know. He sees me turning up like the prodigal son, and he's afraid Dad might decide to leave the hotel to me. No chance. Neither do I want it. Neil's worked hard on the place. There was a time Dad took it for granted I would take over the business but I never felt it was my line, yet when I was young I only managed the odd protest. He never forgave me for leaving.'

'Why did you?'

'The sort of publicity I was getting, was not going to do much for bookings. But you know that, of course.'

'I heard you joined the Marines?'

'Eventually. Did all sorts of things first.'

'And then you were wounded in the Falklands?'

'Only leg wounds.'

'Then you started writing and became a rich man?'

He gave a short laugh. 'You can be homesick in comfort when you've got money.'

'Has your father read any of your books?'

'He's not one for reading. Even if I dedicated a book to him... and I never *do* dedicate books... you can be certain he still would not open it.' He eyed his horse as it pawed at the sand and then looked at Alison. 'Ever ridden?'

'Years ago.'

'Come on, I'll lead you.'

He helped her mount the horse and, gradually,

Alison began to enjoy herself.

Guy started running, then suddenly, to her acute amazement, he swung himself up behind her, jolting the breath out of her, circling her damp body with his arms as his hands held the reins, his taut muscles pressed against her.

They were soon galloping over deserted stretches of beach. Her breasts swung against his hard biceps. Alison couldn't decide whether her heart was pounding madly from fear or from the sense of vulnerability she felt at that moment as his body pressed against her back and buttocks and their hips moved in unison.

Almost against her will she felt an intense excitement growing inside her.

The farther they rode, the more it was patently obvious that no saddle fitted two people.

When he slowed down at last and slid to the ground, Alison's cheeks were on fire.

'That wasn't funny!' She was out of breath and her words were choked out.

'I thought you'd enjoy a burst of speed,' he remarked wryly.

She was confused. Was that all it had been?

'I'll walk back,' Alison mumbled.

'Oh, don't worry, you don't have to ride her again if you don't want to. I've got a car parked where I stable her.' Guy patted the horse fondly when he left her at the stables on the outskirts of Summerland. 'I shall miss her when I go away again.'

'Does Neil ride?' Alison tried to sound matter-of-fact, but his remark was a jolting reminder that Guy wasn't there to stay.

'He prefers what he calls more "aesthetic pursuits",

like ice-skating, dancing. Here borrow this until you dry out.'

He yanked a black sweater from the car. It buried her like a long floppy sack. She hoisted up the sleeves and was about to get in the car when he touched her arm.

'Can we walk for a little while?'

There was something about his earnest expression that made her agree. Alison was astounded when, as they were walking along the country lanes overlooking the sea, Guy brought up the subject of Debbie.

She murmured, 'You didn't want her name mentioned.'

'Believe it or not, I intended to get you on your own after supper to talk to you about her. But it didn't work out that way. I'd like to fill you in on what you may *not* have heard.'

'Please... it doesn't matter.'

'I've discovered it *does* matter to me what you think.' His eyes met hers. He needed to talk. And he needed to talk to *her*.

Guy continued, 'Debbie and I went out together – off and on. One day she rang in a hell of a state and asked if we could go somewhere private. We went over to the lighthouse. We knew we weren't supposed to go over there, but that didn't worry us. We'd been over plenty of times, away from Archie's prying eyes.'

'Didn't he approve of you seeing one another?'

'He didn't approve of her seeing *any* male. Treated her like a precious ornament. No one was allowed to touch Debbie!

'She behaved oddly that day. Oh, I was used to her moods, frivolous, petulant – but this was different.

Eerily so. The minute we went into the lighthouse, she began to act out a little seduction scene.'

He gazed beyond a tangle of hawthorn bushes to the electric-blue sea.

'God knows why I didn't accept the invitation. She was wearing the scantiest underwear I'd ever seen. Perhaps I sensed the air of desperation about her. Or perhaps I liked to be the one who called the tune. I don't remember. But I do remember being puzzled by the strange expression in her eyes. She seemed to be on a different plane.'

Alison could see it was painful for him to recall the incident. But he went on in a parched voice, 'Then she told me she was pregnant. I said, "Whose is it, Deb?" She started laughing. She said in a silly teasing voice, "Well it could be yours if you want." I demanded to know but she just floated around the room, waving her arms, saying, "It's the stars', the moon's, a child of the heavens."

'I wanted to shake her! I asked if that was why she'd wanted me to make love to her? To make damn sure I'd be in the line-up of paternity contenders?'

He brought his hand across his mouth as if wanting to wipe the words away forever.

Alison was silent as they walked along the dusty lane. To one side of them were long narrow gardens leading to a row of cottages, some of them empty. To the other side were shale and marl cliffs with a sheer drop to a golden beach with a grey quicksand collar where it touched slurry. Across the lane ahead of them was an old red and white barrier with its paint peeling and sunshine stuttering through its slats.

'I told her I was taking her back. She refused to budge.' Guy's voice became a whisper. 'I've asked myself a thousand times why I didn't stay and talk with her about her problems. But I said I'd wait for her at the boat... I was sure she'd follow me.

'I was outside when I heard the most chilling sound of my life. A sort of high-pitched chanting. I looked up and saw her on the gallery. I raced up as fast as I'd ever run. I'd nearly reached her when she opened her arms, laughing, calling to me... calling... "Watch me Guy. I can fly!" And... and, she jumped.'

Alison put her hand on his arm. He choked 'I felt as responsible as if I'd pushed her.'

'But – wasn't she on drugs?'

'I should have realized. Stayed with her.'

'We always torture ourselves about what we should have done *after* the event. I know I did after my mother died. We shouldn't. We can't change anything. We can only hurt ourselves.'

He was silent after that, staring out to sea. Suddenly as if grimly determined to change the subject, he said, 'That's enough about Debbie. Tell me about you. Tell me about your project.'

Alison nodded towards the barrier. 'I suppose that's what it's all about.' She went to the barrier and climbed over it.

'Careful!' Guy warned.

She craned her graceful neck to gaze out beyond the jagged overhang where the road appeared to have been sliced across.

'Wow! The road drops to nothing!'

Guy followed her and stared down to the abyss. Around them were slavering biscuit and bronze-coloured cliffs.

'They're being eaten away,' he murmured.

'Springs permeating the cliffs. Tidal surges. With

the greenhouse effect there's a rise in sea level. I see there are coastal defences – revetments...'

'Did you know unexploded bombs from the last war have sometimes been found on these beaches?' Guy broke in. 'I'd think twice about building a house here.'

'But, Guy, don't you know the hotel could be in a similar situation? Given the right conditions, even though they may be freak ones.'

She remembered how worried she'd been when she'd left the library after reading about events that could lead to a disaster on a coast such as this.

'All right, then let me judge for myself. Let me read your thesis,' Guy said.

'I...'

'What's the matter? Not ready to have all those academic theories aired?'

Alison hesitated again. She realized she could no longer postpone what she had to tell him. It would hardly put him in a receptive mood to talk about Honey's job, she thought.

'As a matter of fact, I am. You see, I intend to show my thesis to the Council. I think they should know how dangerous – to my mind – the...'

'Can I read it first?' Guy interrupted.

'Well... yes. Of course.'

'I hope there aren't too many big words,' he said with a wry smile.

She gave a light explosive laugh, as much from relief at his reaction as anything. He put his arms around her and turned towards the barrier. Now, get yourself back where it's safe. I think you must get a kick out of being in dangerous situations.'

She'd crossed over to the other side, when

she heard a crash. She spun round in alarm.

'Guy!' she screamed.

The road beyond the barrier had collapsed in an avalanche of mud and shingle, taking Guy with it.

'G-U-Y!' Her cry mingled with those of screeching seagulls sailing over the cliffs.

She heard his strangled voice. 'Keep away from the edge!'

He was alive! She flew along the lane to an occupied cottage. The owner rang the coastguard. 'The Mobile Rescue Unit's coming.'

Alison raced down to the beach, leaping over slurry settled like paste at the foot of the cliffs.

Guy was spread-eagled part-way down. He hung on to what looked like a clump of weed. Alison bargained with God for his safety. Oh, let him hold on until rescue came! It didn't matter if he went back to Greece *tomorrow*. If she never saw him again. Only, let him be safe.

'How's Mr Guy?' said Cliff's nurse when Alison arrived at the hotel after driving the car back.

'Thank goodness they got to him before he fell any farther. But he has to stay in hospital, as I told you on the phone. He's done something to his arm – and he may have concussion.'

'There's been hell let loose here. We've had reporters bombarding us with questions. Old Mr Kington didn't like that at all. Fancy us having a famous author in the place.'

'How did they find out?'

'It seems someone at the hospital recognized Mr Guy from a photo on one of the books he was reading.

The reporters were asking Mr Kington about some girl called Debbie.'

'That's exactly what Guy wanted to avoid. He said the gossip wouldn't do the hotel's reputation any good.'

'Oh I don't know. A bit of gossip can do wonders for a place. I must say though, it didn't help the old man's temper. He wasn't too happy even *before* he knew about Mr Guy...' She stopped and gazed towards the staircase.

Alison was surprised to see Tracy on the stairs. The girl's expression was taut, cheeks stained. She hurried down, past the two women.

'Tracy...' began Alison.

'Buzz off!' Tracy ran past her to the door.

'They've been quarrelling again,' remarked the nurse.

'I thought I heard your voice!' Clifford Kington appeared in the hallway gripping a piece of paper and leaning on his stick, his cheeks flaccid and grey.

'I came to tell you Guy is feeling a little better now,' said Alison.

'We have been in touch with the hospital ourselves, thank you,' he replied curtly. There was a coldness in his tone that puzzled her.

'He didn't want you to worry about him. Fortunately he didn't fall down the steepest part of the cliffs, but it was very frightening.'

'He'd know how to handle himself in any fall. He fought in the Falklands, you know?'

Did she detect a hidden pride in Guy? Cliff continued, 'He's self-reliant, sure of himself. Not sure of women though. Doesn't trust 'em. And he has good cause!' He glared at her.

'I expect he'll find a woman he can trust one day. Settle down with her,' Alison declared.

'Oh no. He'll never marry.' He left unsaid the words, especially you. But Alison knew he was thinking them. What was wrong with him? He was suddenly so antagonistic towards her. He continued coldly, 'So you were with Guy when he fell? And you the expert who knows all about cliffs!'

'No. Not an expert, Mr Kington...'

'But that doesn't stop you stirring things, does it?' He shook the sheet of paper under her nose.

She backed away, frowning. 'What do you mean?'

'Don't pretend you don't know.'

'I don't know!'

'*This* is only to advise me that a surveyor is being sent from the Council to poke his snotty nose around *my* premises! That's all! *Supposed* danger from erosion of cliffs etc. And you pretend you've had nothing to do with this?'

'I've told you... I don't know...' She stopped. Oh yes, perhaps she did know. Hadn't Simon said he was going to see Archie the last time he came to see her? He must have given Archie his findings about the cliffs. Archie had obviously wasted no time in contacting the Council, probably telling them the hotel was not safe.

'I can see by the guilty expression on your face that you knew. And you didn't have the decency to tell me you were going to the Council... and you came as a guest in my home!'

'Mr Kington,' she said quietly, 'I did not go to the Council, but I have to tell you I *did* intend doing so. I also intended telling you first.'

'You knew I'd had my own survey done!' He waved the paper over his head while the nurse hovered anxiously nearby. 'So do members of the Council. It's fairly obvious some jumped up little toad over there – who knows nothing at all about me! – is trying to carve out a niche for himself. Or herself. Yes, most likely some meddlesome woman who's new, with big ideas.'

'With a hotel full of people, I wouldn't have thought you'd have objected to second opinions.'

'Object? Me? Oh, I don't object at all. The thing I don't like is the underhand way it's been done.' He leaned towards Alison with spittle in the corners of his mouth. The air between them shimmered with anger. He hissed, 'There are folk round here who've yet to find out the sort of man they're dealing with.'

In the silence that followed, Alison heard a small gasp from the nurse.

Neil stood at the top of the stairs, pale and limp. He gave an odd whimper, his naked body folded like a rumpled sheet.

'Drunk again, damn it!' rasped Cliff.

The nurse hurried up the stairs to Neil.

Alison left the hotel feeling miserable. Never in a million years would Cliff believe she would have told him first, before going to the Council.

The evening was sultry. Not a breath of wind. As Alison walked along the moon-pale path she thought, once again, that a light flickered from the lighthouse.

Stars, she told herself.

But she was not mistaken about the helicopter buzzing over the island.

When Alison returned to the chalet, Honey said eagerly, 'Any hopes for a job?'

'It wasn't the right moment to ask, Hon. But I

promise I will when Guy comes out of hospital.'

'Hospital?'

Alison told her what had happened, finishing despondently, 'If I hadn't been stupid and gone past the barrier in the first place, it wouldn't have happened.'

'Come off it. Can you honestly see Guy Kington going anywhere he didn't want to go?'

'His father is none too pleased about reporters homing in on him... among other things,' she added dolefully.

'It's all publicity.'

'I don't think he wants publicity of any kind.'

'Come to think of it, he doesn't advertise the hotel, but he's not short of money is he?'

'No,' said Alison slowly. 'He doesn't seem to be.'

The next day after the midday meal, both of them dragged their aching feet back to the chalet, pulled off their clothes and sank on the beds.

'It's stifling!' gasped Honey.

'Good for next year's bookings.'

'They'll flock here anyway with all the fantastic alterations Archie's got planned. Wouldn't mind a holiday here myself!'

There was a loud rap on the door. Honey grunted but didn't move, except to drag a sheet over herself and nod to Alison to open the door. Alison was astonished to see Guy with his arm in a sling. Her heart leaped. But he was unsmiling.

'You... you should be in hospital...'

'Waste of time. I'm perfectly fit now.'

'Then what's the sling for?'

'God knows. I've only sprained the tendons.'

Honey's voice trilled out, 'For heaven's sake, get him in here before Archie sees him!'

'I'm not the least concerned whether Archie sees me or not. It's his daughter I'm looking for. Can you tell me where I can find her?'

'Why do you want her?' Honey poked her head round the door. She was wearing the sheet like a sarong. 'She's trouble. Come in.'

Guy's face looked like bleached leather. Alison felt concerned about him. He was obviously not fit to be running about.

'Tracy could be anywhere, Guy.'

'The house? Archie's house?'

'You're bonkers. When Archie sees you he'll go mad.' Honey twisted a tighter knot into the top of the sheet.

'Won't it wait?' said Alison, knowing full well he'd do exactly as he intended.

'It will not. I'm probably doing *him* a service.'

'Is this to do with Neil being drunk?' asked Alison softly.

'He wasn't drunk.'

Suddenly the door crashed open. Archie stood with military precision, glaring at Guy.

'What the bloody hell are you doing in my camp?'

'Looking for your daughter,' replied Guy in a deep even voice.

Alison glowered at Archie. 'It's usual to knock.'

He shoved his forefinger towards her. 'The less you say, the better for you. Bloody fine goings-on!' He glared at Honey who stood motionless, her mouth open. The sheet had slid further down to reveal ample cleavage.

Guy rounded on him. 'Don't be stupid, man. For once in your life, listen to somebody else.'

'Listen to who? You? Who killed my Debbie?' ranted Archie.

'He didn't kill her!' Alison faced Archie furiously.

'Oh yes? And what do you know about it, eh? Got his word have you? And you believed him?'

'Archie...' began Honey tremulously, stepping towards him.

'Make yourself decent, you little...' As Archie made to push her out of the way, Guy grabbed him by the shoulder with his free hand.

'Leave her alone. And listen!' His grip on Archie tightened. The two men glowered at one another. Guy hissed, 'I've reason to believe drugs are being passed around – in this camp, centre, whatever you like to call it. Now, do you want your daughter, Tracy, involved in it?'

Archie blanched. His voice became a hoarse whisper. 'You're a damned liar, Kington.'

'Someone close to me is involved. I'm determined to find out where the stuff is coming from.'

'Ah-huh. So now the boot's on the other foot, is it? So now it's *you* who's searching for the answers, just like I did all those years ago. Well, I'll tell you now, you can forget trying to implicate anyone in *my* place. I run a good clean holiday centre – and my little girl knows exactly what would happen to her if she ever so much as touched that poison.'

'I'm not saying she takes it, man! But she might know something about it. Surely, if there's anything going on here you would want the matter cleared up?'

'I tell you, there's *nothing* like that here!' Archie shouted.

'There is Archie,' said a tiny voice. They all looked at Honey. Archie screwed up his face. 'What the hell are you saying?'

'There is stuff here, if you want it.'

Guy let go of Archie and turned towards Honey. He said quietly, 'How does it get into the place, Honey?'

'Don't know.' She pouted.

'But you've damn well used it, haven't you?' barked Archie.

'I haven't! I haven't! Tell him, Alison.'

Alison found herself muttering something incomprehensible.

'Well, has she?' demanded Archie.

'Tell them how you got it, Hon,' Alison said.

Honey ran her small pink tongue over her lips to wet them. 'I was only *offered* it.'

'Who?' urged Guy softly.

Honey became suddenly sullen. 'A bloke I know.'

'*Who?*' This time is was Archie probing.

'A bloke I know.'

'And I bet you know quite a few!' said Archie derisively. He looked at Guy. 'You can't believe what *she* says.'

Alison looked at the woe-begone expression on Honey's face; the ridiculous sad way she clung to the sheet; the helplessness. She cried, 'Don't talk to her like that! You treat women as if we're some lower species!'

'I treated you good! I give you time off to do all that college work.'

'Only because there was something in it for you. Now you've got what you want, I shall be surprised if you give me another job. You couldn't wait to give Simon's findings to the Council, could you?'

'I don't know what the devil you're talking about – but you're right about the job.' He pointed a stubby finger at Honey. 'And I ain't having her back either!'

'I don't need it!' countered Honey. 'I expect Guy can get me a job at the hotel.'

'I most certainly will,' said Guy after the briefest pause.

His words seemed to put new hope into Honey as she faced Archie defiantly. 'I hope for your sake, the police never find out...'

'Watch what you're saying! I'll have you up for slander,' spat Archie.

'All right then, if you don't believe me, try keeping an eye on the laundry van that comes here on a Saturday morning – and that shed where Maurice keeps his boat...' She stopped, realizing she'd said too much. Archie stared at her, then turned abruptly and rushed from the chalet.

'Oh hell; that's done it!' Honey dropped heavily on the bed.

'Where is this boat-shed?' asked Guy.

'You aren't going there now?'

'No one is going to be fool enough to be messing about in there while the beach is crowded,' said Guy.

'Even if you did find anything, Archie would never believe you.'

When Guy left them he was grim and preoccupied.

Honey's gaze followed him. 'He's all man,that one. All man! But I wish I hadn't told Archie about the drugs.'

'You were very brave.'

'Sod being brave. That's what I say.'

That night when Alison was sure Honey was asleep she crept out of bed and put on a butter-coloured dress. She hoped she would blend in with the colours of the sand dunes.

Her sandals sank in the sand. She could hear the soft whoosh of waves on the beach. She positioned herself where she could see the hut where Maurice's boat was kept.

Suddenly there was a sound behind her. She froze.

'What the devil are you doing here at this time of the night?' hissed Guy.

Her body relaxed. She whispered, 'It was me who persuaded Honey to tell what she knew. Now I'm going to find out for myself and corroborate her story.' She hesitated before adding, 'And I guessed you might come out here when it was dark. There has to be a witness if you want to convince Archie.'

'And you think he'll take notice of you?' Guy allowed himself a wry smile.

'I'm better than no witness at all, aren't I?'

He put his free arm gently round her. Even a touch so soft made her nerve-endings tingle. He said, 'There's no one in the hut at the moment and I don't even know if there will be.'

'I'm prepared to wait.'

'Come into this hollow where we won't be seen.'

They were surrounded by marram grass. Their whispered voices seemed to echo in the still night.

'Thanks for going to hospital with me,' Guy said gently.

'If it hadn't been for me, you wouldn't have gone past that silly barrier in the first place.'

'Of course not.' His voice was deeply solemn but she knew he was teasing her.

She blushed. 'D-does your arm hurt a lot?'

'Look.' He took the sling off, flexed his arm gently

and moved it in a slow circle. His bare muscles were long and sinewy. He lifted his hand and stroked her cheek. She told herself it was the oppressive heat that made her suddenly very hot. There was thumping inside her. His thumb traced the outline of her lips.

'You have very inviting lips,' he murmured.

'It... it d-doesn't look as if anyone is coming to the boatshed after...'

The sentence was never finished. He drew her tightly against him. His chest was like iron. Her bones became liquid fire.

His mouth was soft and sensuous; his tongue probed her. She felt vulnerable, like the cliffs with their soft slurry undermining their stability. Her body rocked against him as they kissed. She tried to be silent but she made odd strangled noises.

He held her even tighter. She knew now there was no way she wanted to remember what anyone had said about him. There was one moment in her life. This was that moment.

He stroked her; explored her. The soft sand cradled them. She touched his injured arm and whispered, 'Be careful. You'll hurt it.'

'Nothing is going to hurt, darling. I promise,' he murmured hoarsely.

Eight

It was in the early hours when they heard sounds on the beach. A faint glow came from the boat-shed as three figures disappeared in there.

'I'm going to see what's happening,' Guy whispered.

'Me too.'

'No. You stay here.' Guy crept across the dunes.

She jumped as a voice behind her growled, 'And what do you think you're doing, eh?'

'Archie!'

'Waiting for Kington, I'll be bound!' His sharp eyes followed her gaze towards the boat-shed. 'So that's it, is it? He's come to do the same as me. Find out if Honey was talking out of the back of her head.'

There was a sudden commotion as Guy opened the door. Two figures raced out of the hut. Guy ran after the one who flew like the wind in the direction of the hotel.

Archie charged after the other who headed for the dunes... a man who, Alison thought, resembled the laundry van driver who called at Summerland.

She ran to the hut and stared inside. A candle flickered in a tin. There was a strange smell like there had been in the lighthouse.

From a shadowy corner behind the boat, a bedraggled figure rose slowly to his feet. His eyes were heavy.

'Hi, Alison,' he muttered before slithering to the ground again. Alison gaped.

Archie panted up behind her. 'I'll never catch him. He's disappeared in the dunes...' He screwed up his eyes and walked round the boat.

'Bloody-hell. Jack!'

'Let's get out of here,' he growled to Alison.

Outside there was no sign of Guy or anyone else and Archie insisted on escorting Alison back to her chalet.

She couldn't sleep. Thoughts jumped in her head like sand-fleas. How could Jack and the others have risked so much? But overriding everything were her thoughts of Guy. He had roused her to fever pitch with his expert lovemaking. And afterwards, when she had thought it was all over... The exquisite thrill of how it had been would stay with her always.

The next day, gossip was rife.

Honey chatted excitedly. 'You won't believe it, Ali. Jack has been sacked! After all these years. Why would Archie do that? There won't be any of us left, soon. And that's not all. Janet heard Archie and Rita having a row. Fancy Rita arguing! Archie's found out his precious daughter has been dating Neil Kington. He's packed Tracy off to her auntie's...'

Alison took her project file to the hotel.

'Another baking day,' the receptionist said to Alison. 'The forecast is for a break in the weather, but I can't see it myself.'

Guy was in his father's study. He kissed her gently. She looked into his sad, troubled face. 'What's wrong, Guy?'

'Dad's taken himself to London.'

'Is he fit enough?'

'No way. He left a note. He doesn't want any of us following him... I expect you've guessed it was Neil I chased from the boat-shed? We had a row. Dad heard.' He ran his fingers through his thick wiry hair. 'I'd suspected for some time Neil might be on drugs. When I got home from hospital and heard he'd collapsed I had to find out the truth once and for all. I love my brother. The next time he collapses might be the last.

'Before Dad walked in on us, Neil admitted he got the stuff from a guy who called at your place. Refused to say, who. But he *has* told me Tracy isn't into that scene.'

'Do you think he's trying to shield her?'

'I doubt he's interested enough in women to do that.' He sighed. 'It's all falling into place: his swings of mood, his arguments...'

'And I accused you of not standing up to him. Why don't I learn to mind my own damn business? You can't argue with someone who's high.'

'I shouldn't have tried last night, then Dad wouldn't have heard us. But then I would never have known...' He stopped, his expression grim. 'None of us knows the first thing about one another when it boils down to it. Even our own families.' His eyes were dead. 'Be glad you aren't involved in any way with mine.'

'B-but I am.'

'Alison, you do know I shall be leaving for Greece soon?'

'Oh? You must like it very much.' Her mouth was dry.

'Life is more relaxed out there. The press don't

bother me. The old man didn't like it at all when they swarmed in on him.'

'I expect he didn't want the story of you and Debbie dredged up again.'

'Or anything else that would bring publicity to the hotel,' he said bitterly.

A window pane rattled. Outside a rose bush dragged its nails along the glass as a breeze blew up.

Alison put her project file on the desk.

'I – I only came to give you this.'

When Guy answered the telephone and she signalled she was leaving, he didn't try to stop her.

That evening she wandered despondently along the cliff-walk. The day had been extremely humid but now a wind thraseed hedges; grass rippled in the moonlight. It was daylight bright. She watched the foaming waves hitting at sea-defences, and frowned. The tide was unusually high.

'A-L-I-S-O-N!' came a cry.

Alison stared in the direction of the hotel then started to run to the steps leading to the beach. Tracy was halfway down them, trying to support Neil's dead weight.

'Can you help me? I reckon he's drunk or something!' cried Tracy.

Between them they half dragged Neil's limp body. At the top of the steps he started to giggle.

'It's not bloody funny!' spat Tracy.

'I'm a'right.' He meandered dangerously close to the cliff edge.

Alison was thankful when she saw Guy. He was climbing into the Range-Rover but rushed across when he spotted them. He clamped his sound arm around his brother, almost lifting him bodily.

'OK... you're OK. Lean on me,' Guy said gently.

Once indoors, Neil seemed to brighten up but Cliff's nurse and Guy took him upstairs. Alison heard the nurse say, 'Don't worry, I'll stay with him while you're gone.'

Tracy muttered to Alison, 'I'm staying too. I want to be here when he sobers up. There's no way I'm going back to my auntie's. Dad's punishing me for what happened to Debbie.'

Alison was about to leave when she saw Guy hurrying down the stairs.

'Surely you aren't driving?'

'I have to.'

'But your arm...'

'I'll manage. I've had a call from London. Dad's in hospital. He's had a heart attack. I have to go there.'

Alison managed to persuade Guy to let *her* drive the Range-Rover.

She was surprised he'd brought along her thesis; surprised that he seemed to have read most of it already.

After an acid-yellow streak zigzagged the sky, a clap of thunder made her grip the steering wheel tightly. Tree-tops on either side of them were bending in the rising gale. Then rain started hammering on the roof.

'The weather's broken now all right.' She tried not to sound nervous.

He went on reading and murmured, 'I noticed the barometer falling.'

She was almost driving blind as the windscreen wipers fought the deluge so she pulled into the next lay – by. Guy was staring at her file with a glazed expression.

'This makes a lot of sense, Alison,' he said slowly. He sounded concerned. She told herself he'd got enough to worry about already and said, 'Well, fortunately your father had his own survey done of the hotel.'

'Oh, yes. He had a survey done.'

She was puzzled by his cynical tone. He took a deep breath. 'I didn't tell you quite how distraught my father was last night when he found out Neil was a junkie. Afterwards, when we were alone he broke down completely. It was as if he couldn't stop talking. A pity he left it so late before...' He bit his lip.

He continued acidly, 'It appears my father was in a position to bribe – blackmail – call it what you like, some emminent people in this community. And now – when I read this...' He nodded towards the file.

'I don't understand.'

'You are absolutely right. The hotel *COULD* be in danger. Particularly in conditions like tonight's.'

'But the survey...'

'Exactly. How do we know the guy who did it wasn't one of those in the palm of Dad's hand? That he gave just the report that was wanted? A bent report!'

'It isn't possible!'

'Believe me, anything is possible. I've discovered that much in the last twenty-four hours.' He gazed out at the belting rain and the lightning, then back at her file. 'I've left a hotel full of guests... a hotel that may not be as safe as I thought.

'We're going back, Alison.'

She tried not to speed on the wet roads, but her mind was on the high tide she'd seen that night, the change of wind direction – and other factors that, combined, just might be the agents of destruction.

They saw flashing lights ahead of them. When they slowed down they heard the hum of saws. A sopping wet policeman walked to the side of the Range Rover. 'Sorry, miss, I'm afraid you'll have to divert. There's a tree across the road.'

Guy directed her along a muddy track with more dangerously leaning trees. She only relaxed when she was back driving on the coast road.

They were nearly back at Summerland when she gave a sharp intake of breath.

'Stop!' shouted Guy. But she'd already hit the brakes. Guy peered at the road ahead. 'Who the hell was the imbecile standing in the middle of the road? Where's he gone?'

'Did you see what he was wearing?' she gasped.

'I don't give a damn...'

'He was dressed like a Roman soldier!'

'If some lunatic who's been to a fancy-dress party wants to thumb lifts...'

'But you must have heard the story? The Roman soldier who appears when there's going to be a disaster?'

'Complete rubbish.'

'Then where is he now?'

Guy zipped up his jacket and climbed out with his head down against the wind and rain. He walked a short way along the road and then returned, his expression grim.

'I don't know who that guy was – but he just saved

our lives. Half the road is missing. It's collapsed with the cliff.'

Alison's hands were trembling as she turned on the hazard lights. 'Where's the nearest phone?'

'The hotel. It isn't far now. We can get by on foot.'

They began to run the rest of the way.

'Guy! Look! The sea defences have been breached!'

They only slowed down when they saw the hotel standing strong and safe.

'Thank God!' he exclaimed. They stood for a moment, out of breath, and then ran again until they reached the wasteland beside the hotel. Guy put his arm round her. 'I'll be taking no more chances after this. Tomorrow I'll clear the place and get my own survey done.' He blew into his cheeks. 'Never thought I'd be glad to see it!'

The explosion knocked them both off their feet.

The path at the rear of the hotel between the garden and the cliffs had collapsed. There was a sheer drop to the boiling sea. But Alison's horrified gaze was rivetted on the garden itself. There was a gaping hole where the earth had split open.

She gasped as the conservatory began to crumble into it. She could hear glass splintering through the wailing wind. Potted plants and basket-chairs plummeted to nowhere.

Guy had rushed inside the hotel, ripping off his arm-sling and ordering her not to follow him. But now she flew round to the front of the building and up the steps.

Staff were shepherding guests outside to the veranda. Some had grabbed waterproofs to wear over their nightclothes. Did they know the back of the building was disintegrating?

Alison was helping more guests to leave the hotel when she saw a pale panic-stricken Kedrun trying to wrap a bandage around a guest's finger. Kedrun gave a frantic whisper. 'Guy asked me to see to this man. He's cut his finger. Guy *KNOWS* I can't stand the sight of blood!'

'Would you like me ...?"

'Oh, please, Alison. I'm not feeling so good myself. I'll go and sit in the car for a bit. If you want me...?'

Alison nodded and was tending to the man when someone shouted, 'Where's my little boy?'

She heard Tracy answer, 'I've got him. He's OK.' Then Tracy turned to Neil and snapped at him, 'For God's sake, move a bit faster, you! You must have sobered up by now!'

There were screams as a chandelier in the dining-room smashed to the floor. The receptionist said to Alison, 'I can't get Mrs Bennet to come downstairs.'

Alison finished tying the bandage and went to Mrs Bennet's room.

'I've lost my reading glasses. I must find them. Will you see if they're under the bed, dear?' she said. Alison dived under the bed. A moment later the old lady cried, 'Here they are! Under my pillow. Aren't I silly?'

As Alison escorted her down the stairs, Mrs Bennet bubbled, 'My word, this is going to be something to talk about when I go home. I say! Look at that! There used to be a fireplace there. I hope someone has telephoned the fire brigade about all this...'

Alison did not tell her the lines were down.

Outside, she heard Archie's loud voice before she saw him.

'Ladies and gentlemen! Summerland holiday centre

is open to all of you. Hot baths, drinks for everyone, dry clothes...'

'Alison!'

Alison turned to see Rita, wet and dishevelled, rain running down her anxious face. 'Someone said Tracy's here. If Archie finds out she...'

The hotel seemed to lurch. There was a deafening crash. Then a loud scream from upstairs. Alison rushed back up there. Guy was standing in an open doorway. Tracy was crouched on the opposite side of the room. Except for a narrow joist the floor between them had disappeared.

'Look at me, Tracy. DON'T look down. Stand up.' Guy was talking in a deep soothing voice.

'I can't,' Tracy was trembling with fear.

'Yes you can.'

'I bloody well can't!'

'Stand up!'

Tracy slowly stood up, her eyes wide and staring. She pressed her hands flat against the cracked wall behind her.

Alison saw how taut Guy's shoulder-blades were under his wet shirt. He spoke softly again. 'I know you've got plenty of courage, Tracy. I've seen how you behaved tonight, helping the guests. The time has come to help yourself now. OK?'

Tracy stifled a sob and nodded.

'I want you to edge yourself along a couple of steps and you'll be at the end of the joist.'

'What?'

'Move this way a bit.'

'No! No! I'm scared of heights!'

'Don't look down.'

'I'm going to die!' she shrieked.

Guy murmured to Alison, 'Stand here. I'm going across. Hold your arm out and take a firm hold of her the minute she's close enough. Hang on to the door handle to steady yourself.'

He balanced himself on the joist and after a moment, began to walk slowly across to Tracy. Alison held her breath as she watched him. Somewhere in the distance she could hear sirens. Then Archie's voice whispered in her ear, 'I'll steady her this end. You hold on to me.'

His leathery face had a bleached look about it and was a mass of lines.

It seemed like a lifetime to her before Guy had coaxed Tracy to step on to the joist. He held her waist from behind.

'I can't!' she yelled.

'Course you can, gel,' croaked Archie. He had his arms stretched towards her while Alison gripped his waist.

'Walk to your dad, Tracy. It's only a few steps. I've got you.' Alison heard an unusual tremor in Guy's voice. She tried to swallow but her mouth was too dry.

At last, Tracy began the long slow walk across the joist. But there was a moment when Guy had to release his hold on her – and Archie could not reach her. Tracy froze.

'Come on, gel, Neil's waiting for you.' Archie's voice was no more than a whisper. Tracy wobbled. She stepped forward and caught hold of her father's hands. Archie dragged her backwards with him through the doorway. His body fell against Alison's. He put his arms around Tracy and held her tightly, then turned to Alison.

'Take her outside, will you?'

She saw the tears glistening on his cheeks.

When Alison looked back, he was leaning towards Guy with his arms outstretched.

She thanked God that the hotel had been cleared, when there was the sound of rending timber and crashing brickwork. She watched, mesmerized, as the chimney opened and collapsed with the roof. Slowly the back half of the hotel crumbled into the sea.

It was after that, that the rain stopped.

Whatever else anyone was feeling, Archie was on a high. He continued to rush around informing everyone, including the firemen who'd got the last of the guests out, that his facilities were at everyone's disposal.

Guy was hurrying between guests and organizing where they would like to stay for the rest of the night. There were many offers from other hotel owners and residents of Summerland. Guy would try to arrange transport for any guests who wanted to return home immediately.

Although he was being calm and reassuring, there was an unhappy, tormented expression in his eyes. Alison had once seen him wince when someone accidently knocked his arm. But this expression had nothing to do with physical pain.

'Miss Lacie? Could I have a word, please?'

She turned to see a fresh-faced reporter. He said, 'I believe it was you who predicted this hotel was unsafe?'

'I didn't exactly go around telling everyone...'

'But you did think it unsafe?'

'This whole coastline is very vulnerable. The rate of

erosion is increasing...'

'In your opinion?'

'Of course in my opinion.' She was in no mood to start discussing all this.

'But you aren't qualified?'

'I happen to be studying...'

'Don't you think you might have caused a lot of unnecessary panic, spreading rumours about the hotel's safety? I mean – it did withstand the full force of the worst storm we've had in years.'

Alison was flabbergasted by his remark. But then he continued, 'After all, it did take a bomb to bring it down.'

'What?' She stared.

'From the last war. Been hidden all these years. Amazing.'

'Bomb?' she whispered.

'So have you any comment? It's only natural for our readers to wonder if anxiety about supposed cliff erosion here might have contributed to Mr Cliff Kington's heart attack – and his death tonight in London.'

Alison was in the chalet packing when Archie knocked on the door.

'Terrible business last night. Terrible,' he said.

She wondered how genuine Archie was. He *looked* genuine.

'Who'd have believed a bomb could do all that damage?'

She folded a jumper. 'I don't believe it was just the bomb. I still think it was a combination of factors... oh, never mind.' She added ironically, 'Well – I got myself in the papers after all. It was my ambition once, you know. Huh!'

'Now look, don't you go taking any notice of all that stuff they wrote about you.'

'I really believe there would have been a disaster here sooner or later, bomb or no bomb. But I'll never be taken seriously until I've got myself qualified. And I see now what a heck of a lot of work I've got to do.'

'Well. Them bits of paper make all the difference and it's no use pretending they don't.'

She was feeling far from cheerful but couldn't help grinning. 'Even for a woman, Archie?'

'What I came to say, Alison... well, I was a bit hasty when I said I wouldn't have you back, gel. At the time I was knocked sideways, hearing about drugs and pushers and everything, here in Summerland. I couldn't take that on board. I couldn't.'

He took a bag of caramels out of his pocket and offered them to her. She shook her head. He looked into the bag, then screwed it up without taking a sweet out. 'You know you can stay if you want to? And there's something else. I changed my mind about Guy Kington. He saved my Trace.'

'And do you think, now, he's the sort of man who would have harmed Debbie?'

'He didn't.' He shufled awkwardly.

'What?'

'Seems Jack has been keeping a lot to himself. He said he was on the island the day Debbie died. He saw her fall. He said... he said, she opened her arms and launched herself. Nobody pushed her.'

'Why has he kept that to himself all these years?' she gasped.

'He thought I wanted to protect my Debbie's

reputation. That I didn't want folks knowing she committed suicide. So when I sounded off about the Kingtons, he went along with me. Wanted to keep his job, did Jack. After I sacked him though, he didn't care what he said. He was always a crawler... he... he should have spoken up.' His shoulders were bowed.

'I'm sorry, Archie.'

'Best I know isn't it? Though I'm never going to know everything. Me and Rita have chucked all her stuff out of the attic at last. Found a diary. That was a shock. Seems it was some local lad got our Debbie pregnant. She says nothing in it about drugs so I don't suppose I'll ever know where she got the stuff. *I* reckon it was LSD. God knows where it came from. That bastard, Jack swears there were no drugs in the camp in those days.'

Archie's eyes sparked. 'I'm beginning to wonder if I know owt at all! I'll tell you one thing. I'll make good and sure my new centre is clean and decent for families! I'll vet every bloody member of my staff...!'

Alison felt curiously pleased to see the old Archie coming back to life. As he was leaving, he said, 'Don't forget to let me have your thesis to read.'

'Archie, who did go to the Council about the cliffs?'

'Nobody. It said in the papers – they were already planning to inspect all buildings near the beach. Huh. Funny when you think about it – you and me weren't going to blind 'em with science after all, were we? Still, it won't hurt for me to keep pushing for better sea and coastal defences. So let me see what you wrote. After all, you did it in my time!'

When Alison went to find Guy, she saw him

wandering ghost-like in the grounds of his ruptured home.

'I'm so sorry about your father,' she said softly.

'We wouldn't have got there in time. Must have been fate made us turn back.' His face was creased with sadness, but as he turned her towards him she saw the spark of anger in his eyes. 'I hope you realize that what was reported in the paper, was in no way the truth. Dad's death was not brought on by so called "rumours" about the safety of the hotel.'

'What I said to him about the cliffs could have contributed...'

'Listen, Alison. I'm going to tell you what really aggravated his illness.' He took a long deep breath. 'I found out before he left for London what was on his mind. He's been dealing in drugs – not touching them himself of course – and this hotel was the perfect spot where negotiations could take place. It had to stay that way. No publicity of any sort.'

Alison stared. 'D-did Neil know?'

Guy shook his head. 'Nor me. I'd seen the odd stranger coming to the hotel, but I never dreamed...' He continued bitterly, 'Why? In God's name, why? And who were his clients? Old people? Youngsters?' Then, to himself, 'Surveyors?'

Alison gazed miserably at the stained sky. She could hardly believe what he'd told her. The only comfort she could give was to listen while he spilled out the horror fermenting in him. He continued, 'He went beserk when he discovered his own son was an addict. He spilled out all his sordid secrets.

'It seems the stuff was dropped on the island by helicopter. The laundry-van driver made pick-ups from there. He was in the lighthouse on the day you visited it. He didn't want to arouse any sort of suspicion by being there on his own so he got the hell out of it. Released your boat to delay you while he got out of sight. He's been running things while Dad has been ill; started dealing in the hard drugs – collected his own clients, Neil among them.'

'What was Neil on?'

'He won't say. It could have been just about anything. Dad swore he never dealt in hard drugs – but who's to believe anyone any more? All I know is that I want to see my brother happy and well again.'

'Can anything be done for him?'

'I don't know. I've been told intensive counselling could help. But Neil himself has to decide to go to the rehabilitation centre. He might – when he reaches rock-bottom. If it's not too late, then.

'God! I'll never forgive the old man!'

They walked in silence to the beach.

After a while she said, 'Why did Cliff rush off to London?'

'To meet Mr – or Mrs – Big. Close all deals, he said. There was too much publicity. The local press found out about me and my writing; Archie had got wind of what was going on on his patch. I expect Dad got cold feet.'

'Or was it because he was suffering terrible remorse?'

'Bit late for that! Sorry, I shouldn't bark at you. I've been in two minds about telling you all this, but I won't have you thinking for one minute that anything you said contributed to his heart attack. It was Neil he was distraught about.'

'I still wish I hadn't sounded off about the cliffs, especially when it's said a bomb did all the damage here. It seems I've a great deal more to learn.'

He turned quickly towards her.

'Listen. It's people like you who stir things up, who get the authorities moving. Didn't you read in the paper that intensive investigations are now going on all along this coast? How do you know it isn't because they heard about you and your project?'

She looked at him thoughtfully and then said hotly, 'I still reckon it was all due to a combination of factors and not just the bomb. Look at the coast road!'

For a moment a brief smile hovered on his lips at her renewed belief in her own convictions. Then he turned to study the racing sea. 'I suppose I should take a measure of comfort knowing Dad didn't get involved with drugs until after Debbie died.

'God knows why I believed him when he assured me of that – but I did.' He sighed. 'Some family, eh? I ask myself if things would have been different if I'd stayed here and taken my share of running the place'

'You know Neil liked to be top dog here.'

'I've never seen Dad cry before,' said Guy dully.

The breeze whipped at Alison's cheeks. She rubbed her hands up and down her bare arms. Guy glanced at her and peeled off his sage-green sweater. 'Here – put this on.' Its soft silky warmth enveloped her like an embrace.

He continued, 'I thought it was odd. I found press cuttings about me in Dad's room. And the books I've written. I didn't think he ever read my books.'

'I always had the feeling he wasn't able to show you how he really felt about you, Guy. Perhaps he didn't know himself. But I'm sure he was proud of you.'

'The feeling isn't mutual.' The voice didn't sound like Guy's.

His dark hair blew across his forehead. She saw him wipe the spray from the waves out of his eyes.

She knew he was going through his own private torment.

Suddenly he turned, seized hold of her hand and pulled her with him as they began to run back towards the hotel.

'I can't... I can't keep up with you!' she panted. 'Guy...!' She wanted to laugh and cry and throw her arms around him all at the same time. He turned her to face him, gently rubbing his thumbs across her shoulders. She could feel the warmth of his breath. Her heart began to thud – but not from running.

'Look – I don't pretend to know anything about rocks and things, but I do know a damned good piece of writing when I see it. And that's what your thesis is. Not biased in any way. An excellent report. I see a great future ahead of you Alison. It – it may not be the future you imagined for yourself...'

'Go on,' she whispered hoarsely.

'The reporters *will* get it right. One day you'll get the press you deserve.'

'Even in Greece?' She forced a laugh.

'Oh yes.' His voice lowered. 'And when I see your name, I shall tell everyone... I used to know her.'

He pulled her to him and kissed her long and fiercely. She was not sure if the salty taste was from his lips or her own tears.

When Alison returned to polytechnic she tried to avoid the press but it was impossible. However, her thesis was highly praised by her tutor. At the same time a book was published on erosion written by an emminent professor and Alison was delighted that many of her findings were compatible with his.

After that she worked as she had never worked in her life. It helped to numb the awful ache inside her. This time there was no Simon to help. This time she learned to cope alone.

During the year, Honey wrote to her. Archie's new Summerland Holiday World was to be open all the year.

Before he'd left for Greece, Guy had persuaded Archie to have Honey back permanently.

"And Ali," Honey wrote, "I won't let him down. I'm a together person now. Not as though Archie hasn't got his little red eyes on me! But I got someone else to think about as well. Guess what. I got Brent with me! He's in the crêche when I'm working. Archie let him come. So I'd be a fool to mess things up, wouldn't I? This place is whiter than white what with Jack buzzed off somewhere and the van-driver in prison. He won't beat up any more women like he did me for a long time."

With each letter that arrived, Alison longed for news of Guy.

'Rita is groovy to work for, Ali,' she read. 'She gives me more time off than I had before. She runs her own little gift shop now. Had to battle with Archie, word has it. Ha ha! Good for her is what I say.

'Tracy's still at college. Found another boyfriend! Neil's been in some clinic. He's out now. Him and a friend are going to run a pub in the north. He got the dog back from Kedrun...'

Alison wondered why Guy never wrote to her. Had Honey been right all along? Had she merely been a chapter in his life?

She tried to forget about him but restless nights and endless dreams ravaged her good intentions.

Alison qualified with an honours degree. Simon turned up to congratulate her. He agreed with everyone else that she had a brilliant future ahead of her. In fact, he said, theirs could be a brilliant partnership. He told her he had split up with Renate.

Alison was in a bookshop when she saw a display of books by an author who had won a major prize.

CONTRACT IN MADRID by GUY KINGTON.

Her heart stopped. Guy! He'd written a book about drug smuggling. And he'd used his own name. But there was something else unusual. He had done what he said he never did. He had dedicated a book. She read: 'For my beloved Alison'.

Tears sprang to Alison's eyes. To hell with pride! She flew to the nearest phone. Archie was bound to know Guy's address.

It was sweltering in Athens. As she stepped off the plane the heat made Alison catch her breath. And so many people! Announcements in a language she didn't understand.

As she moved slowly through passport control her pulse raced. Then she couldn't find a trolley.

At last she saw the barrier where people waited for friends and relatives.

'Alison!'

Guy had vaulted over the barriers. He crushed her hard against him until she couldn't breathe. His mouth was over hers. He looked at her and cupped her face in his hands.

'I'll never let you go again!' He kissed her again and her bones liquidified.

A policeman standing talking to the girl from the sweet shop called out to Guy. Guy laughed and answered in Greek.

'What did he say?' asked Alison, her heart bursting with joy to be with him.

'I'll tell you when we're on honeymoon.'

'You take a lot for granted!' she declared – but her smile was bewitching.

That night she gazed at the stars through the open window of his villa surrounded by orange groves. He'd said she could choose where they were to live. That all that mattered was being together. She ran her fingers over his brown skin.

For the first time in her life she knew exactly where she belonged.